THE QUEEN
PROTOCOL

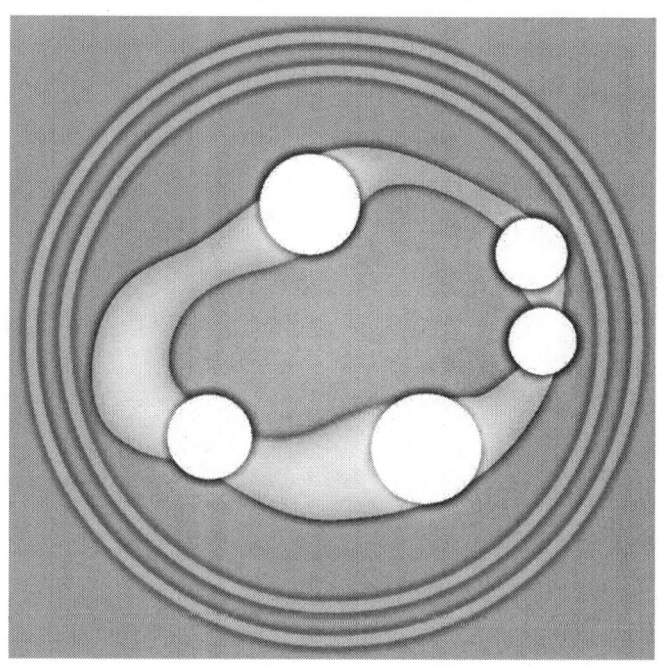

THE QUEEN PROTOCOL

Gregory Benson

Published by Blue Giant Publishing, LLC

First edition.

Print ISBN: 978-1-7340196-2-9

eBook ISBN: 978-1-7340196-3-6

gregorybensonbooks.com

tolagon.com

To Greg and Carol, my father and mother who built within me tenacity and a strong work ethic. They are always in my corner.

Greater love has no one than this, that someone lay down his life for his friends.

—John 15:13

CHAPTER 1

"Faster, Keeper Haflinger, faster!" Crix pointed skyward with both hands as Haflinger mustered up the stamina to carry the boy a little bit faster upon his shoulders. It was worth the effort so that he could hear the joy in the child's voice. They moved briskly through the flowered pass, stirring wild seed pods and tiny insects which swirled upward when the Andor's brisk gallop disrupted their pollen-collecting. Haflinger's bronze legs appeared silver in the sunlight against his sweat-saturated fur.

"Down to the waterfall, and then we will stop and take rest," Halflinger said as steam churned from his nostrils and beads of moisture dripped from his brow. The small child sighed.

It'd been five years since Creedith's massive figure appeared at the front doorstep of the Haflinger Trivot residence wielding a tiny, swathed infant and insisting that the child be allowed refuge. Creedith's relationship with Haflinger had come from a distant courtship, so the likelihood of the child's whereabouts traced to that household would have been doubtful.

Slowing alongside the crackling of water breaking over the rocks of Rivole Creek, Haflinger gently set Crix down. "It's right down that hill. I'll bet since you ran me so hard that you may have a chance to beat me to the bottom." Haflinger started early, instilling a competitive spirit in the child, knowing that his future would demand great endurance and passion.

His little feet sprinted onward, and Haflinger took chase. Crix looked back and let out an excited giggle. Haflinger's wobbly legs maintained a slow stride. He didn't want to pass the child, but as Crix's feet started moving downhill faster than he could keep up, he tumbled, his giggles instantly turning to cries. The out-of-control feeling quickly ended when a pair of strong arms swooped him up and cradled him tightly.

"Not to worry, youngling; I have you. Look, we made it here at the same time." Haflinger turned him around to see the water showering from high atop the emerald green hillside. Clouds of mist billowed up as the crystal streams splashed onto the rocks below. A smile spread across Crix's face.

A large, taloned, four-winged bird circled at the peak of the hill, lurking for prey below. Haflinger put the child down and looked up with interest.

"What is it, Keeper?" Haflinger did not reply. The bird no longer circled but now appeared stationary as though painted into the sky. "Keeper Haflinger!"

Crix reached up to tug on the sizable Andor's leg. Haflinger did not move nor reply. "Please, Keeper, tell me what it is; why don't you talk to me?" The child's voice trembled.

Still, Halflinger did not move or reply. The steady rumble of the waterfall silenced, and the air stilled. Breaking down into a manic cry, the child stepped backward and shot a glance at the sky.

The bird was as black as a windowless room with no lights. It was closer than before, hovering on the other side of the brook, and was at least three meters tall. It spanned its wings, and six boney arms protruded from beneath. Its mouth opened, bearing teeth long and pointed like nails.

Crix's heart pounded, and a sudden chill whisked over his moist skin as he turned to his keeper. However, Haflinger's face was not his. A shadowy veil poured over it with black eyes and pointed teeth. Cast in fear, Crix remained frozen, not knowing what to do or where to run. He continued to stare at Haflinger, and the longer he stared, the more his face appeared to darken. It slowly tilted down and stared directly at Crix.

He took a careful step back, trying to sneak away from the scene until he felt something press against him. He turned around; his view passed by where he had last seen the bird, and he quickly noticed that it was no longer near the brook. Frantic, he tried to dart to the side but was forced back by the pinching of six spiny arms wrapping around his body. A hissing scream broke the silence around him.

"Noooo!" he screamed.

Everything faded to blackness, and then gradually emerged into a murky view of several shadowy figures stirring nearby. It was difficult to discern what the shadows were aside from their laggard movements and long, fluid gaits that stopped momentarily and

3

then started again. There was a sporadic whistle of wind that could be heard but not felt. A thick stench of decay filled the warm air.

Crix tried to reach his arm up, but it didn't move, and the sensation of a wet slimy blanket wrapped around him. He continued to strain while trying to pull his arm up, and he accidentally let out a groan. His voice had a higher pitch, and he didn't recognize it as his own. It was feminine.

The movements halted instantly. "Kerriah . . ." a somewhat familiar voice nearby whispered.

He tried to turn his neck to look, but it wouldn't move. The shadowy figures came closer, and their spectral shapes began to emerge into clarity. Four long, boney appendages propped up a slender torso with two short arms. A gurgling turned to an incoherent chatter and then a hiss. The nearby voice shouted, "No! . . . No! . . . Not her, take me!"

A tickling crept up from the lower part of his body, and a small silhouette laden with glistening black fangs blocked out the already scant light. *Kerriah . . . Krath . . . They're in trouble. Where are they?* His eyes opened. *Was I dreaming?*

"That's it; wake up, you cretin. You will tell me how you came into possession of the blue orb and, more importantly, how it became fused into your useless molecules." The voice was sharp and angry.

As Crix's vision slowly came into focus, two unfamiliar figures stood over him. A reflective lens glided over his head and chest, scanning his body. Crix was clamped tightly to a table and tilted forward. A tall individual's strange, red eye gleamed down at him; half of his face appeared covered in dark, highly reflective metal. The other looked like an older Mendac, pale and wrinkled. The most bizarre aspect of the metallic-faced stranger was his torso, which had six equally polished metal limbs that appeared to move about gracefully and independently of each other. The top two arms had regular hands and the bottom had four pinchers that snapped closed and zipped open as he spoke and focused intensely on Crix.

"Well, speak up as I am mere seconds from tearing its power from your flesh," the slender figure commanded with increased tension in his voice.

"What have you done with Kerriah?" Crix asked; his voice cracked and quivered. Nothing made any sense. Deep inside, there was a scant hope that none of this was real, that he would soon wake up from this nightmare. How did he end up separated from his friends?

The strange figure leaned inward. The bright glow from his red eye glared into Crix's eyes, forcing him to squint. "I assume you're referring to your troublemaker friends that were responsible for the unfortunate obliteration of Dispor. Their flesh is now being fed upon as hosts to the Thraxon warriors born on the quarantined world below. A worthy sacrifice to amend their hooliganism."

"No! Let me go! Let me go—" Crix's teeth chattered and his muscles spasmed as he struggled. The table energized with each of his sudden movements, sapping his strength almost instantly. He tried to call the orb's power, but each attempt squeezed his brain like a vise and punched into his heart, causing it to stop beating for several seconds.

"It's too late for them; besides, you should be concerning yourself with your own welfare at this point. Rest assured, what I have in mind for you will not be at all pleasant, at least not from your standpoint," the lurching figure's voice snapped with a sinister smirk.

Crix's stomach turned sour, and his thoughts spun upon hearing the news of his friends. He struggled to focus, but he did not want to give his captors a hint of weakness.

"Who are you?" His fists and jaw clenched as he spoke.

The figure pushed out a frustrated exhale. "Imprudent boy or whatever you are, don't you recognize your lord when you see him? I am Zearic, Realm Chancellor of the Oro System, Grand Admiral to the Third Thraxon Fleet, and Galactic Marshal to the Marck armies."

"You're Zearic?" Crix's face scrunched.

"That's right. If my appearance startles you, that's good. I want you to fear me. Know that with my transformation, I am your superior in every way. I now control the most lethal invasion force in the known galaxy as well as the Marck armies. You will show some respect for your master . . . boy." Zearic was a hybrid now, with similar qualities to a Thraxon warrior. A menace of his own design.

Crix's eyes turned black with rage before he cut loose with a verbal assault. "Liar! You're none of those things; besides, there's a queen that commands the Marck forces." Crix wasn't sure of this, he only knew of the queen from Plexo's mention of her, but he needed to take that boast away from Zearic. "You're just some traitor that is aiding the Thraxons, of all things!"

Zearic leaned forward and grasped Crix's throat with one of his pincher arms. "You will keep your disrespectful tone in check, or I'll snip your head from your neck right here and now." He tightened, forcing a gagging cough from Crix. "This queen you mention is nothing, merely my pawn. She wants to turn you into her robotic slaves. I just want you to be food for my armies. My way will be much less torturous than hers, so I would advise you to pledge your allegiance to me."

"No! I hate you! My father fought against the Thraxon hoards, and you had him murdered for it!" Zearic released him and took a step back, intrigued as though he had just had a revelation.

"You are the son of the deserter Corin Emberook . . . of course. You were supposed to have been killed. I should have known . . . His illicit use of the orb's power must have altered . . ." For a moment, Zearic stood nearly motionless; his only movement was the fingers of his top left hand, which massaged the thin flesh side of his face. Crix interrupted his pondering.

"Why? Why are you assisting the Thraxons? They want to destroy us."

"Oh, simpleminded fool that only sees things at their face value. Admittedly, I thought as you do a time ago. At least, until the day when I came to a new awareness while conducting interrogations of Thraxon captives. It was a realization that they are infinitely unadulterated, more so than any species of the Oro System. Their sole purpose was to encompass their existence as far as they could reach, and they worked to accomplish this goal without compromise. No matter how many we tortured or what methods we used, none would break . . . ever. None of them would surrender their prime directive. At all costs, their ranks from grunt to general would remain silent for the sake of their conquests." Zearic stared toward the ceiling with his chin held high.

"This is why, all along, we knew so little of them. This was also our weakness and their greatest strength. I admire them, and I will become their supreme leader, and as their leader, I will harness this plan to spread their conquests unopposed from the furthest reaches of this galaxy and beyond," Zearic replied with an ominous smile, his metallic arms gesturing as he spoke. "You most of all should appreciate this, given that your species is so primitive and the oldest of all in the Oro System and yet has gained so little. Yours is a perfect example of a squandered organism."

Crix's mood quickly changed from angry to confused as he fought to assemble in his mind what exactly Zearic meant by this. Zearic tilted his head; his smile widened. "You don't know who you really are, do you?"

Crix tried to regain his composure. "I'm Crix Emberook, son of Corin Emberook, whom many considered to be the greatest of Tolagons."

Zearic gave a disturbing snicker as he paced behind Crix. "This father of yours is not the hero you were led to believe, imprudent fledgling."

"You're wrong; he—" Zearic cut him off before he could finish, all his appendages pointing and gesturing as he spoke.

"No! You're wrong! Corin was not only a traitor to the UMO, a betrayer to the Vico Legion, but also plotted to have the world below us decimated for his own personal gain. He is also not your father at all." Zearic's head tilted as he paused to catch Crix's reaction to this information.

"What?" Crix said with disbelief and mockery in his voice. "You really are as crazy as they say you are."

"No, I am correct in my statements. The then Tolagon Emberook purposefully stalled the council of Gabor and UMO Security Council to gain a child he was not meant to have." *Another child?* Crix questioned Zearic's honesty, but at the same time wondered if it could be so; did he have a sibling he was never made aware of?

Zearic re-emerged into Crix's view and stared into his eyes. "I can tell by the deprived look on your face that you have no idea what I'm referring to." He paused for a minute. "Good. I will gain great pleasure in divulging your roots to you. It's the least I can do." Though Crix gave Zearic little credibility, his desire to learn something of his lineage outweighed his urge to interrupt.

"Your mother was barren and would never be capable of having a child of her own. Much to the dismay of Tolagon Emberook, who, for some misguided reason, felt it was some form of old-world rite of passage to have a son and, even worse, for her to birth it naturally. I thought it to be a pitiful display of weakness to crave such a thing, but the primitive notion so wore him that he came to me in hopes of cheating this genetic flaw in his spouse. Of course, my advanced biological engineering corporation could have

9

aided in this silly ambition, so I agreed to assist with one slight stipulation.

"At the time, the Thraxon forces were amassing for a full and final assault on Nathasia, and Tolagon Ridol was pleading to the Federation for immediate aid. After so many years of fighting this unyielding species, the UMO was reluctant to commit any more resources to save Nathasia from this renewed war. Their armed forces were scant at this point, and they stingily wanted to keep what they had left for their own defenses. As such, there was a growing chorus among the UMO populace that was willing to let it die to save themselves." Zearic stopped for a second. He let out a smug chuckle. "I knew that the moron Ridol would fight to the death to save his pathetic planet. I also suspected that the Thraxons had no interest in the orbs . . . *the fools*, and so Ridol's eventual demise at their hands would allow for me to harvest the yellow orb from the ashes of the besieged planet.

"My arrangement with Corin was simple: stall any UMO aid to Nathasia, and I will ensure a boy child is born of Breata. In his lust for a boy, he foolishly agreed, believing that he could lead the charge and rescue them at the eve of the onslaught, saving the cursed world. His overconfidence in his abilities was his undoing. He sacrificed his reputation and campaigned that the Thraxons were still merely misunderstood and they could broker a truce on behalf of Nathasia. Even though they were being crushed at the time." Zearic stopped and let out a gleeful laugh before resuming. Crix scowled as he realized that Zearic was getting far too much pleasure from telling this story at his expense.

"One thing I will grant him, he spun his audience better than any I've ever witnessed before. He could have told those fools the deepest voids of space were as white as the Halls of Matigane, and they would have believed him. In the end, he failed, of course, and I filled my end of the agreement, giving him his child, though not exactly what he had intended." Zearic stared closely into Crix's eyes as if looking into his soul. His eye twitched as he grabbed Crix's face and squeezed his cheeks in disgust. "You are the byproduct of a filthy Andor, and even though Corin broke his vows as a Tolagon and altered your appearance with the power of the orb, I can still smell the stench of that mongrel breed in your flesh."

Crix jerked his face away from Zearic's grasp and tried to draw upon the orb to undo his shackles, but as he struggled, an overwhelming jolt burrowed down into his bones, to the point of nearly snapping them into splinters. Zearic's maniacal laughter hacked at Crix's eardrums as he winced in pain. "You think I wouldn't have accounted for your temptation to use the orb? The binds that hold you are specifically designed to reflect energy back to where it came."

Crix, still feeling the reverberation of pain from the orb's energy, gathered the strength to ask a question that he must know the answer to. "What do you mean the byproduct of an Andor?"

Zearic released a thrilled grin over being able to give painful information. "Someone that Corin called his friend betrayed him for a side deal. A deal that would ensure the preservation of Troika from the newly formed Marck armies. His allegiance to his brethren was much greater than his supposed friendship with his commanding officer. In the end, he gave me his Andorian molecular extract, which I required to mingle with your mother's. It was the perfect betrayal, and I basked in every thought of it. She did birth you, but before she laid her eyes upon you, Corin took you away from her. Now it makes perfect sense. How could she ever accept you had she known the truth of what you are? That is when he must have done this to you to make you appear . . . well . . . normal."

Crix stared forward vacantly. He searched deep inside himself and could see that, strangely, he always knew this. The main reason he felt like an outsider in Troika was due to the icy welcome he had received from much of its population. But inside, his heart always felt warm and at home there. Who was his real genetic father? Who was the Andor that had betrayed Corin?

"The Andor?" Crix asked in a calm voice, deep in thought. He had to know who his father was. "Who was the Andor that gave you the genetic sample?"

"How should I know? They all look the same," he scrunched his nose, "and have the same stench. I am through with you now; I want the orb, and then you can die and be finally relieved of your pathetic existence," Zearic asserted; his lower arm pinchers snapped and clacked in a jittery stir.

"Tell me the Andor's name, and I will willfully give you the orb," Crix said, though he had no intention of doing so, yet had to know the name.

Zearic drew his head back with a blank expression. "You would give up the orb for something as petty as your mongrel father's name?"

"Yes."

Zearic let a puff of air in rebuke. "Hmmm." He slowly rubbed the side of his chin and then gave a half-smirk. "Its name was Creet." He paused for a second and then stepped forward with his hand extended. "Now, I have given you the name, and you will present to me what I seek."

Creet? He couldn't personally think of anyone with that name in Troika. Who could it be? He must have died during the war, having served with Corin.

"Do you hear me, boy? Release the orb now, or I'll have it stripped out as slowly and painfully as possible as life leaves your worthless body," Zearic demanded, quickly running short on his scarce patience. The lights flickered and went dark. Zearic's feet slowly rose from the floor as the artificial gravity systems failed. He slammed one of his metal pinchers against a nearby terminal.

"What is this nonsense? Get th—" his voice stopped before he could get the next inflammatory words out.

CHAPTER 2

Kerriah!" the strong, familiar voice shouted again. *Creedith?* The fanged creature blocked her view. A stench like smoldering rubber mixed with burned hair filled her lungs. She started to gag just as a blinding flash blasted from behind the smothering figure, causing it to crumble and fall away. More flashes quickly followed the first, each one giving off a brief crackle. Echoes of squealing and hissing came from every direction.

A hollowed voice called out. "Command 8-1 . . . hostiles suppressed. Checking on hostages." A soft-red light shined across her face. "She appears unharmed, cutting her loose." A slender-framed soldier wearing a full UMO tactical battle set stood before her. The insignia on his helmet was familiar, a glowing skull surrounded by the circle of Oro.

Around her stood eight well-equipped soldiers in the same tactical battle sets, most touting smaller subcompact assault rifles and one with a heavy shock weapon. They worked feverishly to cut Krath and Creedith loose from the sticky webbing that held them against the rocky wall nearby. "Sir, the three are here; the Tolagon is missing." The soldier paused for a few seconds. "Yes, Kerriah is with them."

Krath stood nearby, massaging his wrists to soften the aches from his struggles with the Thraxon bindings. "Now, this is what I've been waitin' for. Good ol' UMO battle gear, where is my rig up? I'm ready ta start kickin' some Marck and Thraxon backsides." Cracks webbed across his charcoal-grey skin for having been away from his wet habitat for too long.

One of the soldiers gestured to Krath. "Keep it down; the area is swarming with hostiles," he explained in a light voice from his helmet com.

Krath blurted out, "Bring 'em on; I'm so bliterin' mad right now, I may just gain an appetite for steel helmets and bug guts."

The soldier near Kerriah threw up his palm in Krath's direction in a plea to keep quiet. "Captain Krath, please keep your voice down." He slowly cracked his thick neck and grinned.

"Here she is, sir." The soldier held his wrist up and projected a soft cone of light across Kerriah's face. Her porcelain skin gave off a luminescent glow in the darkness surrounding her. The communication strobe gave her the same visual and auditory awareness as though she was standing in front of the person on the other side.

A slender, gray-haired Mendac came into view. "Kerriah? It's Governor Septin; are you okay?" His muscular cheeks bore the etchings of age, which spanned down to his jaw. However, they were faintly noticeable due to his distracting bright blue eyes.

"Yes, thanks to the unexpected arrival of your soldiers. Do you know where we are? Or better yet, how we got here?" Her jet-black hair still shined against the light, despite a gritty week of harrowing adventures.

"Oh, dear child, you have been taken to Nathasia. We feared that you were killed until unconfirmed reports came back that you had been taken captive outside Dispor. One of our agents discovered that you were with a Tolagon and being taken to the quarantined planet. We have little time to get you out of there. You need to follow Commando Burling and his unit out to the waypoint for extraction."

"Do you have any idea where Crix is?"

"We currently have no intel on the Tolagon's whereabouts. We were hoping he was with you."

Kerriah's face crumpled into a frown and she shook her head. "No. He's not here. We have to find him."

"We will, but first we have to get you to safety. Burling's team is some of our best. I will see you soon." The soldier lowered his wrist and handed her a sidearm.

"Follow us." Stepping over numerous charred corpses of Thraxon larvae and long-legged elder nesters, Burling scaled out of the nesting pit. The Thraxon nest pits were created to feed their larvae from the live flesh of their captives. The pit walls were lined with holes where the eggs were laid and kept until ready to hatch. The larvae grew by sinking their fangs into the chest of their victims, and then feeding slowly over the course of weeks until they formed into a juvenile Thraxon worker or soldier. Late in their lifespans, they metamorphosed into larger egg-laying nesters, where they worked their remaining years to rear their colonies. Their need

16

for living hosts to nurture their young kept them scouring the galaxy for inhabited worlds. The surviving population of Nathasia had, unfortunately, fell to this horrible fate.

Kerriah didn't move. "Wait! We have to find Crix."

Burling looked down at her and motioned her forward. "You heard the governor; he is a mission priority, but we have no intel on where he is currently." A hard pit formed in her stomach. She only took solace on the implication that they are going to find him, but her heart felt heavy as she realized that this was the first time they had been apart in weeks. The trials they'd been through together, along with their hidden feelings, had knit a tightly woven bond between them. She couldn't just forget him or let him go. For her, it was no longer that simple.

"We still have to find him. He has to be here . . . somewhere."

"Don't worry. We're goin' ta get my little buddy back! No way I'm gonna let these nasty clipper face bugs have 'im," Krath's voice boomed from outside the pit.

Burling glanced across his shoulder. "I wish you would keep your voice down." He lowered his arm and tugged Kerriah out of the pit.

The others were already hunkered down outside, except for Krath, who paced back and forth growling to himself. "Ohhh . . . no!" she whispered as she peered across the murky horizon. A lump swelled in her throat as she took in the scene before her. Thraxon nesting pits peppered the landscape. Nesters lurched in and out of the pits as they worked tirelessly to fulfill their sole purpose. In the distance, a low-hovering Thraxon cruiser hung steadily within the planet's atmosphere, half consumed by the black clouds that wisped over its massive hull. She turned to see another cruiser nearby; small pods occasionally blinked upward from the surface and disappeared into the ship.

"I now see why this world was quarantined and kept hidden from public inquiries." Creedith looked over at Krath, questions in his mind becoming clearer, but despair filled his heart with the answers.

"There would have been a full-blown civil uprising had the public known the Marcks were workin' with the Thraxons," Krath grumbled and clenched his fist.

Creedith pulled his mane back slowly with both hands, sweeping it from his face. His eyes intently focused forward. "It makes sense; they have an equal objective in that both sides benefit from our destruction."

Commando Burling knelt and slid his helmet from his head. Black stubble peppered with grey covered his head and face. The well-worn soldier of the Oro resistance was all-too-familiar with combat. The rippled flesh that stretched across his lower jawline and cheek suggested that his face had its fair share of close encounters with energy blasts. He quietly set the helmet down to his side and called the group in. Eager to learn more, they gathered in to listen.

"There's a Thraxon citadel off to the east. The best we can ascertain is that it's impregnable from the surface. We do suspect that this is the Marck-Thraxon collaborative central command.

With no oversight and the quarantine over this planet, they run their unsanctioned operations from here with relative impunity." Kerriah dug her fingers back across her forehead and scalp upon hearing the words. This collaboration had long been suspected, but the idea was so outlandish that it was easy to brush off as just an irrational conspiracy. No longer.

Burling paused for a moment, making eye contact with each of them before he continued. "Now that everyone here is caught up on what's happening, let's cover the immediate directive. There's a small spaceport four klicks to the south that the Marcks are using for supply runs. That is where we are going to commandeer a ship out of here."

Creedith looked over at Burling confused. "You need to steal a ship to get out of here, but how did you get down here?"

"We spodded from the safest distance we could to not attract attention," Burling replied.

"Shot propulsive orbital dive? From what safe distance?" Kerriah's brows rose.

"Four hundred thousand kilometers."

"Four hundred thousand kilometers? Really? I didn't think that was possible. That almost sounds like some crazy stuff I'd try," she said, still uncertain she was hearing him correctly, and that maybe he was adding a little bit of embellishment, though that didn't seem to fit Burling's persona. Shot propulsive orbital dive was a tactical method for landing troops onto a planetary surface from outside its orbit. Soldiers were loaded into special torpedo tubes and launched with precision trajectory. Their launch shells split open once the atmosphere was breached, and the soldier used his individual propulsion system to slow his descent to the surface.

"Yes, we lost one of our own during entry, but it was the only way to get here on short notice. The speed on our launch was so intense that even with all the retention gear, our necks nearly snapped on exit," Burling replied.

"My type of guys, all guts and glory." Krath nodded his approval and cracked his knuckles.

"I'm sorry to hear about your loss, commander," Kerriah's voice softened and she looked at the commando with admiration and sadness.

Burling tapped a clenched fist on top of his helmet. "No need to be. He did his part, and we are all aware that every mission could be the last." It was evident that he was eager to move on and uncomfortable speaking of his losses. The lead commando excelled at adhering to his marching orders and maintaining a precision focus on his team's mission objectives.

"Okay, we keep low and move between these natural crevasses and rises as we go. If you spot a nester, remain low and motionless on the surface until it passes. We have observed that they do not have very keen peripheral vision and fail to notice things that don't move. If you see a Thraxon warrior or Marck, signal one of my units; we will take them down as quietly as possible. Now let's get moving." With that, he secured his helmet and moved out, hunkered down, squaring himself behind cover. The other commandos fell in closely behind him.

Kerriah stood there motionless for a few seconds, her lips pursed and her brows furrowed. She stormed forward, catching up to Burling. "Wait!" Kerriah grasped him by the shoulder just as he was about to embark on their escape plan. "We have a mission here, to retrieve the yellow orb of Nathasia. Our companion Creedith knows of its whereabouts."

Burling's visor slid up, and he looked back at her with skepticism. "That's not possible. The orb of Nathasia was destroyed just before the Marck handover some twenty years ago."

"That's what we were led to believe. It was a cover-up known only by a few," Kerriah continued to cling to his shoulder. Burling was one not to break from his mission directive.

"Look, I understand you may believe this, but I have to deal with what is in front of me right now. Our mission is to bring you back safely to Throwen, and searching for a lost artifact will only put that mission in jeopardy."

Creedith paused and drew back his head, taking in a deep breath of the toxic air, which tickled and then burned as he exhaled. "What she says is true. The orb was not destroyed, only concealed."

"How do you know this?" Burling looked sternly at the Andor.

"I know this because I concealed it."

"If you speak the truth, I agree it's important that we locate it before Zeatic does. However, that is a decision to be made by

Governor Septin and will be weighed when we return." Burling lowered his visor and then started out again.

Kerriah remained steadfast, equally driven. She refused to leave without an opportunity to locate the orb. "Creedith, do you have any idea how close we are to it?" Her eyes fixed on him. She hoped his memory of the time he had spent fighting in the war on this besieged planet would provide some clues.

Creedith looked around. Everything was so unfamiliar, and the world was vast. Much had changed from the last time he was on Nathasia. Specters of black clouds crept out of the darkness surrounding them, and their visibility was scant.

Creedith stared upward. "If I could just see the distant light of Oro, I could calculate our location by the time of year. Between the toxins and the Marck shroud, it is indiscernible. It's located about three klicks south off the Meutor Valley, in a deep well at the base of a dilapidated tower. However, this horizon is not familiar to me, and much has changed."

Kerriah felt desperate, and her mind raced with thoughts. "Is there anything we can do? Do you have any ideas? Anyplace we can start?" She had to find the orb's location or all their efforts were in vain, and they would have lost Crix for nothing. Her thoughts drifted for a few seconds. She couldn't get him out of her mind. *Crix. We have to find him; he can't be dead. I know he's not dead.*

"We have to locate a Thraxon outpost, something where we can gain access to a surface map or positioning system," Creedith replied.

Krath, who had been listening quietly, finally spoke up. "We're goin' ta need their help, tya know." He gestured toward Burling, who had noticed they were not following and stopped. Frustrated, he ordered his commandos to halt. Kerriah knew Burling would follow his orders no matter what she said and felt it was pointless to argue any further. Instead, she had another idea. Burling made his way back over to them.

Annoyed, Burling stomped back over to Kerriah. "Why are you not falling in behind us? We have to get moving right now!"

Kerriah crossed her arms in defiance. "You will have to leave without us. We are going for the orb and then Crix!"

Burling threw his hand up then slammed the butt of his rifle down on a nearby stone. "You are coming back with us now. We risked our lives and lost one of our own to rescue you and bring you back to safety. At least show us the courtesy of cooperation and allow us to complete our mission."

Kerriah crossed her arms and put her chin up. "No. I understand and appreciate your risks and sacrifice in this, but we have lost one of ours as well, and we are going to find him and retrieve the orb. We cannot allow either to fall into Zearic's clutches." She pointed sternly at Burling. "They are both much more important than any of us, and we cannot just let them go. Not if there is any possibility at all for us to get them back. If you care at all about our fight against the Marcks, you know I'm right."

Unfortunately for Burling, Kerriah was possibly more unwavering than himself, and this was something he was not used to dealing with.

23

Burling got up close to her face, and Krath stepped in with a protective growl, giving Burling enough incentive to keep a cordial distance. Burling took a cautious step back. "Look, we are on the same side, and I do agree we need them, but we are not equipped for this right now. If Zearic hasn't located the yellow orb in twenty years, I'm firmly confident he will not find it over the next few days. We can regroup and return with that as our primary objective. Now follow me back to the waypoint so we can leave this place; that's an order!" Burling threw a little old military command into his tone to drive home his closure on the subject. Yet Kerriah remained unmoved.

"Commando Burling, I . . ." she swung her head back to Krath and Creedith, "we do not take orders from you. We are going to get the orb, and if your mission is to rescue us, then you have no choice but to follow and ensure our safety."

Burling reluctantly waved his commandos over. He gave them a quick, confidential briefing. After several minutes, the commando unit collectively looked over at them.

"Fine," Burling spoke aloud. "Since we have not been given clearance to subdue you, we have no other choice than to follow you until you are ready to leave. So what's your plan?" He was firm and professional, yet still had an undertone of mockery in his voice.

"Do you know what sector of this planet we are on?" Kerriah asked.

"Our landing coordinates put us in the Burrianion Sector. We are about twenty klicks from Mt. Pinnel."

Creedith firmly rubbed his thumb across the synthetic edge of his chin. "We are fortunate then, but also ill-fated. In the scope of the vastness of this world, we are relatively near the yellow orb's hiding place. However, between us and our destination is the Sea of Tora, which will need to be crossed." He waited, pausing solemnly.

Kerriah flipped both of her hands in the air. "Okay, then we'll find some sort of boat, and if one can't be found, we improvise one."

Creedith turned to her slowly. His forehead wrinkled with a woeful pain that pushed its way through his thoughts. Memories of lost comrades and sufferings of war clawed out from the depths of his soul. His large brown eyes glistened with hurt.

"The Thraxons poisoned the sea, as well as most of the freshwater sources before we originally routed them from this world. They tried to ensure that a presence on this world was unsustainable and made it much more difficult for us to hold. The water toxins were so vile that it could not be purified, despite all our efforts. I witnessed soldiers literally turned inside out after consuming it. To merely have it splash upon your bare flesh, will cause your insides to liquify. We cannot cross it the way you suggest."

Kerriah stepped back in shock. UMO officials and their military suppressed most of the details regarding the war on Nathasia from the public. They did not want their constituents to fall to fear and panic over such news. Hearing this information made her nauseous. She hated the Thraxons even more now and the Marcks for aiding them.

"We have to go around then," Kerriah said, shaking off the shock of this information.

"No! We cannot. It would take too long on foot, and we do not have the supplies to last here. We cannot cross it, yet crossing it is the only way we can get to the yellow orb, so we must try regardless of the risks," Creedith said. The Andor turned away from the group and shook his head.

Burling stood back with his arms crossed. "The choice is yours, Kerriah. You're running this show."

Kerriah was firm concerning the objective. She felt the rescue of Creedith from Dispor and Crix's disappearance would all have been for nothing if they backed out now, but she also did not want the others' blood on her hands. She made her choice.

"I have to go, and Creedith must come with me as a guide. You guys can head back to the waypoint for departure. We can find our own way out once we have acquired the orb."

"Tya ain't goin' anywhere without me, little one," Krath said as he stepped forward and placed his dehydrated, gristly hand on her shoulder. Patches of his outer membrane flaked off, and the partial webbing between his fingers began to split like dried clay. "Besides, I'm not goin' to risk missin' out on some squashin' of Thraxon bug faces or smashin' some Marck cans."

Burling quickly made it known that he had no intention of failing his primary directive and relayed this to his squad. He let out an exhaustive sigh and looked over at Kerriah. "Looks like we are going to be your bodyguards, so lead the way."

***

The better part of a day passed with careful and tactical movements toward the sea. They reached a long, narrow pass that descended to a massive field below, which was littered with junk and debris leftover from a great battle long ago. A Thraxon cruiser, its hull cracked in two, rested facedown with its aft section a distance behind it. Like a fallen titan with a broken back, the remains of its victims lay scattered about across the wide range; their losses were evident, as was the price paid to ground the great beast.

"This looks like the work of your famed Vico Legion to me, given the insignias on these soldiers' remains," Burling said as he turned over a skeletonized corpse with the nose of his rifle.

"That's right. I remember this day like it was yesterday," Krath chimed in while pointing down to one of the commando's feet, who stood atop a fallen banner that was faded, torn, and half-submerged in the mud. "Step with respect, tya on hollowed soil here. We lost more soldiers than I'd like to explain takin' this cruiser down, and I'll personally see to puttin' a hurtin' on anyone that disrespects these fallen heroes."

Creedith drew a deep breath as he took in the last moments of that day, yet his attention drifted to the here and now as he set his eyes on the burned-out UMO armored division in the distance. "There, we had our backs against the sea, which later proved to be a tactical mistake that we paid dearly for. The sea is just over the horizon."

Kerriah probed intently around the debris. "There must be something here that we can use to get us across the sea."

"Crionic lifters," Creedith said with an unusual glow in his eyes. "These cruisers were equipped with Crionic, or rather magnetic, lifters that would allow them to set down on a planetary surface. As massive as they are, the conventional thrust systems required to lower or lift them would smash anything beneath them for kilometers, making it unsteady to land or takeoff."

"Yes, if we can stabilize them, they will keep us safely above the water's surface," Burling added.

Creedith, a former master engineer in his early years, had no lack of confidence that he could work his magic on the lifters. "I can stabilize them. We just need to find them in this wreckage and mount them on something to carry us over the sea. There should be four in total positioned around the outer points of the lower hull. We only require one but need the controller as well. That should be just below the command bridge. We will also require a power source. I'm assuming one of these commandos has a portable wavelength sensor we can utilize for that task."

"Each one of us. Built into our visor tech." Burling tapped his finger against the side of his helmet.

"Excellent. You should be able to scan through the wreckage and locate some auxiliary power cores. These smaller cores should still have enough residual power stored in them to last a hundred years." Creedith had some occasional downtime during their military campaigns, and he spent most of it tinkering with the enemy's downed ships and equipment to satisfy his technical curiosity. The knowledge intoxicated him as he and Plexo reverse-engineered the Thraxon technology. This data also came in handy tactically as the Legion needed to know where its weak points were.

Kerriah carefully peeled a heap of charred wires and circuitry from the reddish soil and held it up. "What should we be looking for?"

"It will be a large disk, probably ten meters in diameter, and on this particular cruiser model, would have been visible from the outer shell underneath." Without hesitation, Kerriah began crawling through the wreckage in search of a lifter. As she scurried and squeezed between twisted metal, ratted nests of optical lines, and dangling tubes, her memories fled back to her time with Crix in the mines of Dispor. Her heart pounded as she strengthened her resolve in finding him and the lost orb.

"Over here," a voice shouted nearby. "I think this is one of the lifters." Kerriah banged her head on a low-hanging girder in excitement as she rushed out to see for herself.

One of the commandos stood down in a hole and shone his light upward. He waved her down to look. "That has to be it. It's just as he described." A reflection glistened back in his visor and against the smoother parts of his armor. Kerriah eagerly leaped down into the shallow hole and looked upward. Above them was a section of the ship's hull that had cracked away; a silver disk appeared beneath the exposed underbelly of the ship. The disk stood out amongst the gritty and pitted metal parts.

"That's it!" she shouted, excited over the find. That piece of hope was what she was longing for to keep the group rallied going forward.

Creedith jumped down to verify and lightly rubbed his thumb across the surface of the lifter. "That is indeed it. We just need a fusion cutter to free this from the hull."

"Team Engineer Pilar can assist you with that," Burling said. He gestured at her with a chopping motion. Pilar plopped down into the hole, and a nozzle glided out past the topside of her wrist. She pointed it at a portion of the hull that concealed the disk.

"Watch your eyes," she warned as her visor darkened to nearly black. A thin, blue flame darted out, and she began to slice into the weathered metal. She worked surgically to dissect all the components that held the lifter near the ship's keel.

After a while, the lifter finally loosened from the old Thraxon warship. Pilar gently peeled it away with the help of Creedith and a fellow Commando. They then located and procured a controller and auxiliary power core from the wreckage not long after securing the lifter, giving them the critical parts the group needed.

The day weathered on, and the Nathasian air chafed their lungs. The ever-increasing pressure to race against the clock of their depleting resources and their physical tolerance of the planet's poisons pushed them to the point where their muscles quivered and their vision began to blur.

***

With the combined skills and ingenuity of the group, they successfully crafted a crude transport. The lifter mounted to the underside with a control station in the aft section. "Not bad for a bunch of killers that are far better at causin' wreckage and mayhem than buildin' anything," Krath joked as he stroked his plump, three-webbed fingers across the safety rail.

"What do you think? Is this going to get us across safely?" Kerriah bit her bottom lip and nervously sighed, looking for a little last-minute assurance that their creation would not end in their demise.

Creedith's nose scrunched as he looked over the murky water. "I'm more concerned over exposure to the toxins that are drifting up from that sea of death than the seaworthiness of our vessel. Do not worry yourself over our creation. It will work as expected."

They all looked once more across the murky crimson sea. A gloomy mist billowed up from its surface like millions of ghostly fingers grasping for something unseen. The water lapped against the shore, leaving blood-like stains on the mud that was speckled with fragments of rusted metal and refuse.

"Well staring at this is not going to get us there; let's get moving, while we still have courage and strength left in us," Creedith said.

He turned several knobs and flipped some crude switches before pressing a large button with his thumb. The vessel instantly came to life, snapping up several meters from the ground like a sleeping beast that was startled awake from its deep slumber. It held rock steady, and as they climbed aboard, it did not lean or move in the slightest from a weight shift. The only sound the advanced lifter gave off was a faint hum as the power core energized.

Creedith took the controls, which was nothing more than an improvised control stick that stood a half meter shorter than himself. The controls pivoted the lifter beneath enough to steer and accelerate the craft as needed. He pushed the throttle forward, sending the vessel caressing over the toxic sea.

CHAPTER 3

Kerriah took a deep breath. "Here we go," she said to herself but loud enough that the others could hear.

The makeshift craft hovered across the water at a modest forward pace, and the thick, vaporous fingers dispersed like apparitions as they passed. Their throats spasmed shut and their eyes burned as unfamiliar toxins spewed up from the murky surface. The scant light above glistened off the thickening fog as they ventured inward. The sea was quiet. Aside from the hum of the lifter and the anxious beating of their hearts pounding relentlessly through their eardrums, the stillness was haunting.

Kerriah was deadset on obtaining the orb. Her stance was steady, and her mind was calculating. Creedith was focused on the sea. Burling was attentive and remained steadfast on his charge. And Krath was unmoved by the situation.

"I hope if any of tya planned to have offspring that tya already done so 'cause this stink is going to foul up our insides for sure," Krath said while fighting back a wet cough.

No one else appeared to be amused at his attempt to make light of their situation. Creedith continuously rubbed his eyes, trying to find relief from the burning sensation that engulfed them. He needed to keep his vision clear to avoid running them into a rock or debris that hid behind the incoming fog layers. As he raised his left arm to rub away the burning tears, he took notice of the Bracix that covered it. The enhanced alloy was Merik's gift, or as he viewed it curse, to him. So many things happened to Creedith while he was on Dispor. He had changed, but inside, he remained the same.

Kerriah squinted and leaned heavily over the rail. "What's that ahead?" A tall, spectral object reached high in the air from the water and leaned over like a weeping tree.

"No idea." Creedith kept his eyes trained on the possible threat.

"Optical enhance 1-6-3," Burling called to his visor's optical sensors. His view of the object upscaled. However, it wasn't familiar, and he couldn't determine its threat level. "I suggest we stay a safe distance from whatever it is."

Taking heed, Creedith steered the vessel away. As the object faded into the distance, they noticed several more similar objects emerging before them. Creedith tried to steer clear of them as well, but before long, their field of view was besieged with the ghostly giants.

"Well, like it or not, we are going to get a more intimate look at whatever these things are." Creedith prepared them as they moved amongst the lingering objects.

The mist thickened and thinned as they neared the seabound forest of the weeping specters. Kerriah tightened her grip on the rail. As they approached, the objects appeared to lean more into their direction, yet no one had actually seen any discernible movement from them. Burling's team took a defensive stance.

Kerriah's heart skipped as she noticed the strange objects began to appear closer overhead. "Is it just me, or are those things moving?" she hoped someone in the group would tell her she was hallucinating.

The group remained quiet for a minute, and then the voice of a young commando spoke out. "This isn't right . . . We shouldn't be doing this." He turned to Burling. "Sir, we need to turn back; this place is—" Burling was quick to put the junior member of his team back in his place.

"Can that talk, soldier! You need to stay focused on the team and your role; that's it! You got me?" The young commando subordinately nodded and continued to look forward for threats.

A closer look revealed the surface of the uneasy weepers to be spiny and somewhat transparent. Their craft hovered perilously close to several of them as they passed deep into the sea forest. The hair on Pilar's neck stood straight up and goosebumps crawled across her arms as she swung her head around, noticing that the things spanned as far she could see, not only ahead but behind them.

Just as the group started to relax with the thought that the unfamiliar weepers might pose no imminent threat, Burling's voice shattered the silence. "Movement . . . look out!"

From above, a large weeper dipped downward and curled atop of them. Its submerged base still a fair distance ahead. An immense, ghostly-white leaf layered with barbs lowered down and stopped a few meters above the craft. Tiny, clear spots speckled the surface and appeared to turn dark at random.

"Trayco, use your visor optics to get a clear look at it," Burling called out to his commando nearest the object. The integrated optic system in his helmet visor filtered the foreground vapor and zoomed into the object. His targeted view revealed a surface peppered with eyes that blinked randomly. The barbs wiggled and flinched as if they were independent of the main body.

"Well . . . what's the status, Trayco?" Burling demanded a quick update.

Trayco took an uneasy step back. "Sir . . . this . . . you're not going to believe this, but it appears to be some sort of living organism. What could possibly live in this environment?"

Burling cautiously raised his rifle and peered through the scope. "Whatever it is, I'm guessing it's hostile. How else would it thrive here? Stay sharp and ready; if that thing so much as makes even the slightest hostile move, put some pain on it." The rest of his commandos positioned their rifles against their shoulders and stood ready. Krath growled as he grasped a side rail section; his cheeks and jaw stiffened.

The strange leaf lurched above as they moved forward, lingering overhead with an uneasy sway in its movement. Another one appeared, and the commandos found themselves darting their weapons between the two with cautious precision. A crinkling sound of thin plastic unfolding rippled through the silence as the first leaf opened into a flattened position. Its large silhouette casted a brief shadow over their tiny craft.

Barbs darted out from the leaf, leaving a trailing thread behind as they zipped through the air. Each one ticked into the vessel's deck, burying into the metal. The junior commando's body curled forward, and he dropped to his knee.

"Get it off me . . . grrrrhhh!" he howled in pain, one of the barbs pierced through his armored shoulder.

Krath tromped over and grasped the thread attached to the barb but felt the shock of an uncomfortable sting. The sting intensified and turned into a searing burn with each heaving tug as he pulled until his muscles rippled and veins popped. The thread burrowed deeper, and the commando cried out and buckled over.

"I can't get . . . it," Krath growled, battling through the burning sting as he wrestled with the thread. It was thin, smooth, and glided easily through his strong grasp. The pain became unbearable. He let go as the commando cried out again.

Burling pulled a small plasma cutter from his pack and started slicing into the thread, but it took too long. It was like cutting through hardened cable rather than something organic. By the time he sliced through the thread, the second leaf had rotated downward, facing them.

"Watch out!" Creedith shouted as the second wave of barbs shot into the metal hull of their improvised ferry. He snarled as one sliced down his backside, leaving a thin cut before planting itself into the guardrail behind him.

"It's attacking the ferry, not us! We have to get these off the deck. They have us anchored here." As he pushed the controls ahead, the vessel tilted violently against the leaf's grasp.

"They must be feeding off the metal; we have to cut them away." Burling motioned to his team. They slung their rifles and immediately pulled out their standard-issue, compact utility cutters and started working on the now dozens of relentless tendrils attached to their vessel. Tiny power blades glowed as the team struggled to cut through the strange matter. By the time they freed themselves, another leaf had appeared overhead.

"Blast it before it shoots those things at us again!" Krath barked at the commandos.

Leading the action, Burling opened fire and the others followed suit. Its outer layer sizzled with each connecting blast. Dark spots flared across its surface before it curled up into a withered, black shadow.

"Another one!" Kerriah pointed.

The squad directed their fire, and it curled into a black shadow the same as the first. The water began to bubble and vibrate. The strange-looking leaves stopped moving. Almost at once, all the leaves and weepers dipped beneath the surface. The horizon before them was now completely clear.

"Looks like we scared off those nasty chunks of lettuce." Krath leaned over the side to see if there was any sight of them. The water swirled, bubbled, and gurgled as a groan billowed up. The noise intensified, like something coming from deep below.

"Grrraaaaaaaa—" Krath backed away from the side. "I'm not likin' the sound of that. We need to get this tub to shore." He shot a glance over at Creedith. His round eyes appeared larger than normal. Without hesitation, Creedith powered the forward boosters, sending them jarring ahead.

The waters before them seemed to rise then fall away, replaced by a translucent white surface covered with large boils. It was far-reaching, and the occupants of the tiny, makeshift ferry couldn't see the edge. The living surface rose higher and higher, sending the craft into a forty-five-degree angle. Everyone onboard grasped the side rails as gravity turned against them.

Creedith, once revered as the most daring of pilots in Emberook's Vico Legion, pushed the craft to its breaking point, trying to reach the edge of the emerging, boil-covered leviathan. With only the dark and ominous sky before them, they suddenly reached a dropoff as they rode to the top of the elevating beast. Their vessel tipped over the edge, and gravity swung them dangling down the side.

Creedith hooked his legs around the rail nearest the controls so as not to leave them without a pilot. The toxic water dripped and sprayed, falling upon them as they slid past the edge. They accelerated down the side, gaining speed as they plunged back toward the sea below. The spraying water seared pinholes in their clothes and bit into their skin like glowing sparks from hot metal filings. Not able to hang on due to injuries, the youthful commando lost his grasp and tumbled helplessly into the watery abyss below; his body appeared to vaporize as he neared the surface.

"Hang on with everything you have!" Creedith fully engaged the lifter. The vessel sprang off the side of the ghostly mass and smacked into the water below. The forward boost pushed them level with the sea and back in the direction of their destination.

"Now that's what I'd call a good recovery, old pal." Krath gave Creedith a warmfelt pat on the back.

"Don't get cozy just yet." Burling pointed behind them.

A cracking roar like thunder came up from the deep abyss. Looking back, a monstrous beast fifty stories tall and dripping red with toxic slime slowly began to move forward in pursuit of its intended prey. Tidal waves formed as the sea pushed out from its massive form. A grey face appeared, void of distinctive features except a mouth filled with multi-shaped holes that sucked and spouted with rancorous intent as it lurched ahead.

Creedith slammed the forward boosters into full throttle, sending all its passengers onto their backsides. The creature slowly picked up momentum; its jaws gaped open and chomped shut with eager anticipation of its catch. Even against the headwinds of their forward motion, they felt a moist air blast against their backsides as the leviathan's jaws slammed closed. The shoreline emerged like a shadowy savior waving them inward.

Kerriah swung her head around, noticing the creature was gaining on them. "Creedith? It's getting close!"

"Courage, child, I have this," he assured. His heart rate was normal, breathing calm, and his eyes fixed on the prize. Ahead, the coast was near; with a little more chase and some evasiveness, they successfully reached the shoreline.

As they glided across the rock-strewn shore, he resumed a forward trajectory on land until they came upon a wall of boulders. The creature stopped short of the coast and appeared reluctant to pursue them onto dry land. It let out one final thunderous roar of frustration over its lost prey before it slumped back into the sea, disappearing from view.

Creedith stopped their makeshift vessel ahead of a rocky region. Burling unclasped his helmet and slid it off, tucking it under his arm. The other commandos followed suit and removed their helmets and bowed their heads.

"I would like to take a moment to honor the loss of a friend and soldier." His voice was a bit gravellier without the helmet com. Burling had never missed giving respects to his comrades lost on missions; raised in a military family, this show of respect was ingrained in him from birth. Krath and Creedith lowered their heads. Kerriah could not help but remember her own loss.

She touched Krath's arm and he consoled her with a gentle reply. "I'm thinkin' of him, too."

"As a commando of the Oro Resistance, we live by our dictum. We will serve with courage and honor until the day our spirit leaves this hardy shell that we have been graced with and are returned to our father. He served both bravely and honorably." He paused for a minute and then cleared his throat.

The seven remaining commandos uniformly secured their helmets back upon their heads. Burling checked over their shared ration packs. "Lady and gents, we are at the tail end of our meager rations, with maybe a day of water left for the eight of us if we are extremely conservative. I sincerely hope our destination is close." He looked at Creedith for some positive news regarding their proximity to the orb's location.

"The well that contains the orb will be over this rocky hillside, if I recall from what is familiar of this cursed terrain," Creedith replied. From his last memories, this scorched world still had scant signs of indigenous life, and the planet known as Nathasia was, at least, recognizable. Now, this world looked alien to him, as if placed here from the darkest corner of the universe. They began their climb over the rugged terrain, weary and tired.

***

The far side of the hill snaked downward into an uncomfortable murkiness. The air filled with a thick, green haze that turned black as they descended deeper. Their eyes deceived them with peripheral views of spectral images that slithered by every crevasse and nook they passed.

"It smells of death around here," Krath said, squinting from the bitter stench in the air.

They passed a hoard of Thraxon corpses lying frozen in decay. Their last motion appeared to be crawling outward as if painfully fleeing an unseen attacker. Each of their six arms clawed at the coarse ground, leaving behind scratch marks from their struggle.

Kerriah paused and cautiously leaned her head forward. "This doesn't look too inviting. There's a large hole in the back of their heads. It looks like exit wounds, but they are in the same spot on each one of them."

Creedith stuck his Bracix-clad finger into one Thraxon's head wound to get a closer inspection. "These Thraxons were enhanced. This is where their Marck components were added."

"Well, something or someone has forcibly removed them. The question is what or who?" Kerriah said, troubled over what that answer may be. Creedith grumbled quietly to himself in thought.

Krath attempted to pick up a nearby gamma class rifle, but it crumbled into pieces as he lifted it. "Yeah, looks like all their weapons have been gutted." He tried to pick up another one, only for it to disintegrate into powder. "What a darn shame 'cause I would be happy to have one of these handy rights about now."

"Take heed, we should be getting close," Creedith warned and pointed his chin forward. As they moved in deeper, the darkness crawled up around them and a heavy green fog reduced their visibility to only a meter or two.

"There." Creedith pointed to a small fissure that offered nothing but blackness from its opening. The team edged up cautiously. Creedith rubbed his chin as he stared down into the place he'd hoped never to return to. "Get your drop lines out. I have to go down there to retrieve it."

"How far down is it?" Burling began to determine how much line to supply.

"I'm not positive, but I'd say seventy-five to eighty meters."

Burling shook his head. "How heavy are you? According to my visor readings, you weigh three hundred and sixty pounds, and we only have fifty meters of drop line that would be rated to hold you."

Creedith stared down into the abyss then quickly snapped a sharp and serious gaze at Burling. "That's not going to work; the dropoff would be too great, and there would be no way back up. Before, we had Tolagon Corin lower us down via the orb's power." The blue orb's power over mass was beneficial in this regard. He thought the yellow orb's influence over thought and perception would seem to do little good in getting him back out, even if it accepted him as a host, which is a dangerous task in itself.

They remained still and silent for a minute as they pondered their options. Then, Kerriah's voice broke the silence.

"Commando Burling. Do you have any other lighter line?"

"Sure, an additional fifty meters for supplies, but it's only rated for eighty-eight pounds; I know you're light at one hundred and twenty but still too much." The risk didn't matter to Kerriah. This had to be done, and there was no turning back without the orb.

"I don't care. I'm the lightest here, and if we tie the two lines off, I can go the required distance. I have to do it."

Burling exhaled, exhausted at the thought. "I cannot allow you to risk it. My mission objective is to see you safe, not allow you to plummet to your death in some dank hole." He shook his head stubbornly. "No, absolutely not."

However, Kerriah was unwavering in her conviction, and she would not take no for an answer. "It's not about me or you, commando. It's about the survival of all our species. It's about the preservation of the UMO and what so many have already died for. If we don't retrieve this orb or it falls into Zearic's hands, we and everything we know and hold dear is lost. You see, there is no choice. Get the line ready because I'm going down there." She folded her arms and tightened her jaw.

Burling let out an exhausted exhale and ordered his commandos to pull the line from their packs and secure the lighter line to the end of the heavy line. He handed her an empty backpack. "Here, put this on. You need to keep both hands free once you have the orb."

She buckled the empty grey pack over her shoulders and across her chest. The commandos secured the line into a harness around her waist and anchored the other end of it around Krath.

Krath broadened his stance and gripped his hands around the line. "Don't worry, tya ain't goin' nowhere while ty're attached to me."

Creedith leaned forward to give his final instructions to Kerriah. "Don't be afraid."

"I'm not," she replied. Still, Creedith maintained his usual poise and intensity. Kerriah trusted her companions wholeheartedly, especially Krath.

"Okay . . . we are going to lower you down seventy-five meters, and you will touch down to a ledge, careful as it will likely be slippery. Once you have a solid footing, feel the ground in front of you, and you will find a narrow bridge. The ledge is small and the ceiling above low, so crawl across about six meters or so, and you will find an open area that descends briefly to a dead end. The wall before you will have a small opening; inside that opening is the box containing the orb. Carefully remove the box and move your way back out so we can pull you up." Creedith maintained his intense stare until she assured him that she fully understood his instructions.

Kerriah closed her eyes and nodded. Her mouth was dry and her throat sticky and she tried to swallow. The fear crawled up from her belly and wrapped its clutches around her throat.

Creedith grasped her shoulder, demanding her attention. "Now listen real close to me here as this is the most important thing I can tell you." His tone became gravely serious as he grasped the lower part of her jaw to ensure her attention did not waiver. "When you cross the bridge, do not, I repeat, do not, shine your light below. In fact, I would not shine your light at all. Rather, turn it off until you reach the other side."

Her eyes widened. "What are you saying exactly?"

"I would rather not say, and it would be better that you don't know; please, just trust me on this and do as I advise."

46

CHAPTER 4

S he braced herself at the opening and prepared to put her faith in Krath's firm grasp of the line. He stood there like a sturdy tree trunk with a square face as he gripped the cord with both hands. Kerriah knew he would never let go. With her fists closed, she tensed every muscle before leaping into the blackness below. As she dangled just inside the opening, her heart pounded; the harness pinched and pulled tightly around her torso. It was uncomfortable. She could hear the dripping of water echoing and feel the cavern's cold clamminess across her face, neck, and down her spine.

She needed to keep her focus on the task, but anxiety clawed at her. She was never one to struggle with fear. However, this wasn't feeling right. Uncontrollable thoughts started entering her mind; the spinning of words, ideas, and unknowns tempted her to retreat. She realized she might have talked herself into a situation she would not return from; this battle in her mind was maddening. She needed to take captive every thought. The sooner she could procure the orb and exit this hole, the better.

She chose to keep her light off completely until she crossed the bridge and relied purely on her other senses. As Krath lowered her down, the murky light above faded away. All she could hear was her breathing and the synthetic dropline zipping against the rim of the hole above. She stuck her hand out to feel for a solid surface as she descended. The slime coated wall felt gritty and cold to the touch.

Before another wave of angst could pool up from her gut, she felt the floor below meet her feet. Instantly, she dropped to her hands and knees as instructed by Creedith. She swished her hands around to find the edges of the narrow bridge and the opening ahead. The surface was damp and slippery with zero visibility before her. She grew concerned over her ability to keep herself from sliding off the edge. If she were to slip in any way, she wouldn't be capable of grasping anything tight enough to keep from going over the side and into whatever ominous abyss was beneath her.

She stayed as low to the bridge as possible, almost dragging her chest along the way. The cold temperature of the rock and sludge penetrated her clothing, and her body became chilled. She felt completely encased in the obscurity of the cavern; it held her and invaded every inch of her body. Her skin crawled with uneasiness.

The bridge was so narrow that she felt safer sliding her hands forward instead of picking them up as she moved ahead. As she dragged her hands across the surface, a buildup of slime pooled across the tops of her fingers and oozed over the side of the bridge. The excess slime splattered far below as it poured down into the blackness.

A gust of air blew up from beneath the bridge, along with a strong smell of ammonia. She gagged. The dense odor turned her stomach sour, and her mouth watered. It was difficult to hold back retching as the stench was overwhelming. She began to breathe through her mouth, and within a minute, she reached the other side. She flicked her light on to finally get a view of her surroundings. Pink tinted slime seeped from the walls and glopped from the ceiling in long, thin streams like drool from a hungry canine.

The floor gradually descended a few meters. With haste, she moved to the wall at the bottom and noticed the opening; a dim, yellow glow peaked through. All the thoughts and feelings that had overcome her earlier were gone. Her heart skipped a beat.

Without a second thought, she quickly placed her hands into the opening and felt around. There was a slime-coated box inside. She pulled it out and swiped her hand across its surface, smearing away the ooze and revealing a transparent container. Inside, suspended directly in the center, the yellow orb glowed bright like a joyous child.

She could feel the tickle and warmth of a life-like force radiating from around it, almost as though it longed to be removed from this tomb. Her fingertips tingled, and the sensation jittered down her arms and swirled up her spine and to her head. A surge of energy and clarity filled her body. She felt as if she could run faster than ever, jump higher, and push harder. The orb was calling her, beckoning her to join it. There was a wailing voice in her mind . . . *Here . . . I'm here . . . I'm here.* Her head began to throb; she had to put the box down, but she couldn't.

She snapped a glance behind her as a wet sucking and smacking sound echoed out from the bridge area. *What the heck was that?* She needed to leave, but what was that strange noise?

As she cautiously approached the bridge, she heard it again, but louder and nearer this time. Ahead of her was blackness. She thought of her light, she was not supposed to shine it down there, but now she was leaving and needed to satisfy her curiosity.

She approached the narrow bridge carefully, keeping her light high, and casting the beam across it . . . *nothing*. Her heart raced; *What could that be out there?* She pulled up the slack from the line behind her as she crouched back down to cross the bridge. She secured the box in her backpack to hide its light and free her hands.

As she started across the bridge, it was quiet until the sucking sound returned; this time it was shockingly loud and directly beneath her. She slid quickly to the other side and stopped. Curiosity was driving her mad. She carefully pulled her light back out and tilted it down into the depths below.

Red, wavy limbs of algae slinked across the bridge and up the walls, encompassing the entire area beneath her. It drew itself into the direction of the light, and it began to twitch. Its reaction to her light set it into a frenzy, and its movements became rapid. All at once it leaped up from below like boiling grease disturbed with ice. It stuck to the underside of the bridge and splashed upon the walls around her. Its tentacles forked downward at Kerriah in a striking pose. She quickly and firmly tugged the line.

"Pull me up . . . pull me up!" Her frantic voice left no doubt for her companions above that she was in trouble. Her face was mere inches from the red algae before the line snapped her up in short, quick tugs. Beneath her, the flapping and burbling of the algae followed close. She could feel the whips and strikes of the wet algae spinning in her direction. "Faster!"

The tugging turned into a chopping motion, and she moved upward at a greater rate yet; the sound of the algae seemed to keep pace. The tense dropline groaned with each upward jolt, as its limits are tested. Then, a hot spike stabbed into her heel, sending a surge of heat throughout her body. Her face grimaced and her chest arched forward in pain.

A wave of yellow pulsed from her pack, filling everything in her view for a brief moment. *The orb?* She felt a rush of energy shock through her body just before a dim light broke out above her, and she popped up into Creedith's arms.

"Run!" he shouted and took off carrying her over his shoulder at a pace only an Andor's long, muscular legs could achieve. The staunch Andor hadn't seemed to have lost any of his speed in his older years. He pulled ahead of the group, who all fled in a panic up the steep pass. A crimson wave blasted from the hole with the force of a geyser and swirled in their direction behind them. Krath, with his heavier build, tromped further behind everyone like a clunky piece of machinery.

The red algae splattered onto any object in its path, sputtering and whisking from rock to rock at a frightening pace as it advanced toward its intended feeding source. Creedith and company reached the top of the pass and paused for only a moment to get a fix on their pursuer.

For an instant, there seemed to be a comfort of silence before Krath leaped up yelling from below, "Get movin', tya fools. This thing is agitated!" He had a wheeze in his voice as he chugged forward like an old Nathasian rail train. The red algae swirled and sloshed close behind him. The group sprinted over the rocky landscape.

"To the booster craft," Creedith shouted as he picked up his pace and reached the vessel well ahead of the others. He placed Kerriah down and brought it online with forward momentum.

"Hey, wait!" Kerriah waved her arms and limped after him, but he sped forward without her.

The others prepared to board the craft as he approached, but he waved them to the side while gaining his speed into the oncoming algae. Like two rail carriers on a collision course, Creedith did not waiver. Krath, being the closest to the algae, dashed to the side to avoid getting plowed over at the last possible minute. Creedith ran to the rear and dove off the backside. Within a split second, the vessel splashed into the wave of algae. It swallowed the crude ship and swirled around it, momentarily satisfied with its meal.

Creedith fled, waving and shouting. "Keep moving and don't look back!" The group followed him as he led them further away. This predatorial organism would only be temporarily content with the provided sacrifice.

They ran until they were completely exhausted before stopping deep inside a low-lying creek bed. They took some time to regain their stamina.

Burling slid his helmet's visor back to take some deep breaths. "I still can't decide if you lost your mind back there or had a stroke of genius. I think maybe both as now we have no transport back and are stranded here with no rations."

Creedith took no offense to the remark and gave a calm reply. "The organism would never have yielded its chase until it was given what it was hungry for. The sacrifice of the booster craft was necessary to provide us a chance at survival, even if that appears austere at this point." He arose slowly, patting the dust from his weary legs and chest. "We should be closer to the northern tip of the Sea of Tora; if we head southwest near the coast, we should be able to get to the other side and back on a trajectory route to your spaceport, although we will still be far north of it."

Burling slid his visor back down and scanned their southern direction. "We will likely succumb to dehydration long before. We will have to give ourselves up to a simple hope for a chance miracle along the way." He pumped his fist in motion for his unit to fall in behind him. They unenthusiastically pulled themselves up, grasping their rifles. "Let's get a move on it as time is not on our side here," he commanded and then turned quickly around as if he forgot something critical. "You did acquire the orb, correct?" he asked, looking at Kerriah.

Creedith stepped between them. "Of course, she has it."

Burring continued ahead. "Good."

Creedith helped Kerriah up to her feet, who had been sitting silently with her head down. "You have been unusually quiet and still since you acquired the orb. Are you okay?" he said in a low, gentle voice, trying to keep his inquiry private. She shook her head and swiped away the sweat-soaked hair from her cheek.

She got up slowly. "Yes . . . I'm okay, just want to get off this world and find Crix." Creedith placed his arm around her shoulder, and they followed behind the others, the orb still hung suspended in her carry sack. She stepped with a slight limp but labored on to keep her injury concealed.

CHAPTER 5

As they approached the southern tip of the Sea of Tora, they found themselves fortunate to avoid most encounters with Thraxons or Marcks, even though there had been some passing units and nests. Burling was a brilliant leader and almost instinctively found optimal cover for the group and quietly dispatched hostiles that crossed their path. Watching him and his unit work was impressive, and one could certainly understand how they achieved a seemingly impossible feat such as infiltrating the heavily guarded world of Nathasia. However, their lips cracked, and their throats burned from dehydration. They knew that despite their prowess in evading the Marcks and Thraxons, their chances of gaining a way off Nathasia were scant.

Occasionally, Burling would slide his helmet off before squinting his eyes closed and pinching his fingers across the bridge of his dry, coarse nose. The last time he did this, his drawn face glared up at the rusty sky for a few minutes. He closed his eyes and stood quiet as if praying to a god that seldom received his attention. Drawing from every strength and faith he had within, the old soldier kept his poise. His team needed their leader, and his body would have to fail before he would give in.

Krath growled as he raked his hands across his shoulders and down his arms. The burning and itching felt as if Solaran cave mites scurried across them, biting into his flesh up to his neck. Dried layers of skin flecked and peeled away with each passing scratch of his calloused fingertips. He casually shrugged off the discomfort and gave a relaxing glance at Commando Roden before providing him with a friendly smack across his back as he passed by. Roden's tall, slender frame stumbled two steps from the impact and then waved his hand up in a friendly gesture to his oversized companion. Krath loved being a part of a military team once again.

Moving down the southwestern coast, they reached the remnants of a fallen port city. What remained of its tall, narrow buildings curled down at their peaks as if weeping over the devastation below. The team decided to stay outside of the city's main streets and closer to the outlying structures for cover.

Kerriah couldn't help but feel drawn down physically, as she should, but this was unusual for her. Lack of water or food was something she would endure longer than most, yet she felt depleted far more than anyone else in the group. She tried to take her mind off the fatigue and engage Creedith in a discussion.

"Captain Creedith, correct?" Up till now, she hadn't referred to him by his former rank.

Creedith looked over at her and nodded slowly.

"Thanks for saving me, though I'm not surprised given everything I have heard about you. You certainly have a name for yourself. I recall during your campaign that you had more confirmed Thraxon kills than anyone else in either Thraxon wars up to that point." She paused to wince in pain and clinch her thigh. Her muscles felt sore and stiff. The view around her spun and shuddered. She squeezed her eyes closed for a second to regain focus.

"Child, are you okay?" Creedith took notice of her clear signs of exhaustion and discomfort.

"I'm fine." She waved his concern off. He furrowed his brow, tilted his head, and then continued walking. "After the Marcks took over, all I recall hearing about you was that you were a traitor that turned on Tolagon Emberook and murdered him and his family. Obviously a political lie since his child is Crix."

Creedith remained quiet and did not reply. He would not spend the energy explaining himself to anyone. To him, there was no purpose unless there was truth to it, just senseless babbling and wasted thoughts.

Kerriah picked up on his unwillingness to talk. Instead, she just offered her thanks out of respect for the old warrior. "I understand your reluctance to discuss it, but I want to thank you. You deserve better than you were given." Creedith cracked a tiny smile from the corner of his mouth. Though he would not speak of it and was in no mood for idle discussion, he appreciated the honor and thanks.

Creedith's thoughts couldn't help but wander back to visions of the brutal campaign that he took part in on this tortured world. Images flashed in his mind of a world filled with green and blue, one with its industry living in harmony with nature. Buildings and homes were perfectly nestled amongst trees and caressing lakes. Its citizens lived with a spirit of freedom and confidence. Yet the Thraxons had ripped this perfect place to shreds by the time his Vico Legion had arrived.

The beauty of this place rapidly turned into what they observed here today. Death, toxins, wastelands barren of its natural lifeforms, it was a world turned into a hellish nightmare. The surface was now jagged and charred, and the air smelled bitter. There was nothing hospitable in this world. He was there, in the beginning, to witness much of its destruction. He clenched his fists as he walked, staring forward with a concentrated gaze. The memories would always haunt him, constantly squeezing his soul; it left him feeling empty. The memories of its children . . . the ones they failed to protect along with their mothers, fathers, and grandparents.

"Captain Creedith? Are you okay?" He heard Kerriah's voice breaking through his thoughts. "Creedith?"

"Yes . . . Yes, I am okay child."

"Okay, then. It's just that you looked like you were about to get sick and maybe even pass out."

"No need to worry about me. I just have too many memories in this place, and very few of them pleasant. The ghosts here have filled me to the point of saturation."

The continued discussion worked, and she felt a little better. Her thoughts left regarding her own suffering and now focused on Creedith. "I can imagine that given—" Kerriah stopped.

A sudden flash of red glistened off a nearby building and then flickered into the shadows. Kerriah placed her hand against Creedith's large chest to halt him as she remained focused on the area around the dilapidated structure. Then a steady red glow ascended overhead and faded quickly into the shadows.

"Did you see that?" She tried to get the attention of one of the commandos nearby. Before she could, the red glow returned. It flickered quickly and then dissipated again.

There was nothing that would produce this sort of light in the area as she looked around prudently for its source. Dust and loose debris whisked up from the ground, and the winds whistled through the buildings . . . nothing. She had never been one to miss things or see things that weren't there before, yet these mysterious red flares had her off her normal certitude.

"Sir . . . my sensors are detecting a strong power surge nearby, and not from any of us," one of the commandos called out to Burling as he swung his energy detection probe around in a futile attempt to pinpoint the location. The probe's sensors pulsed white to blue faster and faster as the energy reading intensified.

"The Tolagon?"

"Possibly. I can't get a fix on it . . . It's moving too fast."

A deep crimson glow seeped from behind Kerriah and flooded the area beyond like a wave of blood engulfing the air. She turned to look, only to find piercing black eyes staring straight back into hers. A striking female stood before her with onyx hair that wisped like silk in the air, glistening off the crimson hue from her body. Beneath the glow were dozens of strips of liquid. The strips

59

curled and twisted around her skin, then poured to the ground around her. The entirety of her gown stirred across her body and shimmered like water.

Kerriah froze with caution, and the fiery female said nothing. Instead, her eyes glanced over her, sizing her up. The others took notice and fell in behind Kerriah with weapons held firmly at the unknown figure. The woman responded to the group's defensive posture by stepping her right foot back and then crouching down.

"Don't move!" Burling shouted as she raised her hands forward. A crackling sound echoed through the amber glow of the waning daylight, followed by a gust of sulfur.

Kerriah maintained a calm appearance until the ground began to tremble. Blood-tinted spectral figures surfaced amongst them, each giving off an unnatural groan as they poured up from the rocks. The featureless forms were strategically positioned around the group. Their faces had no discernible markings, but somehow, their stare gave the sense of someone screaming without being heard.

A sense of horror momentarily froze everyone in their tracks as their minds tried to process the scene before them. The specters lumbered inward; one of them seized a commando from his flank and effortlessly slammed him into the petrified surface as two others ripped at his body with their hands, peeling off armor and shattering his bones.

"Careful . . . she appears to have possession of the red orb of Solara!" Creedith warned the group after identifying its power based on Commander Corin's description from many years ago.

Kerriah only mildly heeded his warning, having never encountered an orb bearer before, aside from Crix. She took a sweeping kick at the female, but her target flashed away in a blink. Kerriah's neck tingled and clenched as the orb bearer reemerged behind her. With one arm locked behind her back and her throat clamped shut, Kerriah choked and gagged. Her eyes bulged as she struggled to break free of the powerful grip. She could feel her arm dislocating and her knees gave way. While she struggled with the red woman, the featureless minions attacked her companions.

Krath sailed an unforgiving punch into the head of one, only to find a stone slab. Its head shattered into fragments of red, which remained airborne, floating and swirling over its shoulders. Krath winced while clutching his hand as the particles from the head reshaped. Agitated, he snarled as the elemental aggressors continued their hostile advance. The commandos scattered about, firing their blasters into the lurching figures. Sections fractured away as their shots connected, only for their crimson limbs to fully reform themselves within seconds.

Creedith scaled a partially dilapidated wall to get the high ground on his attackers. Burling took an evasive roll into a nearby pile of old, charred metal.

"They appear to be impervious to our attacks!" his voice chirped through his helmet's com. "The only positive is that they are slow-moving. Try luring them into a tight group so we can lob some thermals!"

Creedith pounced down on his three assailants, knocking them from their footing. He grasped two by their legs and slung them nearby one of the commandos. They crashed into a pile and then immediately started to pick themselves back up.

"Krath . . . I require your assistance," he called over to his Hybor comrade.

"I got it, buddy!" Krath reached down and pulled the legs out from one and tossed it into the pile. Its flailing body knocked over the others as they began to get back up. Krath and Creedith were the only ones with enough strength to throw the ethereal beasts as they were heavy and formed partially from the loose ground rock. The two old soldiers snaked around their assailants, distracting them and taking advantage of their lumbering reflexes and slow adjustments.

Kerriah collected what remained of her inner strength and took a knee before rolling forward, sending the crimson female flailing beneath her. She broke free of the red woman's debilitating grasp, giving her a moment to escape. Rearing back, the female shot herself forward, underestimating Kerriah's reflexes as she spun clear of the attacking advance. Having fully committed her attack, she missed her target, crashing into nearby wreckage with a jarring force. Nearly unfazed, she stepped out of the shaken debris, ready to fight. Red gasses appeared to blaze from her eyes, and she stepped forward with her fists clenched. With the backside of her hand, she wiped away an open cut from her cheek while keeping an intense focus on Kerriah.

As Krath and Creedith finished, the pile grew high with featureless beings.

"Get clear!" Burling ordered as he drew a disk-shaped thermal grenade out of his sleeve and gave it a pinch and light tap before flinging it into the pile. The disk glided smoothly into the center of the heap. As it made contact, it sparked a blinding glow and an eardrum piercing shriek as it detonated. The figures drew inward before blasting outward into tiny, burned fragments that whisked away with the breeze.

As the air settled, the group emerged from their cover and began to move slowly with their rifles drawn and fists clenched. The red female's face cringed at the sight of her exploded minions. A yellow flash pulsed from Kerriahs pack, and she felt an immense surge of energy. Without a pondering thought as to what was happening to her, Kerriah took advantage of this unexpected jolt and made a blindsiding charge into the woman. She tackled her midsection and sent her caving to the ground.

As the two struggled, the smell of sulfur wisped up again, and a multi-directional breeze swirled strangely around them. The air felt as though a silky scarf draped across Kerriah's neck. She tried to ignore it as she fought to maintain control of her adversary, but the feeling around her neck stiffened and tugged her off the red female.

All around, the air transformed into birds of prey, each with four wings and long, whipping, snake-like tails that coiled up. These vaporous apparitions blazed red with a ghostly appearance. Dozens hissed and swooshed, dipping down and back up again, swirling their tails around the group, threatening and slicing at them with beaks and talons.

Kerriah gripped her fingers beneath the tail firmly clenched around her neck. As she tightened her grip, her fingers seeped through the tail, causing her to lose her grasp. The red female stood arrogantly back and observed her creations taking their toll on the group. As she paused, her creations became more agile and swift.

Creedith swatted and flailed at the spectral birds as though fighting off bloodthirsty Draylok steed flies as they gnashed and whipped their tails. His actions were fruitless, and it wouldn't be too long before they would eventually tire and fall prey to these airborne marauders.

"Torch them!" he yelled out to Burling, who was occupied with his attackers and failed to respond.

Creedith shouted out louder. "Burling! Use your incinerators!"

"Roden! Your scorcher!" Burling ordered.

The commando drew out his secondary weapon, a rifle that projected outward with four small, pointed nozzles. It came to life with a hiss as he flicked a switch that opened the fuel canisters and released their deadly mixture.

"Blast the air around them," Creedith shouted. The red orb manipulated the natural elements and created the birds from the air; therefore, displacing the oxygen might do the trick.

Roden quickly aimed at his attackers. The nozzles whirled around in a circle, giving off a continuous whine. A hiss was followed by a squeal that cut loose from the scorcher as a blue flame blasted out and consumed the wraith-like birds. Roden swooshed the incinerating flames around until there was no longer any visible threat. The rest of the group ran to break enough distance between themselves and the elemental birds for Roden to safely flame the area, depriving each of their essences and dispersing their gaseous vapors.

A dull chunk of rusted metal sat embedded in the crusted soil near Creedith's feet. Determined to stop the red assailant before she could unleash anymore of her minions upon them, he tore it from the ground and heaved it in her direction. At the same time, he barreled forward like a raging Solaran cave bull. The metal chuck spun directly toward her. She flashed away from the oncoming projectile and then gracefully pushed aside Creedith's oncoming charge. She was too fast, even for him. All around them, the ground shook, and more of the shapeless stone minions emerged, as well as additional winged attackers.

The assault ensued once again. The red orb-bearer glowed with crossed arms, her eyes lit like fire with intense satisfaction as she observed the demise of her adversaries. It seemed an inevitable end for the group as they slowly succumbed to their fleeting stamina.

From high above, a distant whistling approached, shrieking in louder and louder with every second. A blue light emerged, washing out the red. A bolt of blue lightning sent the crimson female mercilessly crashing into the rocky surface below. The impact scattered her creations into their previous inanimate elemental states. A familiar, dusty figure with a bluish glow pulled the limp, unknown, orb-bearer up by her collar. Her fluid dress dissipated, and her black hair draped down peppered with Tolagon white.

"Crix!" Kerriah's tired eyes lit up. The fatigue instantly slipped away from within her when she saw him again. Crix placed the unconscious red woman down and ran to Kerriah's embrace. The two clung together; he held her tightly and sensed her beating heart against his own, and she felt the tickle of the blue orb within him. Her eyes fixed on his, and she was overjoyed. They both felt the intensity of one who has reclaimed a lost love.

"Awww . . . how about tat?" A wide grin crept across Krath's face.

Crix felt a strange sensation warm over him. His skin tingled and went numb. For just a flash, he thought his nose and cheeks had a more pronounced profile with a pale brown reflection.

She pushed away and stared directly at him. "If you ever pull something like that again . . ."

He shook off the sensation and the numbness faded away. "What? You mean . . . get caught by the bad guys?"

"No . . . well, yes. I mean, don't disappear without telling me where you are. I was about to shake the entire system upside down looking for you." It was at that moment that Crix knew they had something, the type of thing that you fight for, that you would without hesitation give up everything else just to hold on to. He looked at her with a smile that could not be wiped away, with a twinkle in his eyes and thunder in his chest. She caressed his hair, taking notice of the Tolagon white hairs that fully encompassed his head. Having him back was like being wrapped in a warm blanket. He was everything that she needed at this moment.

"By the way, how did you escape?" Creedith's voice sliced into the bliss of their reunion.

Crix looked at him differently than before. *Zearic said Creeth. Could it be him?* His piercing eyes had hundreds of questions behind them. He slowly pulled his hand across the top of his head, recalling the painful experience that was still fresh in his mind.

"I got to meet our buddy Zearic, and well . . . let's just say he may have underestimated me a little. I don't think I'm going to get that luxury from him ever again." He gave Kerriah's arms a gentle rub. "Though I'll have to confess that well-timed power failure helped me out. It was brief, but just what I needed."

"Power failure?" Burling asked.

"That's right. It was only for a couple of seconds, which was all I needed for that orb energy deflecting device to de-energize."

"My bet is that's when our EMP missile hit. We used it to disable the planetary shield just long enough for us to SPOD in. It was a risk, of course, as we knew their redundant systems would kick in after a few seconds. I'm glad it was able to assist you as well."

"It certainly did. And you are . . . ?"

"My apologies for the lack of introductions. Commando Burling and these well-trained soldiers are my extraction team. Of course, our extraction turned into an ill-advised treasure hunt, and that's what brings us on this side of the Sea of Tora."

"Well, thanks for helping my friends, and I'm glad I found you guys. It looks like you needed my help." Crix spun around to see the unconscious red orb bearer behind him, his eyes wide with curiosity. "Who is that, and why does she have an orb?"

Kerriah's brow furrowed. "We're not exactly sure. How did you find us?"

Crix shrugged. "It was a combination of favorable timing and some luck, I suppose. After my escape from Zearic, I had to hide and keep my orb usage at a minimum to avoid detection. I eventually found an external service hatch that I could escape the station from. I could hear Zearic's screams of rage and the march of Marck guards for what felt like days before I finally made a quick exit through an airlock using an orb bubble as my escape pod. Lucky for me, it was a low-orbiting station. I'm glad I was able to locate you guys and catch a glimpse of your trouble. I just nudged my trajectory a little to help." Crix's voice began to quiver as he told his story. His mind was still reeling over the realization that they were all together and still alive.

Creedith's brows rose. "Crix . . ." His voice was stern and commanded attention. "You said you were able to locate us during your escape. How exactly did you locate us?"

Crix suddenly looked as though he spotted a ghost. His face dropped and his jaw went slack as he realized that Zearic also knew where they were. He became short of breath as he explained.

"Their sensors were sending alarms all over the station of an orb signature. At first, I thought it was my own but then discovered that it was from the planet below. That's how I knew you were still alive and recovered the yellow orb. The commotion from all this is what distracted them enough for me to make a bold move. I waited until I could drop down on their sensors locked in position. I must have been lucky again . . . or was it . . ." He squinted and shook his head. "No!" He frantically pulled Kerriah away, looking for cover. "We need to hide!"

"Let's get moving, and f—" Burling was unable to finish his statement before Commando Trayco interrupted.

"I'm detecting massive movements encroaching on our position from every direction." He paused to pan the area using his helmet's enhanced visor sensors for movement. Burling snapped into a ready stance. The stalwart leader motioned the others to take cover.

"Trayco, do you have a visual yet?"

"Negative, sir, they are closing in quickly though."

"Of course, with the orbs and all the commotion we just finished with, I'm surprised the whole Thraxon and Marck fleets are not bearing down on us right now," Kerriah said, frustrated with their situation. She continued to wince with pain and clenched her ribs as well as her leg.

"It might be," Crix's voice cracked. His stomach retched at the thought that he might have led them back to his friends after his abrupt escape. "I should have—" Kerriah placed her hand gently over his mouth. She noticed the unwarranted guilt in his face.

"It sounds like they had found us already. I'm just happy you're here, eh . . . errrahhh." She buckled over, clenching her side. Crix clasped his arms around her, catching her before she could fall to the ground. Once again, the numbness crept over his skin, and he noticed his nose and cheeks changed in his view.

He ignored it. He was more concerned about Kerriah. "What? What is it . . . What's wrong?" Crix gently placed her down into a sitting position, and the numbness cleared again. Creedith galloped over and briefly gave Crix a strange look before crouching down to look into her eyes; they were dark red.

"The red orb bearer?" he asked.

Kerriah shook her head. "No . . . I haven't felt right ever since my foot was bitten back in the well."

"The algae?" Creedith turned her foot over and found a tiny hole in the bottom of her boot heel. He pulled her boot off, revealing a blood-soaked heal with an accompanying hole. He dropped his head in thought and uneasiness.

"The algae that I found there was attracted to energized hardware; it never appeared interested in anything organic. Because of this, the algae-infested well turned out to be the perfect place to hide the orb from the Marck forces. I returned to the site shortly after transporting Crix to Troika as I needed to ensure the orb site wasn't discovered. The algae attacked me, and I was nearly suffocated by it until I shed off all the armor and supplies I was wearing and carrying. Most of which were integrated with powered circuitry that attracted the algae, so metal became its target, not me. I was simply in its way. Perhaps it has evolved to broaden its palette for survival. I believe the leviathan we encountered in the sea may have been an evolution of this algae. This is now a world weary of its former self."

Kerriah slowly looked up at Creedith while gripping her foot, trying to stave off the pain. "Why wouldn't it have attacked the orb?"

"I'm not sure."

CHAPTER 6

Burling grabbed Creedith tightly by the arm. "We have to get her back now; that's the only chance she has to survive!"

"Movement! Movement everywhere!" Trayco fell back with his weapon drawn to his shoulder.

"Fan out into defensive positions," Burling ordered, preparing for whatever was coming their way. Hissing sounds whispered from above and eerie figures seeped through the murky sky. Around them, Marcks mounted upon hover disks and Thraxon warriors in propulsion packs dropped into view, too many to count. The Thraxons were unfamiliar, with eyes that glowed and silver limbs that glistened in the darkness while the rest of their black bodies camouflaged against the gloomy backdrop of fog and toxins. The unwelcomed gathering stopped and remained stationary a short distance from the group.

Pilar swung her rifle's optics across the vast range of adversaries. "How come they're not attacking us?"

"Silence yourself. Just keep your weapon targeted on the nearest threat and be prepared." A burst of sinister laughter echoed in the distance.

"Oh no!" Crix whispered loudly.

"Do you know something here that we are unaware of, boy?" Creedith asked while remaining still as possible and focused on his surrounding adversaries.

"Let's just say I recognize that voice, and that's not a good thing." Creedith gritted his teeth and shot a glance at him.

Scores of Thraxons fanned out across the horizon made way as Zearic thrust through atop his chariot-style ship. Dangling below his chariot were dozens of linked arms that snapped and coiled, feeling randomly for something they could grasp and take captive, or possibly worse. Covering his head and eyes but leaving his mouth exposed, Zearic's metallic helmet had a mirror-like polish, which reflected the images of the hoard that amassed around him. His right hand grasped a rod that glowed as he pressed closer to the group. Krath let out a deep growl of contempt at the sight of the traitor. He would like nothing more than to get his hands on that chrome head and bounce it off a few of his Thraxon buddies.

Hovering behind Zearic emerged the red woman, who had returned to consciousness after Crix's pouncing blow. She had awoken without notice during the excitement of the last few minutes, her eyes blazed with fire and her jet-black hair floated through the energized air around her. It was uncertain what level of control Zearic had over her, but for now, she sided with him and his scheme to control the orbs for his own immoral will.

"At long last, I have almost everything I've been searching for right here. I do appreciate you locating the yellow orb for me . . . and of course you." Zearic's jaw stiffened as he looked at Crix with contempt and rage; his rod glowed brighter as if emotionally tied to his ire. His last encounter with Crix left him short of his already scant patience. His rigid scowl turned to a slow grin as he turned his attention to Kerriah, an iridescent, red light glowed over his right eye hole as it provided a more detailed look.

"Now, this is a pleasant surprise. Before us is a true masterpiece of design from the great biomechanical architect, Joric Placater, his finest work indeed." Zearic's scan of her biological and electrical signatures completed, confirming his suspicions.

"Keep away from her. This is the only warning you'll get." Crix stood in front of her, blocking Zearic's view. His confidence had clearly grown since the beginnings of his journey with the orb.

Zearic ignored Crix's warning; instead, he looked through him as though he didn't exist. "He was wise to keep your true identity hidden. The reverse engineering process of your body will be a great aid to enhance my grand army further, to create the truly perfect species."

Crix began to boil with agitation. His body's blue glow intensified, almost blindingly, and then darkened. "That's enough! As long as I still breathe, you will not touch her . . . ever!"

"You're a minor problem that will easily be corrected. Commander, kill all of them except the female. I want her unharmed." Zearic motioned with his rod to a nearby helmet-wearing Thraxon. Its helmet swooped up from its back and formed into a hook at the top. He drew his rifle to his shoulder, and the other Thraxons and Marcks followed suit. They let out a collective hiss and their black fangs gleamed as they prepared for battle.

"Wait!" Crix shouted and extended his arms with his palms out. He couldn't stand by idly while they were mowed down by the combined Thraxon and Marck firepower. He had to do something. He had to save Kerriah and his friends. "Zearic! If you want the orb, I'll give it up to you, and you can do what you want with me, but let them go."

Zearic laughed as he raised his arm up high to pause his force from carrying out his decree. "You seem to be confused, boy, as you cannot give to me what I am already willing to take from your remains. Though it's undoubtedly a valiant effort that no one will remember, now die!" He lowered his arm, and his surrounding force opened fire in a blaze of light.

Crix swiftly threw an umbrella energy shield over the top of them all and captured the initial shots. He gritted his teeth as he struggled under the flurry of incoming blasts that pounded its surface. They were helpless, trapped like rodents in a box, with only minutes till assured death. They each would have their moment. One last heroic act before the protective shield's inevitable failure, and they each adjusted or firmed their stance in preparation.

Then, with a last-second glimpse into the eyes of hope, a small white portal blinked open nearby. Without a second to spare, Plexo was finally able to get a probe close enough to extend his parallaxer into the dark world. Its reach stretched to the absolute limit and the cloudy portal strobed and shook as if barely stable.

"Plexo!" Krath pointed at the bright, stuttering gateway. The sight of this saving doorway ignited them with courage.

"No! You're not escaping me again!" The chaos of blaster fire mostly drowned out Zearic's voice, though his commands were still heard. Three large, mechanized warriors dropped in front of the portal, blocking its entry. Crix and Kerriah both recognized these warriors as they closely resembled the ones from Merik's secret facility on Dispor. The Marck hybrids were organic at their core with weapons and armor fused into their living mass, each different, and each still showing some remnants of their original self. Green vapors seeped from their connectors and joints with each movement as their pressurized toxins escaped. These were apparent efforts of Zearic's unsanctioned weapon development facilities.

Creedith charged out of the orb barrier with every intention to attack the husky aggressors and then slid to an abrupt stop. Through the cloud of gas and smoke that blew up from the oncoming hail of weapon fire, he noticed something familiar about the leftmost hybrid warrior.

"Corporal Guni?" He squinted, trying to visualize the absence of the metal and synthetics to see the original being underneath. Could this be someone from his old unit?

The hybrid focused on him through optical lenses that replaced his natural eyes. Beneath those lenses wrath swirled and rage flared. He raised a segmented appendage that had an insect-like appearance and pointed it at Creedith.

"So . . . if it isn't the wayward Captain Creedith. I see you've had some enhancements," the hybrid shouted, taking notice of Creedith's genetically attached armor. "You should have joined us for the transmutation when you had the chance. We're more powerful than you'll ever be . . . Captain." He laughed with an almost hollowed voice as his appendage fanned open into a dozen razorsharp whips that swirled around with a frenzied threat. Guni slashed the whips at Creedith, chopping left and right as he approached his target. Creedith ducked and then leaped back to avoid getting diced into pieces.

"That maybe so, but you serve a foolish master, and therefore you are beneath me," Creedith scorned while challenging him to take another swing.

"I can't hold this any longer!" Crix dropped to one knee. The agonizing pain ripped through his spine and streams of sweat poured down his brow and burnt into his eyes. His heart pounded faster than he could ever remember, and he felt the full burden upon the orb's shield. Images of dark places populated by ominous beings with silver skin and black eyes began to flash in his vision. The images became so vivid that he was having difficulty deciphering them from what was happening around him.

"You have to, son; all of us are depending on you to hold steady!" Burling said like a gruff old father encouraging his young boy through a difficult task. "Everyone double-time to the portal!" he ordered the others, but as they approached, the hybrids opened fire with their integrated light pulse cannons.

The ground beneath them came apart, and Crix's shield finally failed, leaving them exposed to an overhead barrage of fire. The mix of smoke, ash, and plasma gas left a thick fog that engulfed them as if swallowed by a great beast. Crix grabbed Kerriah around her waist, shielding her the best he could as he charged toward the flickering dim light of the portal.

Using his Bracix-clad arm to block and grasp the spinning whips, Creedith snapped his attacker forward. The hybrid, bulky with armor and weapons, toppled over from the jarring motion. Creedith twisted and drove his shoulder into the other second adversary, sending him and his cannon fire spiraling in every direction. Krath jumped atop the grounded hybrid as he attempted to recover and gave it another stomp down for safe measure.

A hail of plasma blasts ripped through a commando, and another shot seared Creedith's right leg. He wailed and then stammered over to the remains of the dispatched hybrid and heaved it toward their attackers. The incoming spiraling corpse provided a momentary distraction to the onslaught, allowing for Crix and Kerriah to limp through the portal. Burling and the remaining survivors of his team dove through just as the portal started to blink and strobe. Krath charged up to the portal opening and then stopped for a second to observe Creedith still wrestling with one of the hybrids as the Marck and Thraxon forces closed in. Shots blasted into his enhanced Bracix sides, and they began to pulse with illumination as they absorbed the incoming spikes of power. The pulsing power quickly receded into pinpoints and fired back at the attackers. The energy deflecting armor that Merik built onto his body was proving itself to be an effective deterrent.

Krath stood at the mouth of the flickering portal, waving with intent. "Come on, buddy!" Creedith had his arms around the neck of one of the Thraxons, its black teeth gnashed and boney fingers tore at his jaw to break free of his grasp.

"Go! Just go before it's too late! I have this, now go!" Creedith yelled; the portal went dim then flashed open. Krath couldn't reach him in time. He stopped and took a moment to give one final salute in respect to his old comrade before leaping into the portal seconds before it blinked closed.

CHAPTER 7

The blinding light inside Plexo's ship sent Krath's vision into a white haze for a few minutes before he started to see distinguishable shapes form around him. "Where's Creedith?" Crix's voice cried out from the behind the opaque blur. Krath squeezed his eyelids shut for several seconds. "Where is he? I thought he was following you!" He had just found him, and now he was gone. Creedith must have slipped through the portal? His eyes welled with tears. Crix still had so many questions. He needed to learn more about him, who his father was. Was it him? Deep inside, he knew the answer already, which made the pain of this loss so much worse.

He stood over Krath as he lay upon the cold, hard floor. Krath lifted his head slightly to speak, though he was too exhausted to get up. Plexo handed them the light-filtering eyewear needed to see clearly in his ship.

"Boy . . . Creedith . . . he . . ." He stopped to finish catching his breath and his words. His tongue swelled from dehydration, and his throat stuck like paste with every swallow. His body looked like a withered sack of vegetables as he propped himself up on his elbows, wincing, searching for the words Crix needed to hear.

"He's a true warrior through and through. Warriors prevail, they make sacrifices, they inspire us, they kick the backsides of their foes, and sometimes they fall. Creedith did all these things today, and he always will be a true friend of mine. I'm sorry, son, but he's gone." He slowly laid his head back down and his eyes teared up.

Crix dropped down on Krath's abdomen with his knees and pulled his shoulders up by his garments, with his fist clenched around his collar. Crix screamed his frustrations in Krath's face. "No . . . no . . . no! You were supposed to come through with him! Why didn't you? Why didn't you pull him back through? It's your fault! Your fault!" Krath growled and swatted Crix away with one big swoosh of his arm.

"Back off! I know ty're hurtin', but I'm hurtin' too. Don't tya let this out on me. Creedith was the best warrior I have known, and he made his choice. Tya have to live with these losses. Get used to it 'cause there are more comin'," he barked sharply at Crix, who had caught himself by one arm before nearly getting slammed back into the floor.

Crix looked back at him and scowled. "You don't understand . . . he was . . . he . . ." He shook his head. "Never mind." He was weary of explaining something that would likely invoke too much inquiry. He turned his attention back to Kerriah.

"Plexo! What happened? Why didn't tya answer us when you picked us up in that old UMO corvette? And how the heck did we end up in the hands of honey armed Thraxons? I hate Thraxons!" Krath shouted, pointing his dried, plump finger at Plexo.

81

"I am truly sorry about all this. It wasn't my ship that collected you outside of Dispor. Another ship got to you minutes before I arrived. I believe it was a vessel that was already stationed nearby. Perhaps one reserved for Dispor's official use or as the warden's personal transport. Nonetheless, it was a miscalculation on my part. However, I was able to track it back to Nathasia. That's how I found you."

Krath let out a grumble and settled down. He was too fatigued to carry on about it any further. Marcks, Thraxons, and Zearic embodied all the things that boiled his blood, and they all had been shoved in his face over the past few days. He started thinking about the snarl in his belly, hoping that Plexo had something edible onboard.

Crix rushed back over to a raised table where Kerriah rested and placed his hand in hers. She gripped it lightly and turned her head to look at him. Her eyes were dim and drawn. Long, light-emitting appendages scanned her body and drew blood samples and tissue for analysis as Plexo monitored the controls. "Is she going to be okay? Tell me you can help her, please. I can't lose her too."

"I will do what I can. However, she does not have a cell structure I am familiar with. Right now, I am introducing some simulated microbes that should eradicate the hostile organism that is attacking her tissue," Plexo replied softly.

"Is that going to work?" Crix's voice cracked as he caressed her palm and kissed her forehead. "I mean, it has to. We can't let her die. I can't lose her." His eyes darted back and forth between Kerriah and Plexo. He had to do something to help her, but what?

"I'm uncertain. It should work. However, it will not reverse the critical damage to her vital organs." Plexo turned around. Somehow his eyes appeared darker than usual against his radiant skin. "I have to make you aware young Emberook, that, at best, I can stop the progression of the parasitic attack and possibly stabilize her, but I'm not equipped nor have the knowledge to heal her. I can only buy some time." He paused and looked deep into Crix's eyes, whose hair matted against his face as streams of sweat poured down his forehead. The young Tolagon was blighted with emotions and didn't want to accept the blaring reality of what Kerriah was, and at the moment, he didn't care either way. Plexo placed his hand over his face and rubbed his eyes for a second before nudging Crix off to the side in private.

"You must understand that she is not like you, me, or anyone else here." Crix lowered his head and stared down at his feet. Though he listened to what Plexo told him, his thoughts wandered out in search of something that would prove all this detail wrong. "She appears to be comprised of a synthetic matter, not organic. She is by all accounts amazing in design. All her cells are an individual, working, logical unit programmed to function in the same way our cells do, trillions of them working in harmony together, performing every single function of a normal living person. Just remarkable, to be certain. I observed this when you were with her last but thought it inappropriate to mention given the tasks ahead. Whoever is responsible for her creation is likely the only one that can save her." Plexo stopped and stared quietly at Crix for a minute.

Crix's jaw locked, and he shook his head. "This can't be . . . this can't be," he whispered through his teeth. He hadn't yet accepted the truth that Kerriah was not who he thought she was. The signs were there from the beginning, he just chose to ignore them.

"When Zearic saw her, he mentioned Joric Placator." Crix remembered Joric's name from his broader teachings in the Andorian Youth Academy. "Do you think he created her?"

"That's quite a possibility. Unlike Zearic's diabolical perversion of technology, she is the work of an artist, someone with a passion for creating life to its perfection. I suspect it's Joric's work."

Joric was the enigmatic architect of the Marcks and their autonomous control system, who vanished shortly before the Marcks were put into official service. The widespread rumors were that the Cloaks assassinated him. The early insurgent group was known by that name for their use of figment cloaks to elude the Marcks on their hit and fade operations.

"But isn't he dead?" Crix asked, dismayed that Kerriah's only hope was already gone.

"That was what we were meant to believe. Although Joric Placator's whereabouts are unknown, he was under the protection of General Gorag of Solara. It was Gorag's Palic Legion that was given the task of overseeing Joric's work. They were to ensure that no ill fate came upon him before the Marck designs were completed, for there were many who wanted Joric dead. The Thraxons had implanted agents deep within our security zones, which were looking to assassinate the person who could turn the tides of the war against them. There were also the Cloaks who wanted him dead for creating what they predicted to be an oppressive force that would one day turn against us."

Burling quietly approached. "Pardon my interruption. I couldn't help to hear the mention of Joric Placator. He is a priority one directive for us to locate and question. We have sent numerous operatives to the Semptor Region of Solara to seek out Gorag for information as to the whereabouts of Joric. Regretfully, all have failed to report back, and contact is lost shortly after their entry into the region. Not only will Joric be able to save Kerriah but he is the only living individual that knows the whereabouts of the Marck Central Core."

Plexo squinted as he turned his attention to Burling. "Could you tell me what you know of Zearic and the MCC?"

Burling nodded. "Okay, sure. Our intel is, unfortunately, thin on this subject, but here is what we do know. As you are likely already aware, Joric Placator designed the MCC to be an autonomous operating system, which would never require an association or support from any living species. This covered the political requirements. As far as the actual design and whereabouts of the system, we have very little knowledge, but the UMO officials at that time put a significant amount of trust in him. They considered him a genius, and his personality scores all came back with the highest level of ethics and moral character traits. So we feel he's not a party in Zearic's plan, and we suspect he is still alive and in hiding somewhere.

"We also know that Zearic does not know the location of the MCC at this time and has worked tirelessly to descramble the complex communication shifts in the Marck control grid. This

Queen of the Marcks is behind the everchanging algorithm and appears always to be two steps ahead of Zearic's efforts."

Crix cleared his throat. "During my encounter with Zearic, he claimed that the queen was his pawn and implied that he controlled her. How is he even communicating with her?"

Burling let out a forceful exhale. "That's where things get tricky. Joric created a special Marck for this purpose. He named it Aron Dealtic after a beloved mentor of his who died before the war. Aron was to be the voice of the MCC and a direct line of communication back to UMO officials. The only problem was that during the transition, they allowed Zearic exclusive access this Marck, and no one has seen it since. I consider that one of the greatest blunders our corrupt political system has ever made."

"Interesting." Plexo slowly tapped his finger on his chin as he gazed upward. "Hmmm . . . What is your proposal?"

"We have a mutual interest in obtaining the whereabouts of Joric from General Gorag. I feel, with the assistance of the Tolagon boy, we may have success where, until now, we've failed."

Crix's weary eyes sparked with enthusiasm. "You can count me in!" he said, jabbing his thumb into his chest. "At this point, I'll do whatever it takes to save Kerriah and take down these Marcks."

Plexo's head dropped with a sigh. "I've seen the same bravado in Corin, and though I had great admiration for him, I was hoping for a more settled existence for you."

"I understand, but you sent us to Dispor."

Plexo slowly looked up, locking his eyes onto Crix. "Yes I did. Though, it was a rescue mission and one that would procure one of the lost orbs. Protecting the orbs is a primary directive of the Tolagons."

"This is a rescue mission. We're rescuing the whole system."

"I know, but it's a military mission. The Tolagons are supposed to represent peace, and that is what the Emissary's of Eesolan had created them for, to create peace. My brothers and sisters formed the stewardship of the Tolagons for that purpose." His eyes darkened and his jaw turned to a scowl. "Instead, they have been used mostly for war and death. It's not right, not the way."

"I'm sorry. What else can I do?"

Plexo raised his palm. "Your father chose you as his successor to the role of Tolagon of Soorak. That was his right as the standing Tolagon before you. If he had fallen before naming his successor, it would have been up to the council of Gabor. Of course, this was not supposed to be, according to the Emergency Preservation Initiative. No more successors were to be named." Plexo let a quick and robust exhale before posting his hands at his hips. "Your father was never one to listen to politicians. I was dearly hoping for a more peaceful role for you, young Tolagon, but the choice is yours, and like your father, I suspect I already know what that choice is."

"Plexo, you know I have to. Kerriah and pretty much everyone is depending on me, and they need me to be this Tolagon.

That's even if it means putting the role of protector ahead of all other virtues that comprise a Tolagon. Besides, I've already been to Dispor, how much worse can this be?"

Plexo returned an approving smile and placed a gentle hand on Crix's shoulder. "Yes, as I said before, the Dispor mission was required for you to recover the lost orb, and as the Tolagon, it was essential. However, I am aware of your feelings as well. I will do whatever I can to provide you with the support you need for your duties."

"Outstanding!" Burling shouted. "A transport is on its way here to pick my team up and take us back to Command Station Orion on Thale. Meet us in the ship's bay in twelve hours for departure. We will brief you on the way."

With a blank face, Plexo slowly shook his head. "There is still one more concern that I have." He smoothed his hand down Crix's sleeve and took a firm grasp of his hand. He rotated it, taking notice of the subtle blue glow. It was difficult to see in the bright ambiance inside his ship, but being a Luminar, he could still see it. "Interesting." He looked back up at Crix and stared into his eyes. "You must not continue to use the orb's power without training from Gabor. It will overtake and kill you. Thus far, you have shown exceptional resistance to the side effects, but I worry over how long that will last."

Crix's lips pursed as he nodded. "I understand. It's a risk I have to take."

Plexo gently let go of his hand. "Certainly," he replied.

Crix returned to Kerriah's side, and Plexo called a stasis seat over for him to rest in. He sat and lowered his head next to her. She seemed so distant now, so far away from him. His mind drifted back to the small pockets of joy they'd had since their turbulent pairing. Their time in Troika when she caressed his cheek, their embrace in Plexo's main lab, the intimate evening before their departure, cuddling tightly up to each other in the depths of Dispor, giving each other warmth and comfort in an otherwise miserable place, and of course their brief reunion at Nathasia. There just hadn't been a time without the company of chaos. No time to relish in her conversation, to look into her eyes, or enjoy each others' companionship. He didn't care if she wasn't normal; what was normal anyway? *I'm not normal.* She was everything he wanted and had always dreamt of, and he would sacrifice anything to save her.

***

A while later, Plexo located Crix, who had been wandering tirelessly around the ship, lost in his thoughts while the others rested. "What are you doing? I would expect you to be exhausted. You should be resting."

"I can't stop my mind from swirling thoughts through my head. It's driving me insane," Crix replied; his eyes darted all around the room. He was wired even though he hadn't slept in days. "I need answers, Plexo. I barely know who I am anymore."

Plexo gave him a concerned stare. "I think I can help . . . at least a little. Come with me." Crix followed him to a chamber that was so quiet he could only hear a soft hum pulsing through his ears. He began to wonder if the humming was from the orb or his imagination. The room was lightly populated with a mismatch of items, as if for study or collection. The yellow orb that Kerriah had acquired from Nathasia also lay suspended in a cube at the far end of the room. The other items sat atop long, narrow platforms and were surrounded by cool, radiant lights, which did not appear to have a source. These lights were bright and in no way acted as an irritant to the eyes, rather the items they illuminated were magnified and made to appear more brilliant.

"The bracer," Crix said as he observed the Tolagon bracer sitting upon a nearby platform.

"Yes, that is one of the things I wanted to speak to you about. I do apologize for my tardiness on getting this information back to you, but the coding on the bracer was tricky to break. It does, however, contain a map, and the signet does not appear to be a signet at all, rather a key. I was never privy to the Council of Gabor or the secrets of the Tolagon order, even though I am a Luminar. My way was always that of science, and I never welcomed the mysticisms that the order invited, so that aspect was kept from me." Plexo gently placed his fingertips on the signet key.

"The bracer is indeed both the map and the key to the secret location of Gabor. Only the Tolagons and the Emissary Three of Eesolan were ever given these or told of its location. The code would have been impossible to crack by any other, aside from a Luminar. Our native language is impossible to speak or decipher by other species. Luminars have many words spoken in tandem with the principals of light that create sounds that cannot be heard."

"So I can go there to find my answers?"

"Answers, yes. Perhaps not the answers you seek, but answers. There is one more thing, but it's going to be difficult to explain." Plexo cringed as if fighting to get the words out, but Crix saved him the trouble since he already knew where he was going.

"I'm an Andor and not actually the blood son of Corin Emberook, I know."

Plexo's eyes twinkled as he tilted his head. "How did you discover this?"

"Zearic told me."

"I see. It is right that you know, but you must keep a clear focus on the tasks ahead of you. This new way you have merged with the orb intrigues me indeed, and if time were permissible, I would be interested in getting some analysis of it. No one has ever bonded to it quite as you have." Plexo stared intensely at the subtle cobalt glow that radiated from Crix's face and hands. "It's as if it fused to your cellular structure, permanently perhaps. It could explain your extraordinary resistance to its fatal effects and how you have become adept at its use with no training."

Plexo slowly stared down for a few seconds as he spoke. "Very strange, indeed. I'm curious why it has done this with you and no others before you." He looked back up at Crix. "My only guess would be your purity, which is quite possibly greater than any Tolagon before you, and the orbs are attracted to this purity. Just as it draws to good virtue, they detract from corruption and evil.

"This is likely the reason for this red woman that you encountered on Nathasia. Zearic and the Marcks must have finally located its hiding place. This woman, whom I must assume is also virtuous, had controlling possession of the red orb and was able to use its powers to attack your group. My guess is this is a situation where perhaps Zearic has, in some way, manipulated her to gain indirect control over the orbs; for if he were ever to attempt to wield the orb, it would almost assuredly kill him. In the early Luminar experience of orb possession, anyone of ill virtues would be destroyed by the orb during their attempts to control it. I'm sure Zearic was aware of this. Then I can't help to inquire . . . who has trained her to use it?"

"That's interesting. I never really considered myself to be virtuous. It's also hard to imagine how that could be, considering that I'm responsible for not only the destruction of Troika and the entire Andor race but also the deaths of all those poor battered souls on Dispor. I still have so many questions, and if there is one thing I could use right now, it's some answers." Crix's shoulders dropped and his eyelids sagged. The room slowly spun around him as fatigue took its toll.

"Don't be too hard on yourself, Crix. In times such as these, we all find ourselves forced into doing things that violate our own conscience. It is something that I have personally struggled with since the start of this awful war. We Luminars have always used our gifts of science for peace and betterment. Yet here I have found myself responsible for more deaths than I would ever want to explain back home. I sincerely doubt I would be welcomed back at this point." Plexo's eyes lowered and he slowly shook his head.

Crix looked at him in shock over this revelation. "I'm sorry, Plexo."

"Don't be."

They both remained silent in their thoughts for a minute before Crix asked his next question. "What of the Tersik crystal?"

Plexo noticeably perked up with interest over the crystal Crix had left with him before leaving for Dispor, the crystal that Suros had placed such importance of the future of Troika on. Crix felt he owed it to his species to unravel this mystery. He took responsibility for their demise, and this weighed heavily on his conscience. It mentally drained him to carry this burden. Now that he had discovered that he was indeed an Andor, restoring this majestic species was of the utmost importance to him, and the Terisk crystal of Mothoa must be that key.

"Yes, of course, the crystal. I was sincerely hoping you would ask about that. This crystal is easily the most intriguing object I've ever had the pleasure of analyzing. To further my earlier remarks regarding the orb binding to you due to your purity, I suspect that this crystal, and your time possessing it, is also responsible. I believe the crystal has played a part in your advanced usage of the orb without any formal training, even though you only had it in your possession for a brief period."

Crix's eyes widened. "Really?" He raised his hand in front of his face to observe the subtle blue glow. "How would that be? I just assumed it was from a lifetime of having it hidden inside me."

"Let's call it scientific intuition at this point. Your purity is the reason for the orb's bond, yes, but there have been other Tolagons pure of heart before you. The crystal is filled with knowledge that is far beyond that of the Andor species. It contains a knowledge that's from another era and not from this system. It holds a power that wants to be unlocked, much like the orbs of

Cyos. It just requires the correct triggers. The brief time that you had possession of the crystal unlocked a characteristic of the orb which we've never seen before. I have been working on finding its triggers."

Plexo stared back at the yellow orb. "At first, I attempted to energize it with numerous power sources, and each time, it would reject that source and subsequently destroy whatever instrument was the origination point. It was quite costly and frustrating for me. It appeared that it was protecting itself from tampering or from the induction of foreign matter. Scanning it or obtaining a visual enhancement was useless as well. It would always disappear under any of the instruments I tried to use like it was cloaking itself in some way. If I hadn't known better, I would have thought it to be alive. I finally walked away from it for a short while, lost in thoughts. Then I took a great risk that paid off. I charged it with the power from the green orb of Thale." Plexo paused briefly and chuckled as if still relieved over the non-disastrous outcome.

Crix's head jutted forward and his jaw went slack. "What?"

Plexo raised his hand. "I know. I have to tell you I was highly reserved utilizing this option, considering what had befallen the other power sources that I tried. I had to know for your sake and my curiosity. So I placed the crystal in direct contact with the orb's power radiance, and it came to life . . . so to speak."

Crix squinted with intrigue and his tired heart started to race. "What do you mean came to life? Can I see it?"

"What I mean is it illuminated, and it was quite alluring, I must say." A wide smile crept over Pexo's face. "As interesting as

94

that was, it wasn't until you arrived with the yellow orb, that things became really interesting!" He stopped, and his eyes darted back to the orb. "My apologies, young Tolagon, but I couldn't wait."

"Wait for what?"

"I had to see if the yellow orb would give the same or different reaction. When I held the crystal close to it, my mind filled with images, fantastic images of an unknown species that somehow thrive in the voids of space and without the aid of technology, along with early periods of Troika and the Andorian race. The images filled my mind so fast I had to step away from it quickly as I was unable to process the magnitude of information, and I began to lose consciousness. I haven't gathered the courage to get within its proximity since, yet at the same time, that's all I want to do. If that makes sense to you?" The deep blue of Plexo's eyes dilated as he stared at Crix.

"Yes! It does. I need to see it!" Crix's tired body quickly straightened up. He was anxious to see what his ancestors had described in tales and ancient lore about the Andor origins and their creator. He needed to see the fascinating images that Suros displayed to him back in the stone forest. There were so many questions to answer; what was his real purpose? The answer must be in the crystal.

"I cannot advise that right now, young Tolagon. Your mission now is far too grave to subject you to something so uncertain and possibly unstable. It's too much to risk right now."

"No! I have to see it now. The answers that it holds may be important for my mission. I have to know who I am and what I'm supposed to be."

"I am sorry. I cannot allow it. There will be a time for this, but it is not now."

"It's not yours to keep from me, and I want to . . . I need to see it; it's for my species and making them whole again. It's my fault they were killed. My fa—"

Plexo raised his hand toward Crix and interrupted his argument. "Think about Kerriah right now. She needs you to find Joric Placator, or she will almost certainly pass. You need to keep your head clear and get some rest if you're to succeed. The risk of you becoming incapacitated in any way could result in your losing her and at a time that she needs you the most."

Crix settled back into rational thoughts. He began to pace the floor and his eyes shone with tears. Plexo was right; Kerriah was the most imminent concern he had right now, and he could deal with the crystal when he returned. Kerriah depended on him, and he couldn't risk letting her down. "I know." He shook his head with a bit of shame and released a strong exhale. He shouldn't have needed a reminder. "I know. She is where my focus needs to be."

Crix's snapped his attention back to Plexo. "Why didn't I have these visions?" The thought suddenly popped into his head. "I have an orb within me, and I held the crystal in my hands."

"Hmm," Plexo paused before answering. "I'm not certain, but I suspect that it has something to do with the yellow orb's power over thoughts and perception. It possesses the perfect key

96

into the mind required for unlocking the vast information this artifact contains."

Crix stepped slowly over to the yellow orb. He wanted to have a closer look at what had cost them so much to gain. Its soft, golden glow was alluring. He could feel the orb within him perk up as he approached. His fingertips tingled and the hairs on his neck stood up. It was as though the blue orb could sense the presence. Crix came closer; the golden glow tinted his face, overtaking his subtle blue radiance.

"Oh my!" The clang of a metal object hitting the floor rattled the still air as a startled Plexo dropped an instrument he was holding. "Crix—"

Crix swung around alarmed. He stared back in utter confusion. Plexo appeared shocked with his hand over his mouth. "What? What is it?" Crix suddenly noticed his pronounced cheeks and wider, ashy brown nose.

Plexo dropped his hand from his mouth, leaving his palm over his chest. He paced around Crix, being careful not to disturb the scene. "Step away from the orb." Plexo took in a slow breath.

Crix patted his hand around his face. It felt different, velvety, and broader. He looked at his hands; they were larger and topped with short, tan fur.

"Please, young Emberook, step away from the orb."

Crix took a careful step forward. His cheeks and nose flashed back to normal along with his fur-covered hands.

"Interesting." Plexo took a step closer to Crix, his eyes darting back to the yellow orb and then back to Crix. He paused for a few seconds as he tapped his chin.

"Plexo, what is happening to me?"

"It now makes sense." Plexo began pacing slowly as he spoke. "Commander Corin used the yellow orb to change your appearance. Its power over thought and perception coupled with the power of the blue orb had allowed him to create a clever disguise that would last for decades, or longer possibly. He never ceased to surprise me, even to this day."

Crix squinted in thought and then looked back at the orb. "I was born on Soorak. So—"

Plexo raised his palm. "Ah, yes, your question has merit. I can explain it. When the yellow orb was located in the Meutor Valley, there was one thing the Commander was certain of; he was not going to allow the orb to fall into Thraxon or Marck hands. He also felt that he was the only one that truly could protect it. When it came time for your birth, he raced home, taking the yellow orb with him. That's when he used it to conceal your identity. The fascinating part of this is when you near its proximity, it temporarily releases its effect."

Lifting the shroud. Is that what Halflinger meant? How could he have known? Crix shook his head and rubbed his eyes to clear his thoughts. "How long will this last? I'm nervous about my appearance changing. With Troika gone, there's no one else like me out there."

"I'm not certain of the length of time that it will last. I can only tell you that it's finite. It could be another day, or it could be years. I'm actually surprised it's still there after twenty years."

Crix stood silent for several minutes. He had to ask someone the question that burned inside him. "Do you think that Creedith is my biological father?"

Plexo drew a deep breath before answering. "He is."

Crix felt dizzy with emotions; his cheeks flushed and goosebumps ran down his arms. "Really? I knew it! It's strange, but somehow I knew it."

"Yes. Shortly after you departed for Dispor, I ran your molecular code against our UMO military databanks for a possible molecular match. I had your code from the scan I had taken of you earlier. To my complete surprise, Creedith came back positive. I am sorry that we lost him before you had a chance to build a relationship. He truly represented the best of any species that I have known."

Crix dropped his head feeling mentally depleted. Could there be any more surprises? Everything felt surreal to him now.

Plexo placed his gentle touch on Crix's arm. "Go, get some rest. Your adventure has still just begun, young Tolagon; I will be here to assist in any way I can."

***

The morning arrived early with Commando Trayco's voice echoing through the hall. "Tolagon Emberook! Tolagon

Emberook! The transport is ready to depart." He dashed into the infirmary where Crix had slept in the stasis chair near Kerriah.

Trayco was short of breath as he entered. He wore his tightly pressed uniform, grey with bright blue accents around the shoulders and ankles. Two black stripes tinted his flesh, peaking over the top of his collar and ending at his chin. The laser imprint represented "top cadet" in his military training.

"Oh good, we've been looking for you. Plexo advised you would be here. The transport is departing in twenty minutes."

"Where is he? Don't tell me he's still in the sack!" Krath's voice boomed in from behind Trayco. He stormed around the corner and nudged Trayco out of the way. "C'mon, boy! Tya got an important mission ta get to. I'm stayin' back here and keepin' an eye on tya girl for ya; don't tya worry. Now get goin' before I pull tya up by your trousers and toss tya into that transport!"

"Thanks, Krath. I'll be there in just a minute."

"K, then . . . get yer little kiss in and get goin'." Krath lumbered back out along with Trayco, leaving them once again with quietness. The only sounds in their room were the occasional chirps of the medical equipment that monitored her health.

Crix waited for a few minutes, caressing Kerriah's hair, brushing it gently back from her eyes as she lay silent. The holographic monitoring systems spiked, rolling colorful graphs and symbols behind him. Her cheeks were sunken, but she still released splendor and beauty from her core. She was fragile and yet exceptionally resilient. He lifted her hand and gently pressed his lips against her soft skin and gave a tender kiss.

CHAPTER 8

The small transport erupted out of the hangar of Plexo's ship on course for Command Station Orion hidden beneath the watery depths of Thale. Burling snapped out of his seat as the ship stabilized into the stillness of space. "How are you doing?"

"I'm fine, just wanting to get on with this." Crix stared blankly ahead, not making eye contact.

"That's the spirit." Burling crouched down next to him.

"There's not a lot of time, as you know. Our sources have positive intel that Zearic is secretly staging a massive assault with a new hybrid Thraxon military, as well as a joint Marck force, against the UMO system council and the local municipalities. He will then enforce a military martial law on the entire UMO system. We fear this move will spell the end for any native UMO species. We will likely be enslaved, converted into a hybrid, or used as Thraxon chow. Our engagement on Nathasia and subsequent escape may have escalated this plan, so we must get ahead of it and locate that Marck Central Core.

"We will be sending you to the Semptor Region of Solara with a few handpicked commandos to infiltrate Gorag's fortress. You will be tasked with using whatever means necessary to gain the location of Joric Placator. Gorag is the only one who knows of his exact location, but he is not known for giving anything to anyone without a heavy price. To make matters worse, no one outside of his most trusted circle can even get near him."

Burling stopped as the ship copilot made his way back and whispered into his ear. He nodded in agreement. His commandos remained seated alongside each other, lined down the side of the transport. Roden was deep asleep, while Trayco, the communication specialist with the auburn-colored stubble, methodically inspected the internal components of his helmet. Trilla, the gruff, dark-skinned weapons specialist, looked down the sites of her rifle for the sixth time before she finally stepped up and placed it gently in the rack above her. The pointy-jawed engineer, Pilar, glanced up and gave a disarming smile before returning to her tweaking of a portable sentry. She spun a small driver until the adjustment clicked and then confidently slid the tool back into her chest pocket.

Crix couldn't help but notice that while Burling was telling him about Gorag, several times, he would look over at Trayco, who would briefly look back up at him. It was like he was waiting for him to say something more. Crix began to get a feeling that Burling was holding back information. He felt a little disconcerted. He should be honored to join this mission but, at the same time, wanted to be given equal respect, even if he was not one of his commandos. He said nothing, though the look in his eyes spoke of the concerns. Burling, shrewd at reading people, let out a deep exhale.

"Look, Semptor is a hostile environment, and Gorag cannot be trusted. What we do know is that there are still remnants of his Palic Legion that have an unwavering loyalty in his service. He was also given a special force of Marcks early on, which was tasked with protecting his efforts until the Central Core construction was completed. This was a top priority, and the only reason the corrupt politicians of the UMO would have ever agreed to give Gorag this authority was that they could ensure that he would comply with the murder of all those who had knowledge of it once it was completed. That's what he is known for . . . murder.

"However, betrayal is also a well-known trait of Gorag, and the UMO paid for it. Once completed, his Marck force was supposed to be released back to the newly minted Marck authority. They were never turned over as agreed. The information we have is they consisted of a full battalion of eight hundred, of which we do not know exactly how many remain today."

"Has anyone seen these Marcks recently, to know they are still actually in Gorag's service?" Crix asked, trying to get a handle on what he was going to be up against and hoping for better odds. Crix rubbed his knees and leaned forward to show his interest in Burling's answer.

"Yes." Burling's face remained straight as he was about to give Crix the details that would scare most away from agreeing to this mission.

"We have sent three separate special operative squads with the same objective, and each time we have lost contact with them shortly after they have reported encountering these Marcks. The environment creates an added challenge for our units: first, the gravity pulls you down at nearly one and a half times your weight, and second, blistering sand and gravel storms will peel your flesh from the bone if directly exposed. If that's not enough, visibility is zero during these horrific storms that occur throughout each day. These Marcks have been specifically modified to withstand this terrain, and his Palic Legion has been born and raised in this Hell. I can't polish this up for you. You're going to have your work cut out for you here."

Crix straightened himself up as Burling had his undivided attention at this point. "So why are we going on the same mission that has failed so many times already? It sounds to me like a suicide mission at best."

Burling cracked a rare smirk from the corner of his mouth, though satirical. *Okay, so this boy needs an ego stroke, does he?* "Son . . . you're the Tolagon here, and we are hoping you can tip the odds in our favor; besides, what choice do we have? You're our last hope in this; if you fail, we are all going to be overrun with Marcks and Thraxons, and we are simply ill-equipped to stop them. That means that everything as we know it is going to end up like Troika, Nathasia, or likely worse. You got me?" Crix stared down and humbly nodded in agreement. His chest felt heavy, but his heart was dedicated to the mission and its outcome.

"Outstanding!" Burling snapped with the virility of a drill sergeant. The ship shook aggressively back and forth as a violent rumble toppled anything not secured.

"Sounds like we just entered the watery depths of Thale," Burling said.

***

After experiencing thirty minutes of shaking and groaning from the ship's hull adjusting to the deep ocean pressure of Thale, there was a deep clonk.

The transport's rear hatch swirled open and a deck slid out, leading to a platform below. Trapped water streamed off to a drizzle around the opening and a damp gust of air drafted in with a sweet, musty odor behind it. Burling and his commandos hopped up and started lining out. Crix remained seated, lost in the thoughts of what was ahead of him.

"This is it, son, our stop," Burling said as he patted Crix's shoulder on the way out. Crix pulled himself up slowly. His mind was so deep in thoughts that he had trouble snapping himself out of it. What is he doing here? It was only a couple of weeks ago that he was living a relatively carefree life running through the woodlands of Hemlor, excited about his next Annexis game. He just wanted to get through this and start a new life with Kerriah, if she'd have him once she discovered his true origins. How could she ever feel intimacy toward him? Could they even have a physical relationship? Would things change between them once he saved her? If he saved her? His thoughts raced, and he could barely regain his focus.

Crix walked down to the platform below. The transport sat amidst a handful of other eclectic ships that were suspended from the walls of the docking area by couplers. Each connected ship had extended ramps to smaller platforms that led to a central deck below. A large pool of water had the appearance of a massive sheet of round glass at the center of the docking area and was the entry and exit point for the ships. Voices and the clanging of tools echoed throughout the sizable, domed area. Moisture trickled sporadically from the ceiling ornamented in patinated copper bands and markings.

Burling stopped and waved him forward. "This way, son, I have someone I would like you to meet." They proceeded through a circular opening outlined by copper triangles that glistened with beads of sweat. The air felt chilled in the underwater lair due to the cold ocean that surrounded them. This command station was deep enough that sunlight did not reach it to provide light or warmth.

From the docking area, they followed a great hall outlined with Hybor statues that stood nearly ten meters, each made of copper and wearing ribbed armor from their ancient world. Their open-faced helms swooshed to narrow points in the back. Their mouths were wide open and facing upward as if swallowing something substantial. Each wielded a long pole weapon with a double sickle-shaped blade on either side. The large hall ended at another domed shaped chamber, which had an opening in the center and a menacing tentacled creature sculpted into the ceiling. The copper creature's sucker-strewn tentacles snaked down the ceiling to an opening in the floor, its gaping mouth opened at the center and aligned perfectly.

At the far end was an older gentleman with a healthy physique. He was seated at a half-circle shaped desk outlined with strangely shaped sea creatures chiseled into its marble structure. He broke away from his viewing of a three-dimensional display that

106

projected up from his desk once he noticed Burling and Crix entering the room. His heavy chair squeaked against the floor as he quickly stood with a pleasant smile.

"What a welcome surprise to finally have the young Tolagon and the son of the much-lauded Corin Emberook here before us. Please . . ." He waved them over toward two ornate, copper chairs that sat in front of the large desk. "Please,have a seat. I am Governor Septin of Teinol. I can't explain in words how honored I am to have you here, Crix. I have already heard some really great things about you. Honestly, your father's reputation alone would have been enough to welcome you here with honor."

Crix felt embarrassed by the fawning compliments and was not quite sure how to take the remarks regarding Corin since he had recently discovered he was not really his natural father. "Pardon me, sir, but I don't feel all that great right now."

"Yes, I know you have had a tough go here with Kerriah's condition, the devastation of Troika, and the unfortunate loss of Captain Creedith . . . We could have used his skill and leadership right now," Septin said with a half shake of his head and a long face. The governor had his own burdens to carry recently, after getting shaken out of his governor seat from corruption and then taken over by an implanted mechanized political figure under the secret control of Zearic. "I had the utmost respect for your father, and I'm positive you're no less the commendable soldier that he was as well."

Septin leaned his backside against the corner of the desk as he continued. "Plexo informed me that he showed you what has become of the township on the outskirts of my great city of Teinol, where there has been a systematic kidnapping of its citizens and replacing them with these hybrid Marck cyborgs. From what we have recently discovered, my city was one of the first to be targeted for this sick plot as we are considered reformist with a free-thinking populace. All these liberties have been robbed of us. Zearic plans to do the same with all UMO populations. On top of that, he has advanced his plans for a full-frontal assault, a military takeover, all while having this pact with the Thraxons of all things."

Septin stopped and his lips quivered before he smacked his fist solidly down upon his desk. He grimaced as if in physical pain, and his eyes seemed to blaze with fury and indignation. "Please, excuse my emotions here. I am tired and frustrated to the breaking point in all this." He turned and stared at the floor.

A silver emblem of a fern reflected off the high collar of Septin's Jacket, and Crix recognized it from one that was subtlety shown in dark grey on Kerriah's sleeve cuff as well as the commando's helmets. "It's okay, I understand," Crix replied.

Septin gave a subdued smile. "Good. We all have to harness our anger right now and use it to fight this war, but at the same time not let it askew our character." He lifted his head and straightened his posture.

"What about the leadership of the Oro System? I mean, why haven't its leaders stood up against Zearic?" Crix asked. To this point, he knew little about the political situation or politics at all.

Septin rubbed his forehead before resting his hand over his mouth for a second. "We were fools, Crix. All of us, fools. We played along as the war turned in our favor, giving Zearic too much power, which was the very thing we wanted to avoid originally. Now he's so deep in the pockets of most or has them working for him under threat that there is scantly a political system left. Realm Chancellor Litten was a good friend of mine, but sadly, he has been murdered by Zearic's cronies. Zearic has managed to keep it secret using holographic images of Litten and faked public transmissions. However, no one has actually seen him in person for some time now."

Crix shook his head, not realizing how bad the situation was until this moment. "That's terrible."

"Yes it is, Crix. Now it's on all of us to make this right."

Behind them, a sudden hissing sound startled Crix, and he swung around quickly for a look. A tired smile crept across Septin's face.

"You're about to get a little show that I have grown fond of and is the reason I chose this as the place where I like to think and work." He pointed to the hole in the floor behind them.

"You see, this is an ancient Hybor temple that was brilliantly constructed in one of the deepest parts of their world. How they managed to build this wonder with the tech they had at the time is a mystery to this day. Anyway, there is a natural underwater geyser that this chamber was built around, and three times each day it blows from that hole and up through that—" He was interrupted by a loud blast of water that shot up from the hole and out through the mouth of the sea creature above.

"Ha!" Septin let out a short laugh in excitement and said, "Still gets me to this day. An absolute marvel and there is simply no other way to describe it," raising his voice above the roar of the gushing water.

After a long minute, the geyser stopped and the focus returned to Septin.

"Commando Burling, you have already briefed him on the task at hand?"

"He has been briefed, sir, and as someone who has witnessed his capabilities firsthand, I personally hang my hopes and confidence with him," Burling staunchly replied.

"Good to hear and I certainly do as well. Do you have any questions for me, Crix? Anything at all? I'll be happy to answer any questions you have to the best of my ability."

Crix straightened himself in his chair. "So is this the resistance?"

"This? It's only a piece, albeit the central piece; all decisions pass through here, and we have designated this as our Command Control, or as you may have heard it referred to as Command Station Orion. Orion is named after the Hybor Orion temple of the ancient world. We have a series of hidden bases, safe houses, and ships spread throughout the local system that forms the resistance. Our numbers include every species, race, and social class that resides in the UMO. Together, we have all chosen to fight the oppressive tyranny of this so-called Marck unification force."

Crix could sense the deep-seated disdain Septin had for the Marcks, and he was one of the earliest outspoken against it. "Alas, our forces are scant and relatively ill-equipped compared to that of the Marcks, and we always stood little chance against them. However, now that a pact has been struck with the Thraxons, there is scarcely hope in stopping Zearic."

Crix rolled his eyes. "Zearic, yeah. What's wrong with that guy? He has some high-end anger issues."

"He certainly does. I doubt you know his backstory, do you?"

"No. Aside from the fact that he developed some obsessive lust for power that I don't understand."

Septin pursed his lips and nodded. "That's an understatement, but it all stems back from his childhood and his father's obsession with growing his weapons development corporation. Nothing would stand in Raucuss's way, and that would include his spouse and only child.

"You see, Zearic and I went to Long Point Military Academy. He was always awkward and didn't quite gel with the other cadets. I felt bad and tried my best to get to know him and see if he would come out of that odd shell. It worked, somewhat. He opened up to me and spilled some grotesque details of his childhood."

Septin paused to push out a deep breath. "Zearic told me how angry he was with his father, how he would torture him and his mother. When she displeased him, he would use her for live subject testing for some of his early concept weapon designs. Not enough to kill her, not at first. He made sure that it was just enough to inflict as much pain and harm to get his point across.

"All the while, Zearic was forced to watch as he cried and begged his father to stop. One day, he went too far. His latest mind and body altering gas took it too far. The concept was to blast it onto an enemy force and then watch them devour each other. He used just a little shot on Zearic's mother, and she turned into some unrecognizable monster. Her flesh was dripping from her body, and her eyes were red with rage. She attacked Zearic, the only thing that ever cared for her. She began ripping at him with her boney fingers, and her flesh continued to dissolve and spill onto Zearic. His father stood back and laughed all the while. Assuming this was a great way to toughen his child up." Septin closed his eyes and shook his head with a short exhale. "She died from the traumatic effects on her body before she could kill Zearic, but the damage to his mental state was already done.

"I felt terrible for him and thought I could help. I invited him out with some friends from the academy. I stupidly thought that might soften him up a bit. Well, that didn't work out so well. His rigid and unempathetic personality wasn't a good fit. The next thing I knew, he was on top of one with both hands gripped around her neck. I had to beat him off of her." He stopped to clear his throat.

"Well . . . that was the end of our brief acquaintance. Everyone shunned him, and he walked the campus shrouded in darkness. Later, Raucuss died from some mishap in one of his orbital weapons testing facilities. He was blasted out of an airlock. They called it a terrible accident, though Zearic was with him at the time.

"The rumor was that Zearic had a hand in this supposed accident. Knowing what I know about him, I believe that's likely the case." Septin let out one last deep exhale as he finished recalling the exhausting tale. "He's an individual grasping for absolute power because he was so powerless growing up, and he never wants to be that victim that his father made him, ever. In his twisted mind, to not be a victim you must make everyone else your victim. Anyway, that's what we're dealing with. There is no reasoning with him, and negotiations are useless."

Crix didn't blink, and his jaw dropped as he took in the story. "Wow . . . that's really messed up. I sort of feel bad for him, but at the same time, it makes him even scarier. He has to be stopped."

"Everything weighs on your success in gaining access to the Central Core. From there, we can, hopefully, shut down the Marcks for good."

"I am ready. I have no love for the Marcks. They destroyed everything I know. Besides, I will gladly give up my life to save Kerriah and restore Troika if that is what it takes to do so," Crix said as he felt the tingle of the orb inside him.

"I understand Kerriah and you formed something between each other. She is a daughter to me, and I raised her from a small child after we found her lost and abandoned. Later, we realized that she was extraordinary, and in some way, she was different from other children." Septin's neck straightened and the proud parent puffed his chest out. "She excelled past them in her academics, sports, hobbies, virtually anything she set her sights on, she was the best at."

"I will save her, I promise you, and you'll get her back," Crix said with such strength and conviction in his voice that he would have convinced even the highest skeptic.

"Coming from the broken heart of a father, I hope you do, and somehow I know you will," Septin said; his soulful eyes were deep with wisdom. Septin slapped his hand down upon his leg in a sign that he was anxious to move the discussion back to the main objective. "Burling will get you geared up and acquainted with your mission commandos. We need you to be deployed right away. Commando Burling . . . if you would."

Burling stood to attention in response. "Yes, sir."

As they began to walk away, Septin stopped them. "There's one last thing that I need to mention. As you are aware, the Marcks will be probing for orb energy surges. I can even see them enhancing their instrumentation to obtain even the weakest readings considering recent events, which will keep them busy chasing false positives throughout the system. Still, you'll need to reserve using the power of the orb until all other options have expired. We don't want the Marcks' legions converging on you before your extraction." Crix gave a somber nod. Even though he could better control the orb's energy signature now, he agreed to side with caution at this fragile stage. "Good luck, young Tolagon. We are all pulling for you."

***

The long, narrow living quarters of the resistance troops bustled with activity. Everywhere species from the three moons were making preparations for the coming attack from Zearic's

114

forces. Moving gear and ordinance, studying mission briefings and tactics, one would never guess that the odds before them were nothing short of impossible and their futures grim. When they saw Crix there, a spark danced in their eyes, and it was at that point that Crix grasped his true significance. It was not about him or Kerriah or Troika, it was about his role as Tolagon, and that role was not of power but hope, the hope that a Tolagon brought to those he served.

They entered a brightly lit area that was cluttered from one end to the other. The room had military gear and weapons hanging, leaning, stacked, and propped up in almost every space.

"Crix, meet your deployment team," Burling said as he opened his arm to a rugged group of four warriors that stood ready before him, the Hybors Carr and Jex, the Solaran Flotto, and Trayco the Mendac. Nothing was above this group, handpicked as the finest of the Oro Resistance Commandos.

Burling began the introductions. "Carr is your weapons tech, Jex your scout recon, Flotto your demolitions expert, and I don't think you require any introductions to Trayco, your communication specialist and team lead in this mission."

Trayco stepped forward and shook Crix's hand firmly. "I'm honored to have the opportunity to serve with you again, even if it was only briefly before."

Carr had a deep scar which carved a rut in his face from the top of his head, across his lips, and down to the bottom of his chin. His thick, rutted, olive-black skin looked like hammered iron reflecting off the white lighting. He gave a drawn-out, deep growl before he acknowledged Crix with a nod.

"So this is ta one that is goin' to save us all, huh?" His breath smelled like rotted fish, and he intentionally blew it into Crix's face before giving him a satirical grin. He then casually grabbed a rifle leaning in the corner next to him, took a seat, and started to break it down, purposefully not wanting to give the rookie Tolagon any undue respect.

Jex, the more polished and slimmer Hybor chuckled as he walked up to Crix, giving him a hard slap on the back. "Don't mind that cranky old sea dog; he really doesn't like anyone, but I can't imagine going into a fight without him." Jex's deep grey uniform appeared starched and crisp compared to Carr's, and he gave a welcoming smile from the shine of his smooth, moist face. The youngest son of a Thale ambassador, Jex grew up on Soorak and didn't share the same grittiness of most Hybors.

Flotto, with his thick limbs, square head, and large lips, glared at him as if sizing him up for the team. "Hmmff . . . well . . . good to have you aboard, you'll do fine here if you're everything they say you are." His voice was broken and gravelly as if his throat needed to be cleared. He rolled his eyes before taking a seat to resume stuffing mines and grenades into his deployment packs.

Burling smirked. Acclimating with this group was not an easy task. "They are a salty lot and certainly not the most welcoming to greens, but they are the best at what they do. I've put you in good hands, trust me. Now be sure to grab a little chow. Your transport to Solara leaves in two hours. Trayco will help you get suited up and provide a detailed dump of the mission."

Burling stepped out, leaving Crix at the mercy of his new teammates. He found all to be somewhat standoffish except Trayco. Crix wondered if it was the tight-knit group mindset or the species that was making it so difficult for them to warm up to him. He decided to keep his focus on the mission and not to worry too much over it. Trayco gave him an assist getting into a grey battle suit that felt like thick rubber on the outside but strangely breathed like the lightest material he had ever worn over his skin. He felt as though he weighed less and his physical reaction time was quicker.

"Feels good on, doesn't it?" Trayco asked.

Crix stretched his arms out, enjoying the look and fit. He felt like a warrior with the capability to scale up walls. "We call this our agile battle suit or ab suit. Its composition will keep you cool in the aridest environments or warm in the cold. It also packs a base hydro system that will keep your body water-stable by recycling your perspiration. If you feel like you have more energy, it's because of the oxygen fusion that pulls particles from the air around you, drawing it into your skin so you will have an overall lower fatigue ratio."

Crix put his fists up and pumped his shoulders. "This is great! I wish I had one of these for annexis." Trayco squinted, puzzled for a moment as annexis was not known beyond Troika.

"Well, here is the bad news. You're going to lose much of that benefit due to the environmental shell we will have to wear overtop of the ab suit. This is essential because of the hostile environment of Semptor, but it will allow us to travel when the locals are undercover." Trayco picked up a small rifle. "This is called our tac rifle due to its compact size but efficient knockdown power against Thraxons and Marcks alike. We like using it with small units when sweeping out tight areas. It's also relatively easy to learn how to use, and that's why it's the perfect weapon to set you up with."

Trayco paused as he realized how that might sound to Crix and raised his palm in elaboration. "Not that I don't feel like you aren't more than capable of learning how to effectively use one of our more advanced weapons, it's just that we are short on time."

"Not to worry, I understand," Crix reassured. Trayco placed the rifle in Crix's hand and instructed him on the basics of firing and securing it. The basic tactical rifle was lightweight and easy to carry in harsh environments. Crix was never comfortable with guns and had minimal exposure to them. Andors preferred melee and close-in weapons. They had always considered projectile weapons to be dishonorable, though they had used them in recent wars as required. Crix played along with Trayco's instruction, but in his mind, he had no intention of using it.

"The Marck space fleet has stepped up their patrols around the Oro System recently and are stopping ships for even the slightest suspicion, and sometimes for no cause at all, just to flex their muscle. Our transport will be outfitted to look like a mining vessel, and with any luck, we should make our drop inside Semptor unnoticed," Trayco explained. Solara was rich in minerals, and mining traffic was common.

Semptor was one of the original regions chosen by Nathasia as a penal depository due to its naturally grueling elements. The vast landscape was harsh and rocky, layered with small rock fragments that whipped around as the torturous winds ripped through numerous times during the day and night. The dense winds persisted for thirty to forty-five minutes at a time. Bare flesh would be stripped to the bone, and the exposed bone would be pitted and splintered without protective gear.

General Gorag was born and raised in Semptor, and even though his power and influence could have benefited him to a more hospitable region of Solara, he chose to build his palace in the worst it had to offer, sandwiched between the Corvid Mountains and the Sea of Shards. The paranoid leader of the Palic Legion favored the harsh, natural cover this area provided and the lethality of Semptor to keep unwelcome guests away.

"Okay. Have you ever done any sky jumps or high-speed thrust assisted landings?"

"Never, but I've dove into the Barrillian vortex more times than I could count."

Trayco tilted his head back and squinted. "Vortex, huh? Okay, that will have to do. As long as you can keep steady under high-velocity winds, you should be fine."

Crix smiled.

CHAPTER 9

The transport shook as it swooped down into the choppy upper atmosphere of Solara. The crew already felt the dense gravitational pull on their flesh. Their skin sagged as the increased gravity tugged it downward. The bulky environmental shells were heavy and laborious, and now the gravity ensured that this was going to be a demanding trip.

"We are going to drop off right on the outskirts of Semptor when the cyclonic winds kick up; this will give us the necessary cover for our insertion. We will freefall and use our grav thrusters to slow our descent. You will have to kick them in extra hard when your helmet display reads fifty meters. This will help power against the stronger gravity of this world. The wind will blow us off course from each other, but we will regroup on the ground." Trayco barely had a chance to finish when the ship began to quake and jolt violently. The wind and pea-sized gravel hissed and crackled against its hull. An alarm sounded, and the cabin lights turned into a red glow.

"This is it!" Jex announced in his gruff voice. He and the others stood up and gave one last check of their gear before securing their helmets firmly over their heads.

"Here we go, just follow my lead, and if we get separated, stay put and we will find you," Trayco assured Crix, yelling above the clatter outside. They both locked down their bulky helmets, muffling the head-throbbing commotion around them. Crix felt soothed inside the helmet. The deadened sound and gentle chirps of its mission indicators and alert systems somehow took him away from the reality of what he was about to do.

The red light started flashing, and a circular hatch swirled open in the rear of the ship. "Go-go!" Trayco shouted as Jex, Carr, and Flotto dove out without a moment's hesitation and disappeared instantly in a haze of swooshing sand and grit outside. The ship shook with such hostility that Crix and Trayco could barely stay afoot.

"Let's go!" Trayco shouted above all the noise just before he dove into the churning wall of gold.

Crix paused to gather his thoughts. His armored hand squeezed tightly around the security rail above him as the ship rocked back and forth, challenging him to depart. He took a deep breath, held it, and then jumped out into the madness before him headfirst. Instantly, the gusting winds snatched his body like a limp doll and threw him into an out-of-control tumble. He couldn't see anything, and a cloud of golden dust blinded his view to zero. His helmet's tactical display was the only thing visible as he tried to track his altitude from the digits and characters that flashed and scrolled in front of his eyes.

This is insane. His heart pounded and his head fogged over from a surge of adrenaline mixed with anxiety. He quickly discovered that there was little he could do to maintain any control as the vicious winds ripped and slashed at his helpless body. Each time he tried to stabilize himself, the gust reversed the other way, sending him flailing out of control again with a loud blast of sand and debris raking against his armor. He gritted his teeth and snarled with frustration. *You've got to be kidding. I'm really missing the gentle breeze of the Barrillian vortex.*

His visor lit up, and a warning light indicated that his altitude had reached the critical point where he needed to slow his descent. He grabbed for the grav booster controls that ran down the outside of his arms, but the left one broke loose and was bent backward. It dangled behind him, flapping against the hostile wind. With only the right, he wouldn't be able to stabilize his descent, and it would only spin him out of control even more. The helmet sounded off an audible alarm—*the ground must be near.*

Just a little touch of the orb's power; he didn't have to use much, just enough to pull that left control back around. They wouldn't detect such a small use. He would make sure he used just enough; besides, if he died on this descent, the mission would fail anyway. Zzzzzip . . . the control bent back around to his left hand, and he flipped himself upright quickly and squeezed the boosters hard, so hard that he felt all his insides jam into his head. The thrusters howled so forcefully that he could hear them through the pounding gusts of the storm. His helmet crackled with deafening chaos as the fabled rock fragments that reigned supreme near the surface pelted his armor.

He found the surface unexpectedly, and his legs felt like sledgehammers had smacked them. He caved face forward into the ground. *Ouuch! My legs!* He could neither move nor feel them.

The gravity and wind kept him plastered to the surface as the swarms of rock shards whipped by at flesh-peeling speed and deflected off his now much appreciated outer shell. The impacts were so loud that he couldn't put together even a pinch of thought to do anything aside from lay there for a few more minutes and try to maintain his sanity. Slowly, a tingling itch crept up his legs as he began to feel them again. The itching gradually faded into a burning ache. He slowly moved one leg and then the other. His thoughts settled, knowing that at least they weren't broken. He had to get up to relieve the pain. He pulled himself up on one knee at a time and struggled to get on his feet.

Where to go now? He couldn't see anything aside from the golden blur of dust and rock swooshing by, nor could he hear anything except the maddening sounds of the rocks cracking against his helmet. The idea was that they could move during the storms. *How?*

He called for infrared optics from his visor control. Traces of heat signatures appeared nearby, the red and yellow blobs were humanoid in shape and size, *but are they friendly?* He chose to stand his ground and wait out the storm's cycle. It had been going on for some time now and should end soon; besides, he didn't want to walk into something that would worsen his situation.

He waited for what felt like an hour. The tedious standing gave him plenty of opportunities to focus on the additional gravitational weight that strained his tendons and muscles. They already felt swollen and inflamed. He was short of breath, even though he wasn't moving but just trying to maintain his footing. His thoughts turned to guessing how many more of these storms he could weather. Kerriah, Troika, the Marcks, and Zearic entered his mind. He clenched his fists and took a few deep breaths.

The winds finally gave up and the warm blanket of silence wrapped around him. Visibility emerged as the dust gradually dissipated. Behind it, a ruby sky left a burning radiance upon the ground and rocks.

Dome-shaped dwellings peeked across the outskirts of the landscape with one nearby; its once smooth stone outer layer was heavily pitted and cracked from the abusive weather. Like an unwelcome stepchild resented for nothing more than its existence, this was a place that appeared to be scorned and ravaged by this world. Crix wondered where the others in his team ended up or if they were even alive. How could any life be possible here? He decided to keep to the shadows while moving closer to the small village in the distance and, hopefully, get a view of the locals. Trayco said he would find him, so as long as he didn't venture off too far, he should be fine.

Moving with the additional gravity proved to be a challenge for Crix. He felt top-heavy when walking, and each breath labored. He removed his helmet and took a lungful of the settled air. It was hot and parched his throat and chest. His eyes seared red and tears welled up from the dry grit in the air. He let out a hoarse cough as his lungs tried to adjust to the blistering dryness.

As he stood there trying to get a clear view of the surroundings, a nearby voice almost startled him off his feet. "Hi! Can you help me get my drok?"

A small child appeared within a mere few meters without his noticing. He must have been so distracted by the environment that he completely missed her. The Solaran child blended in perfectly with the surroundings, with a tattered and dusted cloak filled with so much grime that it could be easily stepped upon if left out on the ground. Weathered goggles covered her eyes, and her hands were severely calloused for her apparent age. She knelt and investigated a nearby hole in the ground. Her voice was sweet and delicate amongst the otherwise unpleasant place.

"Sir . . . my drok, he's stuck down there. He was running with me to our shelter to escape the crackling and fell into that hole. I couldn't stop to get him out." Other than her goggles and dirty spots, her face looked like that of a typical child, although her brow may have been a little heavier than that of a Mendac child.

"The crackling? Do you mean the storm?" Crix asked, not familiar with the term.

The girl giggled. "Of course, you're not from around here, are you?

"Actually, I'm just passing through."

"Well, can you help me with my drok?"

"Of course, let's have a look at the little fella." Crix leaned over to look down the hole. The moment his head peaked over the opening, there was a rumbling growl like an old engine revving up. Three beady eyes stared intensely back up at him. The eyes belonged to a large animal filled with small, dark spots against course, pale skin and sparse, wiry hair. He raked his taloned feet against the wall, cutting into the rock as if slicing through cardboard.

Crix popped his head back up and looked unbelievingly at the girl. "That's your drok?"

"Yes, he's my best friend. You must get him out of there. I can't live without him," she begged.

"I will help you, but is he going to try and eat me when he gets out?"

Her voice raised with excitement over the notion that Crix was going to get her pet out. "No, silly. He's a good drok. The most he will do is slop your face, but that just would mean he likes you."

"Okay then . . ." Crix looked around for something that could be useful for the task. Unfortunately, the blistered land had little to offer. The only things around were rocks and dust. The hole wasn't too deep, and from the looks of the claw marks along the side of the wall from the drok's apparent struggles to get out, it was only short about a meter or so to escape. "What's your name, little one?" Crix asked.

"Luuda," she answered in her delicate voice.

"Luuda, help me gather up as many rocks as you can, big ones and small ones, any you can get your hands on, then gently toss them down into the hole. If we get enough down there, it will raise the floor high enough for him to get out."

"Really!" She was thrilled and started to gather stones and toss them down into the hole without hesitation. "Make sure you don't hit my drok with any of them," she warned.

An hour went by, and Crix began to second guess his plot; at least the rocks were plentiful, but he couldn't leave this poor girl now. Amazingly, she seemed to show little sign of fatigue or loss of interest. Crix tossed a larger stone down into the hole and turned away to get more. As he walked away, a neck-snapping shove hit him from behind and landed him face-first into the hard surface. The air escaped his lungs, and white spots filled his vision. As he tried to get up, his head was sucked up into blackness and warm slime. It reeked like rotten fish mixed with feces, and the murky, damp walls wiggled around his entire head. He was unable to get a breath. He fought with every bit of muscle he could muster and managed to pull himself downward. With a wet smack and a strong inhale, the daylight emerged again.

"Yaaayyyy! We got him out," the girl's voice cried out in joy. He looked back, and the drok was standing atop him, panting with a wide grin that encompassed its whole face. The three eyes almost vanished under the wrinkles of the foaming smile.

"It looks like he likes you too." She giggled.

Crix tried to wipe the leftover slime from his hair and face. *So this is slopping,* he thought, not exactly what he had in mind, maybe a lick or two at best. The little girl hugged the beast, and it gave her a quick slopping in return. "Thank you, sir." She ran over and hugged Crix as he struggled back up to his one knee and then to his feet.

"A pleasure," he said, though he was fibbing a little bit. "Hey, can you tell me which direction is Gorag's castle?" She quieted, and Crix began thinking that he maybe shouldn't have asked.

"Why would you want to go there? That's a terrible place and won't take kindly to off-worlders like you for sure," she said with a cynical twist in her mouth.

Crix tried quickly to cover his tracks. "Oh, I don't want to go there. I just want to try and avoid it, especially since it's like you said, a terrible place."

"Well, in that case, it's on the other side of the village and then through the sea of shards." She pointed past the village in the distance.

Crix knelt to get eye level with the child. If he were to probe her for more information, he had to come clean with her first. "Luuda . . . I was not honest with you when I said that I was looking to avoid Gorag's castle. In fact, going to see Gorag is exactly my intention. You see, I have a friend who is sick, and Gorag is the only one that has information that can save her."

Luuda looked at him oddly for several minutes and didn't say a word before she finally broke the uncomfortable silence. "I really wish you didn't have to go there; you saved my drok, and you're my friend. Gorag is bad, and he sends mechanical bullies that beat my father and takes our things. I hate him."

"I'm truly sorry to hear that. Believe me when I tell you Luuda, if there were another way to save my friend, I would try it."

She lowered her head, and sadness filled her face, an expression that gripped Crix's heart. She had such concern for someone she barely knew. It was a child's purity that endured the claws of this oppressive environment. He must help her somehow; in some way, he had to do what he could for her. "Luuda, you mentioned the sea of shards. That doesn't sound like a very inviting place, is there anything you can tell me about it that can help me in my journey?" She looked back up at him. Her large, round eyes blinked in thought.

"The shards will cut most things when touched, and they are everywhere. I only know what my father has told me of them. I know that the worms are many before the sea, and they will grab your feet and legs, thinking you're food," Luuda explained.

The cratic worms varied in size from less than half a meter to three meters or more and fed off of small vermin that scurried across the plains of Solara but would, at times, attack larger creatures, cutting off their limbs with their serrated jaws. It was an additional barrier that kept the un-welcomed from accessing Gorag's fortress.

A twinkle suddenly shined over her eyes and she popped up on her toes with excitement. "The wild droks can help you. They eat the worms and will eat them the moment they pop up from the ground. The wild droks run in packs near there, and all you have to do is make friends with them, and they will follow you."

Crix smiled at her virtue and first thought the idea was a little absurd but still listened for her benefit. "So how does someone make friends with these wild droks?"

"It's easy. Just rub behind their ears." She massaged her fingers behind her drok's ears to demonstrate, and it curled up near her, stretching its neck and swaying his head. As she continued, the drok began to purr with exuberance and rolled over onto its back. "That's it; how do you think I got this drok?"

"Thank you, Luuda, I will remember that, and you have been helpful. I have to go now, but I will not forget you, I promise." Crix leaned down, and she gave him a massive waddler beast hug around his neck. He was astonished by such a child's strength, and it was clear that the Solaran people were physically stronger from living in this harsh environment.

CHAPTER 10

Crix said goodbye to Luuda and departed for the far side of the village, being careful to stay out of plain sight. He wondered if his team had lost him. However, before he was able to finish his thoughts, a familiar voice called out over his helmet com.

"Over here, behind the dome." It was Trayco; he was with the other three commandos, and they were lying low behind a collapsed dome structure nearby.

As Crix joined them, he noticed that they all appeared much more at ease. The harsh setting was nothing new to them, and it was clear that this was just one of the many adventures they had shared.

"I was starting to worry a little that something went wrong," Crix said.

"No need to worry, Tulagon. We're professionals and had a bead on your position a while back. Your interaction with that civilian was not advisable on a covert mission like this, and we needed to wait until you were clear of her," Trayco said but did not sound angry, rather more understanding that Crix was not a military trained personnel.

Sirens whirred up in the distance, and nearby sirens joined in like wolves answering each other's call. "The storms . . . secure your headgear and brace yourselves!" Trayco ordered.

After a few minutes, a wall of gold rolled in at speeds that left little hope of escape for those that failed to heed the siren's warning. The initial force of the storm blasted them off their feet from the impact. The cry of the sirens were washed out instantly by the familiar pounding of the rocks against their armor and helmets.

Trayco's helmet tech converted his voice commands to text, which displayed into the team's visors, instructing them to keep close and use thermal optics to keep track of each other. He informed them that they were going to move during the storm to take advantage of its cover. Crix followed the four through the blistering storm, and it was taking everything to stay afoot against the ever-shifting winds. Due to zero visibility, he had to track his team with thermal signature readings from his helmet display. Too often, the red and orange silhouettes would get too far ahead, and he would have to step up his pace clumsily and risk losing his footing.

Keeping up wasn't easy; his leg and back muscles ripped with fiery pain, and his heart pounded against his chest as he gasped for air. He had never felt so out of shape. It was as though he was continuously shoved in every direction while carrying a hundred-pound sack of rocks across his shoulders. After an hour, he thought that there was no way he could continue and, at the same time, wondered how his companions were. Then relief finally came, the winds settled, and the dust seeped slowly from the air, and before them, they could see the skeletal horizon of the sea of shards.

"The sea of shards," Flotto observed, familiar with the namesakes of his homeworld. "This area is rich in mage ore. The stubbornly hard ore wears into thin slices instead of chips. Over many years, the flying rocks have weathered them down to towering shards. Their edges are sharp enough to cut into our armor, so we must take care."

"Did tya see that?" Jex asked, pointing to the ground.

"What is it?" Trayco asked.

"The ground moves," Jex replied, turning everyone's attention downward where the ground's loose, rocky surface bubbled and churned.

"It's the worms Luuda told me of. Look!" A red scaly fleshed worm nearly two meters long popped up from the ground and dove back in like a fish over a calm lake. They carved through the hard surface with the ease of swimming in water. "Stay back! We have to find droks." Crix recalled Luuda's advice.

"Cratic worms. Aye . . . yes, droks be helpful here; they could carve a path through here with the worms they eat. It's amazing how fast droks can digest those critters," Flotto said. "They will live in large cubbies; we just have to look for them. Trying to shoot them all will be a futile act that would create too much fracas."

"We should backtrack to those hills we passed about two clicks back and start looking for a den," Trayco suggested.

***

They found the small hillsides riddled with holes used by creatures such as droks, evidenced by the faded claw marks in the rocky entrances. It didn't take long to run across a live den of droks.

"Looks like I found some, I think!" Jex shouted as he looked down the sights of his rifle.

The others quickly joined him to have a look. Crix carefully shined his light down the hole and noticed about eight sets of eyes staring back up from a large, round bowl inside. "Yep, that looks like droks."

"Let me see tees things," Carr grumbled before pointing his light deeper in the hole to get a better look. A mix of growling chorused up from below, followed by a snarling bark from the alpha of the den.

"Carr, take it easy; we need to make friends with these things not entice them," Trayco said in a scolding tone.

"What? I'm just tryin' to get a peek at the grubby vermin," Carr snarled as he snapped his light back and showed purposeful disinterest.

"Okay, we just need to lure them out, and the little girl showed me how to get on their good side," Crix said.

"I can get them, hole-dwellin' rodents out of there, but there tain't goin' to be much left to make friends with." Carr flippantly tossed a concussion grenade up and caught it casually.

Trayco snapped a glance at his brash teammate. "Can that talk, Carr!"

Crix ignored the remarks and made a kissing sound with his lips while patting on his leg, trying to call the droks out subtly. "Come here, biggens . . . come here." The eight unconvinced Droks remained cautiously implanted in their den. Their eyes flickered from the outside light as they darted around, trying to keep track of the visitors outside.

Crix pulled a piece of dried meat from his pack and held it out, continuing to make the kissing sound. "Hey! That's our rations you're fixin' to feed tose mongrels," Carr protested.

Crix turned sourly to Carr. "No. These are my rations." Then he turned back to calling the droks.

"K-ay . . . but don't tya think tya gettin' any of mine when tya little belly starts to growl later on."

After a few minutes of persistence, one of the droks crawled out with its twitching snout extended forward. It kept its belly low to the ground and its ears tucked back. As it came closer, it paused, then it pointed its nose into the air and gave a snort. Crix dropped the meat on the ground, and the drok emerged into the light of day; its spotted body was grimy with dirt and covered in small cuts and scars, some of which were fresh and some faded. It funneled its lips and reached for the meat stick, slurping the salty snack up into its cone-shaped jaw. The drok swallowed and looked depravedly at Crix as if asking for more. Crix pulled out another piece, and Carr gave out a frustrated exhale, further expressing his displeasure with Crix handing out his rations. The other droks began to move out of the den, seeing that they might be missing out on something good.

Warily, Jex and Carr drew their weapons, and Trayco motioned slowly to lower them. Crix conservatively broke the meat stick up and spread it out on the ground in front of him. As the drok lapped up his offerings, Crix reached around behind its left ear and gave it a gentle massage. The drok leaned inward, trying to get a better rub. It began to purr and shake in appreciation.

The commandos watched in astonishment, and all but Carr broke out meat sticks and did the same. Carr cradled his rifle in his arms and leaned back against a nearby stone, his face scrunched with disgust as he watched. "We should just leave these mongrels and make our own plasma trail of worm carcasses. We don't need this." He pulled his rifle up and aimed down the sight at one of the droks.

Trayco glared back at Carr, his brow furrowed. "Carr, we can't just go shooting the place up, you know that. It will draw too much attention to us." He was losing his patience with his brash-tempered comrade.

"Being trailed by a pack of oversized mutts is not goin' tya draw any?" Carr spouted off, and everyone ignored him.

***

After enough time passed charming the wary drok pack, they felt ready to make for the Sea of Shards. They kept close, and the droks followed. The eager beasts snorted and snarled at the ground like they could smell and even hear the worms ahead.

"Up ahead!" Jex shouted, observing the worms squirming to the surface and then swirling back under again. Once the droks gained sight of them, they charged forward and began jamming their snouts into the ground. The husky beasts snarled and shook their heads before slurping their prey up like noodles.

"Wedge formation, I'll take point. Keep pushing the droks forward," Trayco ordered, pointing and waving onward.

The group nudged ahead and remained close as the droks tirelessly engulfed the worms with no apparent loss of appetite.

Several worms found their way through the droks, and one of them snaked up around Trayco's leg. He shouted several unsavory words as he bashed down on it with the butt of his rifle. His armor crumpled against his calf and thigh. Sliding the long blade of his pouch knife from its sheath, he began stabbing and slicing at the constricting attacker. It reared its head back and hissed, looking for a vulnerable spot to strike. "Get it off me!"

A quick blast of green flashed over the worm and cooked it instantly. It dropped limply from Trayco's leg as Carr lowered his rifle from his shoulder. "Damnit, Carr!" Trayco shouted and then quickly sighed. He annoyingly kicked the crusty carcass away and peeked up at a wide grinning Carr. "Thanks for the assist."

"Are you okay?" Crix asked, noticing that Trayco's armor crinkled around his leg.

"I'm fine." Trayco nudged the charred worm with his foot. "I can't believe the strength of these nasty critters. Our armor was needed for more reasons than we thought."

As they advanced toward the Sea of Shards, an occasional worm managed to slip by the greedy droks, and the group proactively neutralized them with controlled rifle blasts. After a short time, they reached the shards, which rippled the horizon with their jagged silhouettes. They gave the appearance of a choppy ocean turned to stone, and it was easy to see why the area received its name. A collective lump swelled in their throats as they approached the unwelcoming sea. As seasoned commandos, they knew the site was a tactical nightmare.

Beneath their feet, the ground felt like metal as their boots clanked with each cautious step. The worms' jaws could not penetrate the dense land and the droks stopped and began barking. "I think this may be the end of the line for our friends," Flotto said as they walked past the droks, who were frozen in their tracks. "They fear the threatening postures of the shards, so they will not enter the sea."

"Bye, my friends, you've been a great help." Crix gave one a gentle brush with his hand. As the team entered the Sea of Shards, the droks' nervous barks turned into whining. They began to pace for a short time before scampering back in the direction of their homes. In his mind, Crix gave a warm and thankful hug to Luuda for her innocent wisdom.

The eerie profiles of the towering shards shimmered against the daylight. A chill slithered down his spine as the life-like forms gazed staunchly over the unwelcome trespassers. Many of the shards curled near the top, with a jagged edge running down the weathered sides, while others exposed a piercing tip, stabbing into the skyline as if to frighten off the beasts of the air.

Dust swirled up, and broken rock fragments scurried across the ground like small insects taking cover. "The winds are upon us again. We'll need to make haste as we are not going to be able to move through here once the storm returns," Jex warned. He scanned the group and took a side-step; his large frame grazed against a nearby shard, which sliced into his protective armor. "What the heck?" he complained aloud as he rotated his arm to inspect the damaged metal shell.

Trayco took a quick look at Jex's damaged metal shell. "I concur. We need to keep alert and close with rifles ready. I don't like the limited visibility, so utilize your visor's thermal enhancer." He then pointed forward through the cluttered sea. "Let's move out."

They swept their rifles carefully around each passing shard, and the further they ventured, the more unsettled they became. The wind squealed through the serrated corners, and the group darted anxious glances at even the slightest of movements. A dangling fragment broke off overhead, and Carr sprung back to avoid being guillotined. He crashed into Crix, who somehow kept on his feet and narrowly missed stumbling into a razor's edge directly behind his position.

Trayco stopped and turned around toward Crix. "Don't lose your footing!"

Jex peeked up from his rifle. "Yeah . . . We'll keep that in mind."

Beads of sweat trickled down Crix's forehead and across his brows. His glove plonked against his helmet as he tried to wipe them dry. His eyes squinted shut once the salty trickles seeped in with a burning sting. To add to his misery, keeping track of the team proved troublesome as they disappeared with each cautious step through the rugged maze. The densely packed shards brought back memories of the stone forest of Mothoa. Crix's vision swirled, and a hard pit formed in his gut when he glanced upward at the lethal edges that towered above. He struggled to keep his mind off the possibility that a piece of mage ore could fracture, fall, and slice through his helmet. There was no place to stop among the shards, no place to rest.

Like the sudden commotion of a clumsy intruder, the riotous winds whooshed and the crackling impacts of stirring rocks echoed in the distance; the dreaded storms approached again. The alarms from the nearby townships were too distant to hear from their location, and they were caught off guard. "Brace for impa—" Trayco couldn't finish his command before the flailing rocks blasted into them, turning their limited visibility instantly to zero.

They had to stay afoot, and the unseen, razor-edged shards inhibited any movement. Trayco felt that even a meter or two would be too risky for the team. Clear thoughts drowned into the deafening roar of violence as their armor drummed and clacked from the impacts. Crix stood and stood, wavering at times from the shifting winds and trying his best to ignore the scorching pain that flamed up his legs and into his neck.

"What was that?" Something heavy jolted against his side, shoving him against the wind gusts and flying debris. He remained still. *Someone is moving around.* Maybe one of the other guys, but why would they, when they were so tight against the shards, why were they risking it? Disconcerted, he checked his thermal readings, indicating that everyone in the team was still in the same position.

CHAPTER 11

The pounding of the Solaran storm slowed and finally dissipated to a gentle breeze and light dust. Visibility slowly returned, like a fog lifting on a chilly morning, and Crix could see his companions emerge into his view, but there were an additional four silhouettes. *Jex, Carr, Trayco, and Flotto . . . who are the other four?*

Trayco snapped his rifle up to his shoulder. "Marcks!"

However, these golden-stained Marcks were different. A red insignia of a gemstone displayed across their chests appeared to be the only thing that wasn't weathered and worn on their armor. They had a single, round eye emanating a cool-white light that glistened against the settling dust as they rotated their heads. A vented opening protruded where a mouth would have been expected. The Marcks looked as though they had wandered this terrain for a long while, appearing more mechanical than the other ones they had seen before and, at the same time, more threatening. Instead of rifles, they grasped bronze-tinted swords. Each curved slightly at the tip.

There was an uncomfortable pause between them, and Crix felt a bead of sweat trickling down from his forehead once again.

He was hesitant to be the first to move. Then one of the Marcks began to draw both its swords back.

"Bust 'em up!" Carr shouted with a raspy voice, which sounded like an old motor. He opened fire, sending a Marck flailing backward, sheering in half against an unrelenting shard. The others joined, firing their weapons. The remaining Marcks whirled their curved blades, deflecting what shots they could or crumbling under missed blocks and evades.

Crix swung his rifle around and aimed at a Marck thrusting and chopping at Jex, who was currently on his heels trying to keep clear of the spinning blades. As his blue sight reticle quickly contracted into a small circle and strobed on his intended Marck target, a large sword unexpectedly swooshed down. Crix's rifle popped, flashed, and split into two useless pieces. He stumbled backward, his right shoulder crashed into a shard, cutting through his armor and slicing into his flesh. The wound burned hot, and almost instantly, he felt the wetness of blood soak beneath his battle suit. He was in a void, trapped in a slow-motion of thoughts and reactions. *What happened?*

The Marck bolted ahead, chopping with both swords in an alternating sequence; the blades buzzed and whistled like two Hemlor stingers protecting their nest. Without a weapon, Crix backed up close to the edge of a shard. As the Marck plunged his blades forward, every hair spiked across his skin, and he darted to the side. With his intended target gone, the unyielding Marck drove both his blades simultaneously into the massive shard's edge. The blades snapped off, and he continued to stab wildly at Crix, the broken edges swishing past his head.

He continued to duck and maneuver around its attacks. Merely a split second of mistiming would end his journey. He looked around for a weapon, an escape, something to better his current predicament when the Marck's center eye ruptured forward, sending glass-like fragments spraying out. The Marck sparked and flashed, then dropped to its knees before haphazardly landing on its face.

Trayco stepped forward, remnant fumes still curling up from his rifle's barrel. He proudly placed his foot upon the Marck's back. Behind him, Carr had a Marck's arm locked against its neck with its clenched sword still in hand. He forcefully pulled the sword across its neck as he ripped its head back. The Marck's head popped and flashed before rolling off its shoulders and clanking to the ground.

Trayco swung a glance at the downed Marcks. "Threats neutralized."

Carr smashed his boot heel into the Marck head, caving in the metal plates. "Tya see boy, tat's how it's done. Send these abominations back to the scrap heaps and rust piles they belong in." Flotto remained silent as he nudged a Marck torso over to get a better view of its insignia.

"Gorag's Marck's, I take it?" Crix took note to Flotto's interest in the Marck; he nodded quietly in agreement.

"Let me patch that wound," Trayco said, noticing Crix's blood oozing from the sliced armor on his back. Crix removed his helmet and backplate as Trayco pulled out a pencil-sized object from his pack. "This is going to sting a little, but just hold still for a second." From its tip, a thin beam of white seared into the wound; the flesh folded over itself and sealed the injury with just a faint appearance of a scar. Crix noticed that Jex had a deep cut across his chest with burgundy-tinted blood seeping through the sliced metal.

"What about Jex? He looks like he could use a little aid as well."

Trayco smiled and shook his head. "You're right, but he's not going to let me. I think it's a Hybor ego thing."

Carr scowled. "Hybors don't fuss over scratches; that's for mommas and their babies."

Trayco moved forward, taking point, and then gave a chopping hand motion to his team. "Let's keep moving and stay alert."

***

They painstakingly wove their way through the web of sparkling mage ore formations, and before long, they reached the edge of the sea. A dusty mountain swirled in gold dominated the horizon. They moved carefully through the last rows of shards, and before them awaited a unit of twenty Marcks with a mix of rifles and blades similar to the Marcks they had previously encountered.

"Back!" Trayco ordered, waving his team back deeper into the shards. "Marcks, twenty or more!"

Carr perked up. "Let's get at 'em!"

145

"Negative! We'll get cut to pieces. Besides, this cover is terrible. We need to fallback and see if we can get a flanking position."

A voice that was not a Marck yelled out from a distance. "It's okay. We are not here to fight you. Please, come out, and I can explain."

"Who the heck is that?" Jex asked.

Trayco peeked his rifle around a shard, using its visor-integrated optics to get a safe look. "I don't know, but if they think they are going to play us for fools, they are highly mistaken."

Crix stepped forward. "Maybe we should at least see what he has to say." At that moment, clanking metal and the winding of servos motors echoed from every direction behind them.

Jex spun around and stared down his rifle's sight. "We're surrounded, and they're closing in fast!"

Carr lumbered back a few steps to gain a better vantage of the incoming Marcks. "It's a friggen trap!"

Trayco swung his rifle around. "Great. So much for plan B."

"Well?" Crix persisted. "I can go out and talk with them."

"Absolutely not!" Trayco cut him off quickly. "You're our VIP on this mission, and it's too risky. I will go out."

Carr let out a low, rumbling growl. "Trayco, have tya lost yer freekin' mind?"

"Please understand, if we wanted to kill you, you would already be dead. We know why you're here and are willing to assist," the voice yelled out again.

"Keep your sights on the leader; if anything--and I mean anything--looks wrong, drop him where he stands. You got that?" Trayco said before he cautiously stepped out and placed his rifle down at his feet and his hands in the air.

He approached an older, well-weathered Solaran clad in eclectic armor and a blood-red cape. "Good. Now, as you can see, we do not intend to kill you; rather, we are willing to assist in your mission." The Solaran motioned for his Marcks to lower their weapons. His sun-baked face was heavily wrinkled, and the sagging skin didn't move as he spoke.

"Your Marck patrol we ran into earlier had a strange way of showing a willingness to assist us."

The Solaran smiled and took a deep breath. "Please understand that their primary orders are to keep trespassers from crossing the sea . . . for public safety, of course."

"Psss . . . public safety . . . right," Trayco whispered to himself.

"You seek General Gorag, correct? I can take you to him as he is expecting your arrival."

Trayco dipped his chin back and squinted. "Expecting our arrival? Who are you anyway, and why do you have these illegal Marcks?"

147

"I am Tolta Brea, Principal Emissary for Gorag the Great and Core Lieutenant of the Palic Legion. These Marcks were gifted to General Gorag by the Galactic Marshal for his service in the protection and oversight of building the mechanized force that eventually saved the UMO populace." Tolta attempted to straighten his old, thick-boned back and neck as he slipped his hand inside a chest pocket, resting it there. His pride for his leader showed through, as did his zealot allegiance to the former Palic Legionnaires.

Trayco posted his hands to his hips and looked back at his group still hiding in the shards and then again at Tolta. His eyes squinted. "So what now? You just take us to Gorag, and he gives us what we want?"

"I know you're not foolish enough to believe that; of course, General Gorag will expect something in return. I feel that is only reasonable." Tolta tilted his head, awaiting Trayco's reply.

Trayco paused in thought. "I don't suppose you're going to tell me what that something is, right?"

"I'm afraid that I'm not privileged to that information. You must come with me to discover what he has to offer."

Trayco turned to look back at his awaiting companions, then back again to Tolta. "Let me confer with my team."

"Very well, don't take too long. General Gorag is gracious, yes, but not known for his patience."

***

Trayco expressed his reservation of the scheme. However, given the present circumstances, he felt this was the best chance they had at this point. This would at least get them close to Gorag.

"Trayco, I think tya have been consumin' too many of those pretick canes, and tya mind is goin' soft. I trust these Solaran slugs as 'bout as far as I can toss 'em into the nearest gammac corridor," Carr protested as he pointed his thick-webbed finger at Trayco and then toward the Marcks.

Jex pulled his rifle up and aimed in the direction of the Marck force. "I'm with ya, Carr . . . I say we just throw down with these low-tech cans and see who emerges as the strongest."

Trayco looked over to Flotto. "Flotto? You have been quiet in all of this. What are your thoughts?"

Flotto curled his plump lips and looked back at the group. "I say we go with them. Gorag has his faults, but he is also a businessman; I feel we can strike a mutually agreeable deal."

"Haa! Of course, tya do," Carr barked, implying that the fellow Solaran was biased.

Crix popped his neck, tilting it back and forth, trying to loosen the tensed up muscles. Trayco looked over at him next. "Your thoughts?"

"Let's see what he has to offer."

"Okay. I say we go despite my reservations. They are obviously aware of our presence here, and fighting through Gorag's force would just be foolish bravado," Trayco said as he squinted at Carr and Jex.

"Well, tat's just great! So now we just stomp in as willin' captives?" Carr grumbled; the scar across his face turned to an "S" shape from his scowl of disapproval.

CHAPTER 12

Following Tolta and escorted by twenty Gorag-controlled Marcks, they entered a mostly hidden mountain pass that snaked up to a sturdy-looking castle high above. The ground was pitted and unkempt, but the Marcks filed their way up like marbles through a polished tube.

Along the path, they encountered other Marcks standing guard. These guards vigilantly watched the group move their way up to the castle, each one with the gemstone insignia of Gorag blazoned upon their chest. The four, tall, castle towers pierced through the thick, dusty sky. The two bulky forward towers were outfitted with rotating cannons, meant to keep both ground and aerial attacks repelled. Elevating further up was a pair of thin, loftier towers whose tops vanished from view into the hazy clouds. Gorag's menacing castle nestled into the mountain like a Monoglade child in its wild-eyed mother's arms.

It appeared to be only accessible from the front side unless someone could scale the extreme elevation of the mountainside behind it.

The intensive climb up a sharp slope peppered with barbed rocks took a toll on their endurance. The group heaved breaths of thin air, and their inflamed muscles scorched against their aching bones. Solara was a solid chunk of metal and stone, and its gravity took an unforgiving toll on the group members not used to its abusive nature. The sight of the castle gates peeking through the gritty air gave salvation that the burdensome trip was over, but behind this relief was the fear of what lay ahead of them.

The golden gates of the castle had huge bolts lining the outer edges with the now-familiar gemstone insignia stamped outside. The walls were thirty meters high and lined with both Marck and armored Solarans atop. This, however, was already expected in a castle occupied by Gorag. What was not expected were the towering Marck guardians that stood on either side of the gate. No one in their group had ever seen a Marck like this, outside of early design concept drawings.

The guardians were basic in appearance, with rounded, clunky armor and squared eyes and mouth on a dome-top head. They stood nearly twenty meters tall. Like mystical giants come to life, their primary defense was their thick armor, and their offense was brute hammer-like strength. They stood motionless with caked-on dust and grime packed in and around their joints and outer shells. It appeared as though they moved little, if at all; perhaps they were there only as intimidation. However, as the group approached the gates, the giant heads ground slowly inward, and their square chins dipped down as freed clumps of dirt poured down from their necks. These titans were keeping track of the unfamiliar guests. The Marck giants turned and grasped two large levers beside them. Their bulky arms pushed the levers forward, and the gate began to labor upward. The gates groaned, and the ground trembled as they moved upward. The watchful Guardians turned back toward the group as they proceeded into the castle grounds.

Inside the castle courtyard, the walls were lined with Marck soldiers bearing swords, pikes, and other melee-style weaponry. Iron bars secured arched windows that overlooked the area. A single golden statue of Gorag stood proudly in the center. He wore a crowned helmet and chest plate that was partly covered in ornate robes that drug the ground. His large hands wielded a spiked scepter guarded across his chest. His face appeared as though crafted from a youthful version of himself.

Above them, a charged, shadowy grid of steaming, red thermal energy protected the courtyard from the storms. Rocks and debris snapped and flared as they contacted the shielding barrier. The gates behind them slammed down, shaking the walls and ground. They continued ahead past the courtyard and over a smoke-stained, stone bridge that led across to an inner portion of the castle. The smaller palace within the castle was more ornate versus the battered exterior host, shadowed with twisted iron décor and pointed archways.

Tolta stopped and turned to the group. "You will now remove your armor and any hidden weapons you may be carrying."

"No way," Carr protested.

"Visitors are not to enter the palace armed or armored. They are to come in peace. This must be agreed upon or . . ." Tolta motioned up at the guards around the walls and they pointed their rifles down toward the group in response.

Jex looked up and let out a deep exhale. "I don't like this."

"Just do it," Trayco ordered as he started to unclasp his armor. The others reluctantly followed, leaving a pile of protective gear at the palace entrance.

"Good. We shall proceed then." Tolta waved them forward with a smile.

A heavy, black portcullis creaked upward as they approached the main entrance of the palace. They passed through the dimly lit gate guarded by two Solarans clad in open-faced helmets, chest armor, and rifles casually shouldered. They pounded their fists on their chest in salute as Tolta passed through.

Dank, musty air mixed with an odor of burned flesh curled their nostrils as they entered. The ambiance felt uninviting. Screams of pain and terror echoed through the rows of blackened archways before them. There was a general sense that this was a place that most visitors were drug into rather than invited.

As they followed the Marck escort down the long-arched hall, shouting and banging lurched ahead of them. The hall opened to a large, brightly lit area. Gorag's lair was enormous, eclectically adorned with bizarre brass and black instruments of weaponry and torture. There was an apparent show of someone sadistic and nefarious that called this place home. A crowd of Solarans gathered around a sunken section of the gritty, stone floor. They shouted and pumped their fists with excitement and, in some cases, anger. Long, black spikes hung in clusters above the pit area. The spikes flashed and threw down random beams of white light that made a resounding pop, leaving their eardrums wrenching in pain.

Gorag sat in the back of the room, his ornate throne reclined and perched high above everything else. He wore thick, burgundy robes that draped off the sides of this throne, and he had a fiery gemstone that replaced his left eye. The brilliant gem glistened from nearby lights and created red prisms that danced around the room as he moved his head.

He took notice of the entering group with a brief moment of interest and then turned back to the activities in the pit below. Seated behind him were his prized harems of Solaran and Mendac females adorned in a display of scantily attire. They relaxed across an eclectic peppering of crimson and onyx silk couches. Most of them appeared amused with the activities and giggled amongst one another, while a few looked drawn and quiet.

The entering Marcks parted and retreated, keeping formation to the backside of the room while a pair remained directly behind Crix and the others. Tolta proceeded ahead as they stopped short of the pit. Inside the deep pit, a husky Solaran and a Hybor were mounted into skeletal devices of worn, black steel. The contraptions wrapped around their bodies from their fists to their feet. They tromped heavily at one another, flailing and kicking viciously like two ravenous animals fighting for survival.

Light beams popped and hummed all around the fighters, and they tried desperately to avoid contact. The Hybor's heafty fist cracked into the Solaran's chest, giving off a flash of spark with a sizzle of flesh. The Solaran staggered back, his skin melted from the blow. He screamed in anger then charged headlong into the

Hybor, sending him smashing into one of the light beams; his body flashed white then turned to vapor, leaving only the skeletal suit clanking to the floor.

The surrounding crowd roared with excitement. A rumbling bass of laughter bellowed from Gorag as he expressed his pleasure with the fight's outcome. The light beams deactivated, and the pit arose slowly, level with the floor of the crowd. Several guards unclasped the Solaran fighter from the caged suit and escorted him before Gorag. They shoved him forward, and he took a knee in a show of reverence.

Gorag motioned him to rise. "You have given us a good fight and vanquished another vile Hybor. Now its foul lungs no longer pollute Solaran air."

Carr growled loud enough that several of the Solarans close by turned around to look, then scowled at the sight of a Hybor. Gorag paused for only a second and then continued. "You have pleased me, and therefore I pardon your crimes of murdering a citizen of Semptor. Go now and be free, for Gorag the Great is merciful." The Solaran smirked and ran off past them, never once looking back as he left the throne room.

The room's occupants now turned to the group that entered during the fight. Tolta spoke to Gorag. Crix and the others couldn't hear what he was saying, but Gorag looked at them with an unpleasant scowl. "Come closer so I can see you better," Gorag said with a profoundly irritating snarl.

CHAPTER 13

The two Marck guards pushed them forward. Gorag's body appeared as one that had, for many years, enjoyed the overindulgences of pleasures that had been at his disposal. He slowly tapped his fingers across the throne's armrest; his slouching posture gave the impression of one that would not be easy to satisfy. "Sire, I present to you the Tolagon and his companions as promised," Tolta said, swinging his arm outward in a presenting fashion.

"Why are there two fowl Hybors stinking up my throne room? Why have they been allowed to live? Explain yourself, Tolta, and be quick about it." Gorag's eye appeared to light up the gemstone with fire as his ire ignited.

Crix glanced at Jax and Carr and then back to Gorag. "We were told that you would help us if we came peacefully. Are you not one to keep to your word?" Tolta's eyes opened wide with shock over the disrespectful remark.

Gorag scowled resentfully. "That is so, at least until I saw the company that you keep. Now there is a price that must be paid. One that will be paid in blood and suffering."

Trayco's face flushed, and sweat beaded up across his forehead. He cleared his throat. "So what do you want?"

"I want you to fight and kill both of your Hybor companions; then, and only then, will I let you live. After that, I will consider aiding you in your quest."

Without a second of delay, Trayco answered. "No chance of that. We all leave here or none of us."

The sagging flesh around Gorag's face stretched up into a menacing grin. "Very well, then." He pointed to the Marcks behind them, and they immediately drew their swords and plunged them into the spines of Carr and Jex. Both cried out dread-filled wails while trying in vain to reach back to stop their attackers. They squirmed as the Marcks held the blades in their backs, twisting them, grinding them into their bones, and severing flesh and nerves.

"No! You bastar—" Trayco screamed out loud. The shock of losing his longtime comrades smashed into him like an Armion freight carrier, but he quickly pulled himself back and tried to keep his poise in front of his adversary by not showing his emotions.

Crix squinted and lowered his head, trying to block out the horror that he couldn't stop. His heart raced up with each passing second as their voices continued to screech and howl until they went silent. Everything in the room blurred and then became crystal clear. Crix began to have tunnel vision, his jaw clenched.

Jax and Carr's lifeless bodies lopped down upon the stone floor like sacks of wet towels. The Marcks dragged them out of the throne room, leaving a glistening smear of burgundy shaded blood.

Crix tried to remain steadfast and not allow the fear within him to show through. He stared coldly forward, his dry mouth and throat stuck together as he struggled to swallow.

"Now that the first offer has expired, I can at least speak to you without the stench of those disgusting Hybors rotting my throne room." Gorag looked directly at Flotto with a sharp smirk.

"I am here to serve you, Lord Gorag," he said, bowing low.

Gorag waved his scepter in a blessing gesture. "You have done well, Flotto, and have earned your place here amongst my Legionnaires."

"What?" Trayco hissed under his breath. Flotto had served with his commando team for several years. Trayco clenched his teeth as he thought about Flotto treacherously leaking information back to Gorag this entire time and might have led to some of the previous commando teams' casualties.

Gorag squinted as he turned his attention to Trayco. "Surprised, are you? You shouldn't be. Solaran's loyalty will always be with the sovereignty of Solara. What do you think has been the root of all the centuries of warfare between our worlds? That political nonsense of disputed sector control and commerce disagreements was all a ruse to hide the real underlying reality."

Trayco glared at Flotto with disgust. He had served as a commando of the resistance for a long time; now his thoughts flashed back and questioned every action, every word, and every mission he was on to find signs of the concealed agenda. Crix remained calm and tried to keep his focus on Gorag. He needed to devise a plan on how to escape this horrible predicament. *Keep him talking.*

"What has been the root of all the conflicts then, Gorag?" Crix asked with a touch of sarcasm behind his question.

"What?" Gorag asked, surprised by his audacity. Crix ignored his tone and elaborated.

"I mean, you're telling us that millions have died and peace has been nearly impossible, for what? Generations of blind loyalty? Come on, I don't believe that, and you don't either." The words just poured out, and even Crix couldn't believe his own actions or where this boldness was coming from.

Gorag scowled in frustration over his continued outward disrespect, something he wasn't accustomed to. He turned his head until the red glare from his gemstone eye reflected directly into Crix's eyes, forcing him to squint and turn away.

"You may be the youthful Tolagon, but your vulgarity is only shadowed by your apparent lack of wisdom. I should have you struck dead where you stand for questioning me in such a way." Garog let out a strong exhale. "You're fortunate you caught me in a gracious mood so, I shall give you an answer. The real answer is because we hate you and everything you represent. The whole of our world was populated by the criminal discards of Nathasia long ago. Do you truly believe we have forgotten this? It's ingrained into the marrow of our bones, this world, with its oppressive gravity and hostile winds were supposed to be an eventual death sentence for our ancestors, but we adapted and now call this our paradise. It has made us stronger . . . superior to your kind. Hybors are good for dying, your kind is good for slaves, and we do not want you here unless it's serving one of those two purposes."

Gorag stopped to feel his face; his skin drooped further down and his natural eye sunk deeper into its socket. He swiped his hand across his face with a harsh cough and quickly grasped a nearby golden lever adorned with an image of a horned beast at its top. He pulled the stiff lever upward, and a transparent container slid down slowly around his reclined seat. The occupants around him took a cautious step back as a hiss preceded a murky green gas that crept down from above and filled the cylinder. Gorag shook violently and let out a horrid growl as his hulking, silhouette shadowed through the gas. Trayco and Crix peeked discreetly at each other, both with the secretive hope that whatever was going on underneath that cylinder resulted in his demise, but at the same time, they still needed him alive.

The gas gently whisked away, sucked back into the unseen above. Gorag's appearance had changed. His skin pulled tight, and his eye looked youthful and plump. A sinister grin filled his face like the odious doll that a child would feel compelled to hide in a closet to keep from having ill dreams. The conduit glided up, and Gorag sat erect, seeming more muscular than before. He took a deep breath and let out an explosive exhale.

"Poray gas?" Trayco whispered. *I now see what the real problem is.* At one time, it was used to enhance youth, athleticism, strength, and aggression of UMO soldiers during the first Thraxon war. Unfortunately, it was also responsible for causing psychosis and eventual death from its passing effects. The gas would rapidly deteriorate the user's mind and body when not administered in persistent treatments.

161

Gorag stood and flexed his muscles. "That's better, much better." He motioned at a pale, gaunt-looking Mendac slave, who held a decanter of spirits nearby. The slave hurried over ready to fill a cup, but Gorag was not interested in the spirits. Instead, he grasped the slaves head with one hand and squeezed; the slave let out a painful whimper as the cracking bone echoed through the chamber. The head collapsed under the pressure of Gorag's squeeze, and the slave's legs buckled before he tossed his limp body away from his throne.

Crix turned away in disgust. *Monster! What a horrible monster; I would rather find a way to rid everyone of this plague, but I have to get the information we need from him or Kerriah and the UMO are lost.* He mustered up the necessary courage to ask the question directly and firmly. He had to, even in the face of such an atrocity.

"Gorag, we were told you knew of our mission and would help. I realize you hate us, but if Zearic and the Thraxons have their way, we will cease to exist, including you. We need you to tell us the location of Joric Placater; apparently, you are the only one with knowledge of his whereabouts."

Gorag snatched up a large gem-encrusted scepter and smashed it angrily down on the ground in front of him; gems loosened from the impact, zinging across the room in several directions. "So you think that Gorag the Great will just give you this type of information for free? Arrogant fool! If you want something from me, it will cost you."

"The resistance has resources at its disposal. How much do you require for this information?" Trayco asked.

"I have more than adequate currency and have little need for yours. I desire your blood. You will fight to the death in the Vapour pit," Gorag snarled, hungry for some more death as he stared at Crix.

Crix sized up a nearby husky Solaran that had scars and sear marks on his skin. His appearance was one that had been a part of this pit fight before and emerged the victor. He bit into his lower lip to keep his nerves settled.

"Why are you looking at Kannag? That is not who you will be fighting," Gorag barked; for a second Crix felt a slight relief, only for a second. "You will fight each other, and one of you will die; only then will I consider granting you your request."

"No! No deal," Crix shouted without a second thought. In his mind, there was no way he was going to kill Trayco, so they would have to find another way.

Trayco stared gloomily at Crix. "It's okay. It's not about me, and I have always been ready to lay down my life for the cause. Now is that time."

"But—"

Trayco raised his palm, quickly stopping Crix's rebuke. "I'm only a pawn in the greater plan that you have to finish."

"I can't do it. I can't kill you . . . I won't," Crix whispered aloud.

"Well? What's your answer? Are you going to fight? This crowd needs to see someone die," Gorag's voice boomed from his throne. The gathering around them stirred and grumbled with their craving for death.

"We will fight, but how do we know you will keep your word?" Trayco asked.

"If I feel adequately entertained by your death brawl, I will tell you the location of Joric. I don't see what good that information will do you anyway. Hmmm . . ." Gorag scratched his chin as he stared at them, pondering their request. He smirked. "It will likely lead to a death worse than what I am offering you now."

Crix gave Trayco a sideways glance. "That's not very reassuring." He had to find a way out of this. There had to be another way.

"Don't worry; we will give you the show you're looking for. The victor will be expecting the information we seek after this is finished, plus the return of our gear and safe passage out," Trayco said.

Gorag grinned and then clapped his hands together in anticipation. "Good! Get them in spark suits and lower them into the pit."

"Let's give them their show," Trayco said, patting Crix on the back as he stepped forward. The skeletal spark suits rattled down from above as they approached. Crix looked at him with a long face. How was he going to do this? He couldn't murder Trayco; he was a good man. Machines and bad guys were easy to kill, but Trayco was neither. He labored through the emotional tidal wave of what was about to transpire.

THE QUEEN PROTOCOL

Two muscular, bare-chested Solarans tore off the top of Crix's ab suit and smeared a thick layer of black grease across his chest and arms. He noticed that these two Solarans had a buildup of grease and blotchy patches of grime that coated their bodies. A pungent odor of sweat and bodily excrements curled his nose as they circled, clasping and snapping metal latches. Across the pit, he could see the same happening to Trayco. The suit clasped around his arms, neck, legs, and down to his feet. A large, sweaty Solaran locked a handwheel into the back center of Crix's suit and turned it. The metal bars squeezed around him with every creaking rotation. His muscles bruised against the metal cage as the Solaran continued to turn the wheel. Sour breath and a laugh blew against the back of Crix's neck. It felt like he was enjoying making it uncomfortable as he cranked it in tighter and tighter.

Crix grimaced and flinched as the metal bands pinched into his skin. "Okay! That's tight enough." The Solaron peeked around the cage and smirked back at him with mockery in his eyes.

The Solarans scurried out of the pit like rodents. Crix stared across at Trayco. The cruelly fastened metal bands made him look more like a tortured cyborg pieced out of scrap than himself. The pit area rumbled and shook as it slowly dropped back down, giving its spectators an elevated and safe view from the ensuing violence.

"Light them up!" a voice called from above. It wasn't easy to see the crowd, but Crix could hear their voices starting to shout with excitement. The suit began to vibrate and hum gently, then picked up tempo and intensity over the next few seconds. He felt an itching in his armor-plated hands. It must have been the power surging through them; the same power that burned the chest of the Solaran in the match before. The exoskeleton rattled for a second,

165

and then he felt a sense of weightlessness; suddenly, the dense gravity of this world no longer burdened his sore muscles. He looked down and noticed that he stood on his toes. The power flowing through the cage appeared to be giving it an antigravitational spring upward. He was so light on his feet that he felt like a seasoned fighter.

An announcer's voice broke through the shouts of the crowd. "There are no rules in the shock pit; just kill your opponent or be killed. If you want to please the great Gorag, then brutality is your only friend." Crix could hardly understand him over the barking of the spectators shouting in their last-minute wagers. "When you hear the horn, fight!"

Crix's heart raced, and perspiration trickled down his back and forehead. How did they end up here, like this? Trayco appeared focused and leaned forward, ready to pounce ahead like an ebb tree tiger waiting for the perfect time to jump at his prey.

I can't do this—Before he finished his thought, a deep bellowing horn sounded off like a great beast calling its mate, flooding out all surrounding noise for a few seconds. Crix looked up to see the leering crowd above screaming and shaking their fists; their voices pierced at his nerves as the horn faded. In his forward view, there was a swirling light from Trayco's fist that blinded him for a second, just long enough to get blasted in the side of his head. The bars and accompanying plate metal from the spark suit absorb most of the shock, but he still felt its sting. It was a jolt that he could feel down to the roots of his teeth. It was an impact with a kiss of electricity.

The post-impact waft of burned ozone filled his lungs. He staggered back as Trayco sent a continuous barrage of right and left blows that met his lower abdomen and side of his head. His neck cracked over and sent him down to his backside; the smell of charred hair turned to a stench of scorched flesh. His skin seared around his abdomen and left ear, burning and feeling like his skin was dripping away.

Trayco kicked Crix's side; a shocking reverberation cut through the metal skeleton, eating at every disk and tendon in his body. The crowd above stirred into an angry frenzy over the one-sided match. Trayco stomped down on Crix's chest; the metallic heel clattered and crackled as the energy arced into the bars covering his chest. "Get up! Come on!"

Someone above tossed the severed head of Carr down upon Crix; it clonked off his chest and clomped over on its side, staring directly at him with dried, opaque eyes. *Savages! I can't stand the sight of them, but I have to do this for Kerriah. I can't just lay here to die. There are too many depending on me, and I'm not going to die here for their entertainment.* Crix rolled over back to a kneeling position.

Trayco swung for another forward kick; this time, Crix grabbed his heel with both hands, and he lifted his leg, tossing him backward and slamming him down into the hard floor. The crowd roared with pleasure. He leaped upward and drove his metal foot down into Trayco's rib cage, minimally collapsing the protective bars. He felt the stinging shock echo up his leg as his foot impacted. He picked up his fallen opponent by his limbs and swung him around for a time or two before sending him sailing into the pit wall.

Trayco got back up slowly, shaking off the blow. Crix took a storming charge, but just before he reached his target, a blazing pole of light drove downward directly in front of him. He dug his heels in and skidded to a narrowing stop, his eyes fixated momentarily on the light beam. A closer look revealed that the light consisted of tiny spheres that swarmed like frenzied insects. The swarming gave the light a gentle flickering effect.

Trayco got back to his feet again and tried to circle behind Crix while focusing on the light pole. "Come on, Tolagon! Let's see what you've got." He beckoned him with a wave.

Crix took the bait and surged forward, leaping at him with both fists aimed directly for Trayco's head. At the last second, Trayco sidestepped and slugged him, sending his momentum out of control. His flailing body narrowly missed one of the lethal beams before smacking against the hard surface and spinning to a final stop.

The crowd stirred into a jubilant frenzy over the action; Trayco glanced upward. *Now it's time.* Carr and Jex had made their sacrifice; now, it was his turn.

Crix leaped up and took a hammering strike into Trayco's lower back; the shock of the power suit jolted through the protective cage and raked through every nerve and burned into his eyes. He tried to spin around, but Crix clamped around his throat. Trayco reached back and clenched a bar on Crix's cage; stepping back, he tossed him over his shoulder and quickly mounted him. He pressed his fist down at Crix's face while he pushed against his attack with his forearm. There was a blinding light from the electric charge that popped and swirled from his fist with the smell of thick ozone.

Trayco grunted, and his forehead scrunched as he bore his fist down. "You have to kill me. You have to make it look convincing. Don't make me take my chances by killing you. You're our best hope." A light beam suddenly shot down next to him, startling Trayco for an instant.

Crix felt him loosen his pressure. Taking advantage of the momentary distraction, he shoved Trayco's arm into the beam. The UMO commando let out a horrific scream as his arm appeared to demolecularize with the tiny spheres swirling up to his shoulder. Crix, taken aback, pushed him away from the light beam, severing the contact and leaving Trayco without an arm. Blood poured from the wound; Crix repeatedly blasted his fists down on Trayco's injury, searing it closed with power-infused heat-blasts from the spark suit. "N-No . . ." Trayco gasped.

CHAPTER 14

The cheers from the crowd silenced, and they began tossing garbage into the pit and shouting obscenities over the act of mercy. Crix looked at Trayco and squeezed his eyes shut. *I almost killed this man of honor and loyalty. A warrior of faith and integrity, all of which are qualities that no one here possesses even the tiniest speck. Why should he lose his life for their pleasure?* He stood defiantly and gazed up at the crowd.

"No! I won't kill him." The light beams retracted, and the floor rumbled back up to the crowd's level. Gorag's face reeked of scorn, and his fist clenched around his scepter.

The guards removed Crix and Trayco from the spark suits and shoved them down before Gorag. "What shall I do with you now, imprudent child? My subjects demand your blood." He grinned; the evil stare pierced into Crix's eyes. "And I demand your blood as well, so there is little hope for either of you." Gorag stood, his unusually large frame towering over the average Solaran. "They shall be fodder for the heydromac! Let it feast on their living flesh." The crowd cheered at the proclamation. "I will sift the Tolagon orb from his feces!" Gorag slammed his scepter onto the ground, displaying his grand authority over the one-sided verdict.

Crix felt a sharp pain stab into the back of his head, and his face planted into the floor. His feet rose, and his body was dragged swiftly across the warm, stone surface. His blurry vision went black as they shoved a sack over his head and cinched it tightly across his neck. The restricted air sapped his remaining strength.

The sudden clatter of rickety metal ahead ended with an abrupt crashing down behind him. He felt his body moving upward as the continuous squeak of an unoiled wheel became the only discernible sound. The warm, humid air slowly gave way to a cold, crisp breeze. Crix's head cleared enough to feel the bite of the cold against his skin. As he laid against a steel grate floor, his body shivered, and he attempted to curl up for warmth. Before he could get into full fetal position, the rugged tread of a boot slammed against his neck. The hard rubber pressed into his muscles, pinning his face into the chilly grate.

The squeaking wheel stopped, and the rattle of the metal broke the brief silence. The heavy foot lifted from his neck, and his body yanked up from the metal grate. His stomach dropped as he slid down smooth stone before losing his breath on a coarse surface. There was a thump next to him, followed by a groan. *Trayco?*

Crix shoved his thumbs under the tight bands around his neck and pulled. The sack wouldn't come off until he pushed his chin into his neck. He ripped the band across his chin and nose. Daylight burned into his eyes for a minute until they adjusted.

"Trayco," he said.

He heard laughter above him. Two husky Solarans pointed and chuckled to each other before turning around and stepping into a rusty cage. Within seconds, it disappeared from view and into the castle below.

Crix pulled the sack from Trayco's head. He squinted and recoiled from the bright outside light. Crix looked around at the rocky bowl that surrounded them. "I think we're atop the mountain. Above Gorag's castle."

Near them stood a lone tree, stoic and weathered, with four boney branches weeping down its sides. Crix stared at the odd-looking tree for a minute, trying to figure out how it grew way up here. Having spent his life in Troika, he had seen many types of trees, but this one was different. Its top came to a point, with Crimson veins webbing down to its base and seeping into the soil below. The sound of Trayco wheezing with each labored breath took Crix's attention back to his fallen companion.

He clutched him by the arm and hoisted the weary commando to his wobbly feet. The air was thin, and he felt a bit of nausea stirring in his stomach, along with a twinge of dizziness.

"Whatever is up here, we have to find a way to kill it," he whispered to Trayco, but he didn't reply. "We can't just wait here getting weaker." Crix glanced around for a way out. The word "Heydromac" remained in his head.

They sat in a deep bowl of rock and dust. Above them, stone spikes of grey with fingers of saffron oozed down their tips. "I can raise us out of this pit, but I need to get a better view of what we're dealing with." Trayco's head hunkered below his shoulders. He tilted his head to the side and stared up at Crix with sunken and tired eyes. His legs wobbled and collapsed. Crix snapped him up before he hit the ground, placing his arm around his neck. He dragged him over to the tree and carefully set him against its murky trunk.

Crix couldn't help but notice the bitter scent of decay nearby. He curled his nose and shot a few glances around, trying to locate its origin. "Just take it easy for a few minutes." Tracyo looked to be barely hanging on to consciousness as his eyelids slowly fell shut. He remained quiet and firmly clutched the shoulder where his missing right arm used to be.

"I have to find us a way out of here," Crix said. He squatted down for a closer look at Trayco's face and then placed his hands on his shoulders and gave them a firm shake. "Stay with me, Tracyo." The commando's chin dropped to his chest. "Dang it." Crix stood back up, staring at where he had last seen the Solarans that had thrown them down there. "I'll be right back. Okay?"

He called the power of the orb and lifted himself upward. *Where is this heydromac?* Concern dug at him. As he neared the top, he noticed a row of small, black lenses along the rim. *Cameras. They're watching us.* They weren't obvious, concealed amongst the rocks.

He could see the empty shaft where the elevator came up. It was just a black cavity now, going back down into the bowels of Gorag's lair.

Trayco's weary voice screamed out from below him. Crix swung around. The tree's weeping tendrils sucked into Trayco's flesh. They pulsed and pumped as though draining whatever it needed from his body. "Trayco!"

Crix darted back down, determined to pull him from the clutches of the creature. The top of the tree peeled down with hundreds of whisking strands blooming out. A boney white head emerged from inside the strands, dripping with red excrement. It let out a deep, gurgling groan and two dimples formed on its pale flesh. They appeared to be eyes, and though unusual, Crix could see suffering within them as they curved downward in sync with the groaning.

The tree's base sucked upward and three legs slithered from beneath its trunk, pulling itself from a deep hole underground. The strands from its head swooshed around, grasping at Crix. Trayco's body lifted from the ground. With his insides now consumed, he hung like a dirty rag, merely an empty sack of skin hanging from the heydromac's clutches.

Crix's face blanked white with horror. The heydromac cast the limp flesh to the side and rose, eye-to-eye with its next assumed meal. Its face sunk into pale, rippling flesh. As Crix tried to shake off the panic of Trayco's demise, a strong tug on his leg forced him downward. He slammed to the ground and sucking limbs followed, striking into his chest and abdomen. Crix let out a frightful shriek as the orb strobed, and the limbs snapped back up from the unfamiliar shock.

He couldn't rise back up. The view above him darkened with limbs and swirling strands. He scurried on his hands and knees for the ominous hole that the creature had emerged from. In his panic, it was his only chance. He fell in, tumbling deeper than he had imagined, with grit and loose soil raining down. The hard smack onto the sticky ground below peppered his vision with pulsing spots of light.

The heydromac's mouthless face appeared over the hole for a moment, then glopped away, followed by boney strands feeling their way through the opening, slithering down the sides, reaching for their prey. Crix scampered across the floor, still on his hands and knees, trying to find a path out. A sharp stab drove into his back, and he arched in pain. Another piercing pain jabbed into his leg and arm. In a terrified response, he unleashed the orb's power. A blinding light occupied his vision like an apparition and then began to fade.

The heydromac's jellified arms lay pasted to the surface around him. The orb's powerful shock of energy stole the life from them as they attempted to extract Crix's insides. A loud thud, along with a rumbling across the ground, brought Crix back up to his knees again. He had to be ready for anything. However, there was only silence. He winced as he grabbed the back of his leg and tried to turn around. The wetness of blood ran down his back and leg.

Using the orb to raise himself from the hole, he dropped down near the heydromac. It lay motionless across the surface. Its once-whisking-strands splayed out flat and lifeless. Crix took a few careful steps closer to the shapeless head. As he neared, it burbled up, forming a bulbous shape. The head turned, and Crix leaped back. Beneath the mostly featureless face, he sensed sadness as its flesh rippled down and it let out a wet, gurgling groan. Crix pushed his arms forward with his fists clenched. Deep from within, he felt all his remaining strength leave, and he let out a powerful orb blast, smashing the heydromac's head into sludge against the rock beneath.

He dropped to his backside and looked around. *Trayco.* There was only a splat of blood-soaked flesh slid down the side of the rocky bowl. Crix turned away and cringed. Then he scowled and turned back at what remained of the slain creature. His heart sank. This heydromac was nothing more than another victim of Gorag's blood games. Who knew where they found this thing or what forsaken home they had ripped it from.

The squeak of the elevator wheel snatched his focus away from the grim scene. Crix snarled at the thought of facing the cold-blooded criminals again. His body pulsed blue as he levitated himself up for the unpleasant reunion. The rattling of the rusty bars emerged slowly from below. From the shadows appeared a faded, turquoise crate filled with Marcks and two Solarans. Their eyes peeked up through the bars as they neared the surface.

Crix planted himself near the entrance and took a few cautious steps back, ready to confront them while they were still bunched up in the elevator. His body glowed and his eyes blazed as the crate emerged and the doors clattered open, ready to strike with everything he had.

Several sudden thumps and a somewhat familiar growl turned his attention over his shoulder. *Gorag!* Vice-like hands dug into his ribs, and the Tolagon felt his body jar upward. His stomach left him before he was slammed back down into the unforgiving surface. The breath escaped his lungs, and everything around him went quiet for an instant. Before Crix could put up a defense, Gorag's scepter blasted down upon his head.

Somehow, he couldn't seem to escape the darkness. In his mind, he could hear voices, one hauntingly familiar. "Make an example of him . . . to all that think they will come here and impose themselves on us." The voice faded into silence. Time stood still, and Crix couldn't tell if the next voices came from a dream.

"Sire, we cannot extract the orb from him."

". . . Be there after the storm, to recover it from what remains . . ."

CHAPTER 15

His arms ached and his wrists throbbed. A burning, yellow light made his eyes water and tears pour over his face, which seared from insistent swelling. He squinted to catch a view of his surroundings and felt relief when he realized he was outside, but the relief quickly faded. Chains dangled from a hook far above him. The clasps around his wrists cut into his flesh and burned as sweat seeped into the fresh wounds. His body swayed from the shackles with the catch of every brisk gust of wind like a shabby flag. This time, he could not draw upon the orb to save him. A heavy helmet fastened upon his head kept his thoughts mixed. He couldn't focus enough to call its power. As he tried, a high-pitched squeal screamed into his ears and nausea bloated his stomach. He vomited and heaved over and over uncontrollably.

The storms! They had placed him there, helpless, to be stripped of his flesh and bone. Nearby, chains dangled from several tall poles that were currently vacant of their victims. This was a place of doom and despair which Gorag used for public executions so the political eyes could bear witness and submit to fear. How long had he been hanging there? To Crix, it felt like quite a long time. His wrists bled and shoulder burned behind the cold tingle of circulatory loss.

The storms could be there anytime. His arms felt dead, the cuffs around his wrist cut in deeply when he moved, and blood trickled down and webbed out across his bare chest. His breaths were short, and his head was light with a faintness that almost soothed him as he awaited the inevitable. Thoughts of Kerriah filled his mind, and a powerful, nauseous pit formed in his stomach. The bile scorched his throat as it heaved from his mouth again, dripping down his chest. He couldn't even capture a last moment of reflection over those he cared for or memories of his past. He could only stare down at the contents of his stomach below with a foggy mind devoid of thoughts.

His chin rested upon his chest as he heard the sirens in the distance warning of the stalking storms that would come to devour anything aside from stone or steel. The winds kicked up the dust around him and coated eyes that he was unable to rub.

If this is what's to become of me, then take me now; relieve me of this suffering. He winced as the cumbersome helmet screamed into his ears again, and his gut hurled. It wouldn't allow a single thought without consequence. Misery and sadness, disappointment, and nothingness filled his heart and mind; the dark lonely feeling of not being able to reach something that you have longed for but can't remember. He was frustrated, defeated, and disillusioned. Broken, he heard salvation.

"That's him," a tiny voice from far below announced.

"Stand back," said a low voice from further away.

The chains rattled and clanked. A sudden vibration shook through them again and again. The tension from the chains released, and Crix felt weightless for a couple of seconds, then the ground met him with a stiffening impact. Large hands grasped quickly around his waist, and he could see the dry, hard packed soil moving by as thick legs covered in heavily weathered boots strode along with a sense of urgency. The wind roared, and the smaller pebbles began to blister against his back and rattle his head just before he heard a heavy door slam shut, and then the sounds of the punishing storm were muffled in the distance. The sturdy dwelling insulated the audible chaos from the storms surprisingly well.

He was plopped down upon thick bedding, and a cloaked face stared over him. "You're safe for now," said a distorted voice as though coming through a filter. He pulled his cloak back, revealing a riveted helmet with a vented mouth that protruded outward.

"Who are you?" Crix asked, his voice faint; he struggled to focus on his unfamiliar rescuer.

Before answering Crix, he turned two round fasteners on the sides of his snug helmet and pulled it off, placing it gently on the table. A strong face, muscular, with many years of wear, squinted for a more focused look at Crix.

"I am Fershold." His hair was wiry and grey with streaks of black that matched his facial hair.

"You already have met my granddaughter, Luuda." He placed his hand on the back of a small child and guided her forward for him to see. It was the girl he had helped a day earlier. She gave him a big smile.

"I knew I would see you again; I just knew it," she said.

"She was out playing and noticed you up there on the hook of treachery. She came and told me of your helping her." He unbuckled the helmet from Crix's head and slid it off and then placed his hand on Crix's forehead. "Lucky for you, as I would have normally left you there to be stripped of your flesh, but Luuda insisted we save you, and that pure heart of hers can be very persuasive." He dipped a cloth into a bowl of water and wiped Crix's face and forehead, carefully cleaning off the dirt and swabbing his wounds.

"The hook of treachery?" Weary and drained, Crix took a moment to scan the room. The dwelling had a round ceiling with reinforced metal bands scaling from each side. Aged, tan leather-lined the ceiling inbetween the bands; it had a lived-in, warm feel.

"The hook of treachery means you personally defied Gorag, and he keeps that special place to make a public example to others who might get an idea of doing so themselves." Fershold drew water from a bulb-shaped, copper tank into a cup and then lifted Crix's head for a sip. Crix took a small sip, then a larger gulp. "Slow up there, I know you're dehydrated, but you're going to cramp up gulping it down like that," Fershold said, pulling the cup back. "I'll get these wounds mended up the best I can." He pulled a brown box out from under a stack of ancient-looking books. Fershold appeared to live a primitive lifestyle that had forsaken any sign of advanced technology of the era.

He opened the box up and pulled out a vial of milky fluid. "Drink this." He pressed it up to Crix's cracked lips, which immediately retracted from the pungent odor. "It tastes rancid, but it's an old Solaran elixir that will soothe your pain, your mind, and promote healing." Growing up in Troika, Crix was already accustomed to ancient remedies common in its traditional society and swallowed it down without questions.

"It's good to see a youthful Mendac that will accept an old-world tonic so willingly. I trust these solutions over the twisted and perverted machines that invade our bodies under the guise of healing that we have today. Most are unaware of what these things are really doing to them. Luuda and I keep things simple and trust in the pure and natural for our daily needs." Fershold swabbed his wounds out with a cloth dipped in a creamy, yellow substance. "Now, can you tell me what you are doing in Semptor and what you did to end up in the precarious situation we found you in."

"We need information that only Gorag has."

"We?" Fershold said as he pulled back from tending to his wounds. Crix raised his head. "The resistance. This information would possibly save all life as we know it in the UMO . . . and . . ."

"And what?"

Crix paused before answering. "To save Kerriah."

Fershold gave a warm smile. "Ahh, a female, one that you must be fond of, I presume. There is no shame in that. I once had a love as well and would have filled canyons to save her if I could. The wars stole her from me, and she only exists in my memories now." He cleared his throat. "Enough of me, though, what information is so important?"

"The location of Joric Placater," Crix mumbled; his eyes felt like they were sinking to the backside of his head and his body went numb. He lowered his head back into the soft bedding.

Fershold said nothing more and finished tending to Crix's wounds and then settled back into a sturdy, cozy chair. He watched Luuda as she sat on the floor playing with two dolls shaped like Solara's indigenous animals; he picked at his beard, lost in deep thought.

He picked up a bottle of emerald-colored spirits and poured a short glass. "Tell me, young Mendac, why do you have that azure radiance seeping from your skin? I don't believe I've ever seen anything quite like that before, and I've seen quite a bit in my time."

Crix lifted his head, taking a lengthy stare at Fershold. This steadfast soul who took care of a gentle creature like Luuda must be trustworthy. "I am Crix Emberook, and most will know me as the son of Corin Emberook, third Tolagon of Soorak. The blue color you see is the orb of Soorak. I was sent here to gain the location of Joric Placater from the only individual who apparently knows of it, Gorag."

Fershold raised one of his bristled eyebrows at Crix. "A Tolagon, huh? I was under the knowledge that your kind was disbanded after the Marck handoff; your very existence is a violation of the UMO stabilization pact." He sat up and leaned over with a scolding look in his eyes. "And what exactly are your intentions once you locate Joric?"

"To learn the location of the Marck Central Core and take control of the Marck forces before they are used to enslave and murder all intelligent life in the UMO system."

Fershold let out a raspy chuckle as he settled back into his seat and took a savoring sip from his cup. "So you're going to just march right into the Marck core and take control of it? Do you have some massive military force somewhere that has been hidden from public knowledge? Besides, I suspect wherever it may be, it will be impenetrable."

"There is a small resistance that consists of highly trained personnel capable of the task. With my help, we can stop the Marcks."

"A Tolagon," Fershold said quietly, almost as if just to himself.

"Do you have definitive proof of this so-called Marck plot to overtake their creators? I thought a failsafe system was put in place and that the core was coded to be benevolent concerning UMO law-abiding citizens," Fershold said, taking another sip of spirits.

Crix winced as he propped himself up to his elbows, and he looked at Fershold with disbelief. "You can't be serious? How long have you remained secluded here?"

"A good while now," Fershold replied, still seated comfortably in his chair.

"The Marcks have become an oppressive force that's responsible for terrible violence against UMO residents. They even laid complete waste to Troika and its citizens. The failsafe you refer to has failed already, and what's worse is Zearic and his Sinstar Corporation are somehow in league with them.

"And that's a whole other twisted tale; he has secretly joined forces with the Thraxons to build an elite hybrid species. They are united and planning to overtake us as we speak. We are out of time. All of us will be killed or converted, including your granddaughter. I will do whatever I can to stop this." His lips twitched with disgust, and his eyes filled with heavy tears that he fought back. His fingers gripped into the coarse blanket beneath him.

"They have taken everything from me, everything that I've known, and everything I loved." As he finished speaking, the storms' roaring outside settled to a gentle patter against Fershold's sturdy structure.

"The storms have subsided, and soon they will be looking for you, as well as whoever dismantled the two Marck sentinels that stood guard. They may come here looking for you, so you must be concealed." Fershold got up from his chair and took a long stretch with his arms extended overhead.

Crix's wobbly legs struggled to get up as he almost toppled a small table trying to catch himself from falling. His heart raced in panic as though he just remembered something important. "Oh, no! The extraction! What time is it?" he asked out of breath over the thought.

Fershold quickly grabbed his arm to assist. "I don't bother with keeping accurate time these days; I have no desire or need for it, but I can tell you it's the thirty-third cycle of the 6,088 year. Being that this is the fourth storm that blew through today, we're likely at about midday."

"I have to go. I have to be at the Arpol Ridge before the day's end. If I miss the terminal extraction, they are to assume that we've been killed." Crix stirred up to his feet but felt somewhat dizzy from the elixir that Fershold had given him.

"Whoa . . . settle down there. You're not in any condition to go anywhere right now, and Marck patrols are going to be scouring the area for you."

"I have to let them know that I did not get the information from Gorag and that they have to give me more time. If they think I'm dead, then all is lost!" Crix struggled and shouted into Fershold's face, but the strong Solaran wrestled him back over to the bed.

Luuda stopped playing over the excitement and grasped her grandfather's arm. "What's wrong, why is he so upset? Can't we help him, granddad?"

Fershold placed his large hand atop her head. "We will do what we can for him."

He paused, stopped, and listened as Crix attempted to plead with him again, only to be quickly hushed by a wave from the crusty old Solaran's hand. Fershold then walked over to the front door and unbolted it; it creaked slowly open and he stuck his head out. He quickly closed the door and re-bolted it.

"Marcks," he whispered. "They are here sooner than I had expected."

He stormed over to a metal door and slid it upward, exposing a small, cluttered storage area with shelves filled with bottles of fluids, tools, and some protective outerwear. He kicked a hidden plate at the bottom of the wall inside the storage area. The plate triggered the floor to fold down, revealing a ladder bolted to the side of a rock wall that led down into a dark space beneath the dwelling.

"Quickly!" He waved downward. "Hide down here. Do not make any noise or movement until I open this up."

Crix, groggy, struggled down the ladder and into the cavity below. The trap door slammed shut, leaving him alone in the dark with only the gentle glow of his orb's radiance. His eyes slowly adjusted. He could see the shadowy silhouette of a rifle, a hanging gun belt with a blaster pistol, a UMO pilot's helm, and military-type uniform hanging on a peg in the corner. It displayed an insignia of a long-handled melee weapon with a ball at the end surrounded by electric bolts. The insignia was familiar. Crix suspected this might be the Palic Legion's standard, having noticed its faded motif stained upon Gorag's palace courtyard walls. *Fershold's was Palic Legion?*

Foot stomps clonked back and forth across the floor above. Muffled voices became louder and then turned into shouting. The sudden jolt of something heavy clattered down, and he began to have conflicting thoughts regarding Fershold's command of staying put until he opened the door. What if he needed Crix's help? He could save Luuda and Fershold if they were in trouble. They were at risk because they had chosen to help him, so why shouldn't he try to save them?

The commotion stirred up again, and underneath it, he could hear Luuda's faint sobbing. At least she was still there and alive. He had to do something. He couldn't stand by while they were harmed.

His sweaty hands grabbed the cold bars of the ladder and he began to climb. He pushed on the door above, but it wouldn't budge. It must have a lock that was triggered by the hidden wallplate. He looked for a release anywhere from his side, but before he could find anything, the door popped open and the light above glared down.

"I thought I told you to stay put down there?" Fershold stood above Crix with his hands on his hips and a most disgruntled scowl. "What are you doing up on the ladder?" He tugged Crix up by his arm and out of the secret space. Crix gave his eyes a quick rub before observing the dwelling's contents turned upside down and Luuda's face red and swollen with tears.

"What happened? I wanted to come help but—" Crix started to explain himself, but Fershold cut him off.

"Gorag's despot Marck police force is what happened." Fershold's eyes darkened with contempt as he began to speak of it. "I don't know who he thinks he is sending those contraptions here to bully us like this. It wasn't always like this. There was a time I would have fought and died for the leaders of Solara—no longer. Corruption and self-satisfaction are all that matters to them

anymore. There is no honor as there was in generations past."
Fershold's face scrunched in disgust, and he spat on the floor.

"So you served with the Palic Legion?"

Fershold gave a sideways grin. He had expected this
question. "That's right. Obviously, you have seen my old uniform. I
was once the pilot of Gorag's personal cruiser and a sworn soldier
for his feared Palic Legion." He uprighted the overturned tables
and then took a cloth and wiped the tears from Luuda's face.

"I was loyal as I was conditioned and trained to be. When
Gorag decided to keep his provisional Marck Legion, violating
UMO Central Command orders, and then use those very Marcks to
ravage civilians and illegally rule with an iron fist, I knew I could no
longer be a part of his terror group. So I decided to fake my death
and take up a new life." He paused and stared at Luuda. "I even
tried to kill the general that I was sworn to serve and defend." He
paused again, this time longer. Crix remained quiet and stared
attentively at his host. Fershold could see his need to hear all the
details.

He picked up several items from the floor and continued
with the rest of his story. "I tried to kill Gorag by overloading his
ship's quantum drives and force pressurizing the reaction, causing it
to self-destruct outside the Nathasia System's Quadril Gammac
Corridor. I intended to kill him and then escape by stowing away in
a livestock cargo container I jettisoned just before the explosion,
then change my identity and go into hiding.

"I must have floated around in the darkness for weeks on a
gamble . . . a prayer, before being picked up by salvagers. This

specific livestock container had an efficient life support system, but by this time, they were on the brink, and I was severely dehydrated after exhausting my water rations. They didn't ask too many questions and were mostly concerned over their take from their pickup. I gave them a false name, and I eventually found transport back to Solara, where I was to start a new life."

Fershold stopped and rolled his eyes and shook his head as he recalled the next part. "However, I then learned the news that Gorag was still alive. Apparently, on the day of our departure to link up with his legion to oversee the newly built Marck armies' initial release, he had made a last-minute change with his shadower. He was good. In fact, I failed to realize it wasn't Gorag, even after speaking directly with him shortly after our departure."

Crix tilted his head. "Shadower?"

Fershold smiled and nodded. *Did this boy's schools not teach him anything?* "Shadowers were a group trained in the art of disguise and widely used during the war to protect high-ranking officials. Most of them I could spot close up, but not this one. As I said, he was good . . . real good. I still don't know why Gorag made that decision to this day. Why did he switch without telling me?" He pounded his fist on the table. "I was scared at first and hid so deep in a drok hole that I didn't know when the days passed and night fell." He looked over at Luuda, who had resumed playing with her dolls, and then he leaned in to whisper to Crix. "I had to feed on the poor creatures to live, and I can tell you that they don't have a very palatable taste." He cleared his throat and resumed a normal tone.

"After a while, I no longer cared; I changed my identity and decided to make my home in the place that would be the least expected, right under Gorag's nose. For years I lived a simple life with no care for what was going on with the war or politics; I kept to myself until, one day, when I was searching for coriadic diamonds in the lowlands, I heard screams in the distance. What I found was a family's dwelling being ransacked by a patrol of Gorag's Marck thugs."

He stopped to look over at Luuda, then motioned Crix to lean in a little closer and whispered again. "When they finished, they started torturing the residents and putting them to their swords. That's the first time I saw Luuda. A baby carelessly cast to the side screaming, left for dead. The soulless metal devils didn't even bother to give her a quick death after they burned her home and murdered her parents. I took her in, but I wasn't going to dishonor her parents by pretending to be them. Instead, I told her I was her granddad and that her parents had died of an unfortunate accident."

Fershold walked over to Luuda and placed his hand atop her head. Tears welled up in his steel-grey eyes. He took in a forceful sniff, fighting them back. "She is all that matters to me now and all I live for. I want to give her the best I can."

Crix placed his hand on Fershold's elbow. "I have been hidden away from the worst of this for most of my life until recently. I've discovered that the war has taken the best of almost everyone I have met so far." He stepped back with a serious look. "You must see the importance of my mission. We have to take control of the Marck's central core, and Gorag is the only one that knows the location of the person that knows where it is. I have to link up with my extraction team."

Fershold glanced over at Luuda, then stared at Crix for a few seconds. His face was drawn and tired in appearance. "It's no use going to Gorag again. He will never tell you what you want. He would hold onto it even if it meant his own death, just to spite you."

Crix threw up his hands in frustration as anger filled his eyes. "Then all is lost; that was our only hope at this point."

"No," Fershold said softly.

"No, what?"

"No, it's not the only hope. I know the location of the Marck architect." Fershold appeared weary over the thought of becoming involved again, yet his passion for Luuda forced him for the sake of her future.

"What? . . . How?" Crix tilted his head forward and his jaw dropped.

"As I told you before, I was his pilot and, as such, was the only other person besides Gorag that had to know of his location since I had to navigate there for his consultations. Everyone else that had been exposed to that knowledge had their minds wiped or were killed." Fershold was relieved to finally tell someone this information, yet still hesitant.

He took a good, hard look around at the broken glass and damaged belongings scattered about his humble dwelling, and he knew that Luuda would never be safe there. In his mind, he had a difficult choice to make. He calmly kicked his helmet that had been knocked to the floor from the Marck scuffle, and it tumbled across the uneven inlays before thudding into the wall nearby. Crix stayed silent. Fershold settled deep into thought as he watched Luuda play, as if though she hadn't a worry in the world.

"I'll show you where Joric Placater is, but in return, you have to give myself and Luuda safe transport from here and relocate us on Soorak. I want Luuda to grow up with as normal a life as possible, with friends, and a formal education center. For her to have life without fear of Marcks or Gorag's thugs storming down our doors. If you can truly do what you're saying you can do, then I will help in any way I can."

Crix slowly rubbed his eyes, blinked several times, and blew out a hefty breath of air. "That's a deal. We need to get to the terminal extraction point by sunset. We'll either take control of the Marcks or disable them, but one thing is for certain, we are going to need your help."

"I will take you there, but first we have to get you concealed from the Marck patrols." Fershold began gathering up a helmet, protective armor, and padded cloak. Everything a typical Solaran from the Semptor region would need to go about his daily tasks in the hostile outdoors. "Here, put this on so we can see what we're going to be working with." Fershold slapped his hand atop the pile of gear he had stacked together.

Crix fastened on the pitted pauldrons, chest plate, leg armor, and cloak. The heavy cloak wafted a small cloud of dust as he clasped it together. The metal helmet's visor had a narrow slit for the eyes covered with a thick, cloudy lens, through which he could barely see with it pulled down.

Fershold stepped back and took a good hard look at Crix. "Nope, that's not going to be enough." He turned down his dwelling's illuminators enough to see faint blue bleeding from behind the visor.

He grabbed an old, cracked jar from a cubby and scooped out a glob of grey grease into his hand. "Put your visor up." Crix hesitated for a second, then slowly raised his visor. "Close your eyes. I'm afraid you're not going to be able to have any visible portions of your body, including your eyes. Your orb glow is giving you away, and we can't take that risk." He smeared a heaping layer of grease across Crix's eyelids, sealing them shut.

"Now what am I supposed to do? I can't even see to walk, fight, or anything."

"I will lead you, and if you're questioned, you were blinded during an accident while working in an orbital fusion relay station." Fershold turned to Luuda, who had stacked enough tools, parts, and junk to make a small home for her dolls. "Luuda, get your impact gear; we're going on a trip."

She smiled and hopped up from the floor. "Really? We get to go on a real trip!"

"That's right; make sure you get some of our dolls to take with you."

"Yah! We are going on a long trip!" Her voice elevated with excitement.

THE QUEEN PROTOCOL

Crix felt around until he found Fershold's shoulder. "Just so you're aware, I don't know a thing about orbital fusion stations."

Fershold smiled back at him. "I know that, young one, but you have it in your blood somewhere."

"What?" Crix asked.

Fershold ignored the inquiry and continued to prepare for their journey. He gathered up a small pack of gear, and Luuda had a few dolls in a tied-off bag that she dragged behind her. Crix kept his hand on Fershold's shoulder as they headed out into the wake of the dusty, golden sunset toward the Arpol Ridge.

***

They were not far into their trip before Crix could hear the clanking feet of Marck patrols in the distance approaching. He felt a sharp pull from Fershold as he changed course, attempting to keep their distance. The clanks from the Marcks faded further away until they eventually silenced. Storm sirens sang out in harmony across the region and blew past them with their steadfast warning cries calling out to all in Semptor.

"The storms," Fershold said with a calm coolness in his voice, one that had seen and lived through more than he would care to speak. He pulled Crix down to his knees. "Huddle together, keeping your head down and backs to the storm. We will use each other to protect our faces and heads; the less of yourself you can expose, the better off you'll be." The three of them knelt with their heads bowed into one another.

The storm's distant crackling viciously slammed into them with the force of a cargo transport pounding into the atmosphere. Even with the armor and padding, there was a painful vibration that nipped into their bones. Crix was amazed that Luuda remained still even when the storm began to push her over and Fershold yanked her upright again.

**

The storm passed, and they stood up, kicking the loose rocks from around them, but some unwelcome guests had taken advantage of the storm's cover.

"We need to see your marks," a hollowed voice ordered.

The identifying marks were the way Gorag kept track of the citizens of Semptor, and all were required to have an implant placed in the top of their right hand. The implant told of their residence and name. Fershold had taken a fictitious identity before the law was put in place.

The Marcks scanned his and Luuda's hands, and then Crix felt a push against his chest. "What of this one? Does he not speak? Remove your helmet!"

"Please . . . he was blinded in an accident while working on Orbital Reactor Station Thirteen over Soorak; his eyes can no longer take direct sunlight," Fershold tried to explain.

"Can he not speak either?"

There was a long, uncomfortable pause before Crix spoke. "These two are my only family now, and they care for me in my disability." It was all he could think to say at that moment.

A deeper and more authoritative voice spoke up in the distance and slowly moved forward as he talked. "Lost sight, you say. Then why did he not get optical implants?" Piran Defel, the long-trusted lieutenant of the Palic Legion, still bore the standard on his crimson cloak.

"My master warden, do we look like the sorts that can afford expensive optical implants?" Fershold said as he raised his arms, displaying his tattered cloak. "We are meager scavengers, loyal to Gorag the Great."

"Hmmpph." Piran Defel's face was boney with mottled skin, evidenced to his exposure to Semptor's harsh elements for too many of his years. Gorag trusted him, but Piran never impressed him enough to gain a higher position outside of commanding Marck patrols, which had kept him in the field for decades.

Piran squinted and veered his head side to side as he tried to stare through Crix's visor. His pungent breath crept through his crooked grey teeth. "You can raise your visor; the storms have passed." His voice rose.

"I feel more comfortable with it down, thanks."

"It's his disfigurement from the accident, revered one. The sun's light will burn his eyes. Additionally, his loss of ability to support himself has been disgraceful, and he was once one of great pride."

Piran scowled as he scratched his chin. He tilted his head back haughtily and then shoved Crix with a single hand, forcing him to stumble slightly backward. "I don't like invalids or foreigners and would rather you not be here breathing our air, so I advise you leave, and if I ever catch sight of you again, I will have you stripped and left for the storm. Now go before I place your filth beneath my boot."

Fershold bowed and then quickly escorted Luuda and Crix away with a slight spry in his step. "That was close," he whispered to Crix. "You could not see, but there were at least two dozen of Gorag's Marck elite guards around us. They really want to find you. Fortunately for us, Piran Defel is about as egotistically dumb as they get, and I find it strange that he still lives."

***

The sun began to dip into the dusty, orange horizon, and their pace intensified with the possibility that they might come short of their deadline. The sound of droks howling in the distance announced the late hour, and the shadow of Arpol Ridge appeared in the range ahead. Crix could feel the temperature becoming cooler. "Are we almost there? It feels like we are about out of time."

"We are going to be close on time, but the ridge is just ahead. You said at sundown, right?" Fershold downplayed the grimness of the situation, and Crix sensed it.

Crix raised his visor and scooped the grease from his eyes to have a real look. "No! It's too far for the time we have. We are not going to make it like this." He started to remove his protective impact gear.

"What are you doing? The storms will be here anytime, and you'll be de-fleshed."

"If I don't make that extraction, then de-fleshed is what I'll be hoping for." It took several minutes to remove the bulky gear, but as the chest plate fell to the ground in a deadened clank, he lit the orb within him, and a blazing blue pierced through the waning light.

"Have you lost your mind? You're going to get us all killed displaying your orb light like that!" Fershold snapped as he and Luuda both covered their eyes from the intense light.

"No, I'm going to save us, hang on." Crix surrounded them in the orb's power and lifted them from the ground; Luuda squealed and giggled at the sight of floating through the air. They hovered a dozen meters from the ground. Crix tried to stay low enough to keep from being sighted from far away, yet clear of lower obstructions in their path. The ground zipped by faster and faster as they picked up speed, and the ridge quickly engulfed their view. Its crescent-shaped elevation arched like a giant over the barren land, and the conspicuous sky turned a sordid, deep purple as the second sun dipped behind the rocky peak. Fingertips of cold air danced across their bodies as the evening breeze whisked in. Crix's eyes peered ahead, and his adrenaline surged. He couldn't fail now.

CHAPTER 16

As the high ridge's shadow covered them, there was an unsettling sensation of enormous eyes staring down. "It's sundown; where is your transport?" Fershold asked with doubt already starting to form in his mind.

"They'll be here at the shadow of its base. We just have to give them a few more minutes."

"We're too far away from the nearest township to hear the storm sirens. However, it will come from the other side of the ridge. If we stay ready and keep close to it, we will have a minute to assume our protective position, like before," Fershold said, pulling Luuda in closer to him.

Crix stood firm and looked skyward. "No need to worry about that now. I'll protect you from here."

As soon as he finished his words, echoes from the storm poured in from the ridge's far side, and the winds swooshed down upon them. The thunderous clopping of rocks pelted off its stone face and spilled down from above. A gas cloud spewed up around them as Crix discharged the orb's power. The cloud quickly dissipated into a thin, blue, protecting globe, and the wind suddenly calmed within its barrier.

The rocks showered down from the clifftop and swerved in from the sides with the menace of an angry swarm. Crix endured as the storm raged. He dropped to his knees, gritting his teeth with strain and exhaustion, and at one point, Fershold covered Luuda thinking that he would lose the ability to maintain the barrier.

The storm finally began to settle just as Crix reached the limits of his strength, and the remaining dust feathered out into a thin mist. He released the barrier and laid with his back flat on the course ground drenched in sweat; his chest rapidly pumped up and down, trying to catch a solid breath of the dry air.

"Granddad?" the little voice sang up gently from the silence.

"Yes, Luuda?" Fershold replied as he bent down to wipe the sweat from Crix's head and make sure he was okay.

"Who is that big guy behind you?" she asked. Fershold felt his stomach sink into his legs. Somehow, he knew before he turned to look, and what he dreaded was unfortunately so. *Pershon.*

Pershon was the longtime giant Solaran champion of Gorag. This menacing brute was the one Gorag deployed over the decades to finish a job whenever his core forces fell short. Pershon had never failed his objectives and was widely known for his ruthlessness.

Pershon had a muscular physique of rippled flesh fused into a shapeless trunk of a neck. A steel cap covered his block-shaped head, and his face appeared to fit inside painfully, manifested by his curling lips and gritting teeth. A pair of black, ribbed hoses snugged tightly across his shoulders from a tank mounted to his back and fused into the lower portion of his neck. The giant placed his foot atop a rock and leaned in toward Fershold. His shins appeared even larger than average with metal boots that came to a spike past his knee.

Fershold observed the Poray gas tank and immediately knew no negotiation was going to happen here. If Gorag sent Pershon, then there was only a single objective: killing his given targets with cruel intent. As the remaining dust settled behind Pershon, there was a mix of Marck and Palic Legions on foot, with some on cyro-magnetic attack transports, which leveled off at ten meters as they emerged from the clouds. Their fixed pulse cannons trained down upon them. The small craft's silent magnetic hover systems concealed their approach.

"Ahh . . . the traitorous Captain Antelic," Pershon said; his voice was sharp and broken, a voice that one would expect to come from a large drok if it were to speak. "I've always known you were scum and that our paths would cross eventually. That mishap with Gorag's transport and your disappearance was too obvious. He was not on the ship that day for good reason." Pershon's chiseled face wrinkled into a wide grin.

"That's right. We suspected your mixed loyalties already. Your destination was a meeting with yours truly, but that was denied when you staged your death. After a long twenty years, I finally get to have my pleasure with the only job that has ever escaped me." He cracked his knuckles and then pulled a sizable mace from his belt.

"Why do you need all your friends here with you just to take little old me, Pershon? I mean a big, notorious, heavy hitter like you doesn't need backup, does he? I feel so disappointed with our meeting already." Fershold knew that he couldn't defeat him physically, so he started to work on his ego instead.

"Don't mistake the company as weakness, you pathetic worm. They are here only on Gorag's order. He wants to ensure the Tolagon has no escape."

"So it's the Tolagon that you fear then, is it? I can understand why this boy, who's barely into adulthood, would be scary to you, I suppose. Just look at the lunacy in his eyes which tells of the countless victims of his wrath. Hmmm . . . I would be frightened as well if I were you. Maybe you should just turn back now before he unleashes his fury." Fershold was getting into the moment but held himself back from stepping too close.

Pershon angrily pounded his mace into the ground, sending rock fragments blasting in every direction. Luuda began to sob from the display of violence. "Scared? I will show you what it is to be scared, you scum-sucking sack of drok feces." The enraged goliath turned around to look at the force amassed behind him.

"Turn away! Leave us!" he shouted with an eardrum pounding bark. At first, the legionnaires appeared hesitant and torn as they turned to look at each other. Even the Marcks' postures relaxed as their logic systems attempted to decipher the conflicting order. No one moved.

The voice of a nearby legionnaire, who still wore decorations of war and the rank of battle master, expressed his contempt for the command. "We do not answer to you, Pershon. This order is from Gorag."

Pershon squinted with a shade of insanity covering his face as he turned to the one that gave the reply. His ego was in question by all that surrounded him. He screamed out with a thundering crack that echoed off the cliffs. Metal coated his spiked teeth and spit stretched into strings from the top and bottom rows as he bellowed out his frustration. He turned over his left wrist and pushed a hidden switch, sending the maddening Poray gas flowing directly into his throat. He took a deep breath, and his chest puffed outward, drawing in as much of the dispensing gas as he could in a single inhale. His muscles flexed, veins bulged, and his eyes blazed red before he flung his oversized mace into the cyro-magnetic attack transport that the emboldened battle master occupied. The ship's hull cracked open and burst into smoldering fragments.

The other legionnaires and Marcks open fired on Pershon. He leaped aside while pulling a twin-barreled rifle from his back and unleashed a flurry of concussion shots that sent the other attack transports spiraling out of control. He tossed the rifle down and charged the ground forces like a raging Solaran cave bull. He shrugged their connecting shots off as if they were pesky bites from nighttime insects. He tore mercilessly into the Marcks and flung their torn-off body parts into the Legionnaires. Within minutes, the landscape laid littered with bodies and metal parts. Pershon stood alone, his body laden with charred blast marks and dripping red. However, his bloodlust looked far from over as his enraged eyes turned back to Fershold.

"You see, I don't need these puny things to help me. They are nothing, just as you are about to become."

Fershold noticed Crix standing firmly before him; he had both fists clenched and the orb gasses swirled around his body. He would always be ready to defend against what would appear an impossible foe, an unbearable task, placing others' safety before his own. Fershold now realized how vital Crix was, that this single individual could change the tides of the oppression that had plagued their system for so long. Only a hero's heart would stand with such poise in the face of death, and a hero's heart was what they had long awaited.

"If the transport arrives, get Luuda away from here; don't wait for me," Crix said as he elevated himself from the ground; dust kicked up and the air whipped and curled from under the young Tolagon.

Pershon laughed as Crix elevated into a defensive posture. "Prepare to die in agonizing pain, boy!" He charged ahead like a reckless juggernaut void of fear or thought.

Crix took a beast fighter's pose and swished to the side at the last minute, allowing Pershon to crash into the lower ridge behind him. The ground shook, and Pershon screamed with rage as he flung boulders at Crix in a pummeling barrage. His agility, assisted by the orb, kept him safe from the spiraling menaces. Crix darted down upon Pershon's head, riding his shoulders tightly as he dug his fingers deep into the giant's eyes. Pershon let out an ear-piercing wail before ripping him off his back.

Crix crashed violently into the hard ground, taking the breath from his lungs and sending shockwaves through his spine to his toes. His sight blurred momentarily, and he could hear the voices of Fershold and Luuda shouting faintly in the distance. A hefty object from above approached quickly, and it blocked out all visible light. Pershon's boot heel crashed down on Crix's chest. His bones cracked, and whimper of breath heaved from his mouth.

He had nothing left. The giant picked up an enormous rock with the intent of turning Crix into a greasy splat underneath its weight. A sudden rumbling filled the landscape around them, and a warm, swift breeze whisked across Crix's face, snapping him out of the dizzying coma. He observed Pershon staring upward into the sky with the rock held low.

The transport . . . finally. Crix was exhausted, ripped with pain, and longed to leave this place and its strength-sapping gravity, but he had to allow Fershold and Luuda to get aboard safely. He struggled back up to a knee and dusted himself off before giving his eyes a good, firm rub for clarity. The transport circled above like a bird of prey looking for its next meal. The sight of its low flight wings extending from its sides gave Crix the little boost of confidence that he needed.

He wearily dove at the distracted behemoth, but Pershon was fast and saw him coming. He took a crouching sidestep and threw a right hook. Crix took it in his shoulder. The blow sent him spinning back into the ground once again—the hard surface mixed with unforgiving gravity robbing him of his renewed strength.

The transport opened its assault on Pershon with a hail of fire from its cannons. The shots ripped into his flesh and the ground beneath. The giant collapsed faceforward, like a great tree falling from loose soil. The cannons quieted, and Crix cautiously got back to his feet and wearily looked upon Pershon for any sign of life. He remained motionless as the transport dropped down for its pickup.

Fershold and Luuda both stood back waiting to board while Crix took a careful inspection of his fallen adversary. It wasn't easy to accept that he had died so quickly. The giant remained motionless, looking harmless for the first time in many decades, his reign of terror extinguished. Crix nudged him with his foot; the burned flesh stunk as the smokey tendrils seeped up to his nose.

He squinted over the repulsive odor and gave him a solid heel stomp for safe measure. A muffled laugh came from the ground and sent him leaping back in panic. Pershon lifted his massive body to his feet and immediately triggered another dose of poray gas. Black scales of charred flesh flaked off, revealing new skin beneath. The passing effects were all the juggernaut needed as he snapped back into an attack stance

Without a second thought, Crix took flight and darted around behind him. He ripped the hoses from Pershon's neck with both hands. Gas wisped and hissed from the tank as the giant swung in a manic rage to squash the pesky fly that was getting the better of him.

Pershon leaped upward and snatched Crix's leg, yanking his body downward. He squeezed both of his vice-like arms around the young Tolagon's ribs. Crix winced as the air escaped his lungs, leaving him with only seconds to react. He stretched his arm up and shoved it into the gaping hole in the giant's neck, sending an orb blast directly into his brain. Pershon's eyes ruptured from their sockets, and he dropped to his knees, limp and lifeless, before finding his final resting place.

Crix noticed that Luuda and Fershold were already safely aboard the transport and hastily joined them to embark off this world, which he would not miss. As they drifted away into the sky, Crix looked down through an observation window and couldn't help but feel saddened by the loss of the soldiers that had accompanied him there. The dedicated warriors' bravery and blood were necessary to get there, and deep inside, he knew it was a sacrifice he would be facing soon. He clenched his ribs and closed his eyes tightly. His body was in pain, throbbing from his head to his legs. He tried to stay focused on the tasks ahead to keep his mind away from the burning discomfort, but every breath sent shocks across his battered nerves. A familiar voice quickly broke his thoughts. "Good job, buddy."

"Krath?" Crix looked back and noticed Krath standing there outfitted in a black and grey gunner suit.

"Who else would tya think? If there's goin' to be any rescuin' of tya, I'm goin' to be first in line to do so. Besides, it gave me an opportunity to test out these barrage cannons on those baddies. I'd say they worked darn good."

Crix jumped up and gave him a firm hug. "You are a sight for sore eyes, Krath. I really needed a familiar face right about now."

Krath hugged him in return and then nudged him back some. "Alright . . . alright there. I don't want to be givin' tya the wrong impressions here. I like tya, but tya need to keep all that stuff for Kerriah."

"Please tell me she's still hanging in there."

"She was doin' okay when I left, a little lackin' of words just like before tya left. That was a day ago, and we've been under a communication silence with Plexo's old boat since. Tya will have to ask Septin or ole glow rod when we get back. I just provide the good looks and companionship."

Crix was eager to get back to Plexo's ship to find out for himself and let her know that he had thus far kept his promise.

CHAPTER 17

Upon their return to Plexo's ship, Crix had just one thing at the top of his mind. "Kerriah . . . is she okay?" Crix insisted on an answer to his question first, but Governor Septin's evasiveness steepened Crix's concern. He needed assuredness that she was okay, and then he would debrief them on the mission and explain who the two pedestrians were that they picked up.

The old politician placed his hands on Crix's shoulders and looked squarely into his eyes. "Son, you know that I had taken Kerriah into my home as my daughter, and I know she is important to you . . . Dammit . . . I don't care if she is synthetic, living, or whatever, she's a daughter to me." Septin called out a chair from the floor and tugged Crix over to sit. "Take a seat and unwind for a second."

Crix settled into the stasis enhanced seat; all the pains from the past days were screaming out at him now.

"As I was saying, Kerriah is something special and will always be so, no matter if she's in our lives here and now, or just an imprint she's placed on our hearts and memories. She's been an inspiration to all of us, and I know what she is to you, especially through your recent trials and missions." Septin took a long breath, but Crix began to feel ill over where his words were heading and impatiently interrupted him before he could continue.

"Governor, can you just tell me if she is okay or not? I really need you to be straight with me."

Septin's face looked long, and he gave an exhausted sigh. "You're right, young Tolagon. It's the least I can do. Son, we lost her last night. I would have never believed it; she was always such a fighter and would heal so fast that at times I thought I could see her wounds heal right before my eyes, but the red algae that attacked her just took too much." Crix's face appeared void and pale—soulless. He just sat there like an empty shell, and the world around him silenced as he stared down at the floor. Septin took a long pause before he spoke again.

"She did mention you before her passing." Crix's eyes moved upward to meet his. Septin brought a closed fist from his jacket's pocket. "Here."

He opened his hand, revealing a small, red, oval-shaped amulet with four rings that touched at their center edges. Two rings were larger on the top and the bottom, while two were smaller at the sides. The amulet pulsed dimly in his hand, and as he handed it off to Crix, it stopped momentarily and then began to pulse again, but a little bit brighter.

It felt radiantly warm in his hand and was smooth to the touch. Crix felt the warmth seep up through his elbow and into his chest and then down to his knees before giving his heart a tickle.

"What is this?" he asked, curious over what would give him this feeling.

"I'm not sure, to be honest. It's something Kerriah has always had and always kept to herself. She had it concealed in a small indentation under her belt and asked me to give it to you specifically, so there you are." Septin settled back with a little more relaxed posture, likely relieved to get this off his conscious.

"I remember when we first found her as a child; she was cradled in the arms of an embattled Marck, a foreign design, one by the likes of which we had never seen before. It was during the Marck transitionary handoff. I was the junior command of the Hadon Legion that was flushing the Thraxon swarm from sector thirteen and had just finished exterminating the last remnants of Thraxons from the Negmor moon. We were preparing to hand off the sector to the newly appointed Marck Legion that was to be assigned control of that sector.

"I led an exit patrol for one last sweep of the Voltar Mountain just before the handoff when we observed the signs of active small arms blasts and light detonations down the lower side of the southern pass. We hurried with caution in case it was some of our own in trouble from a possible Thraxon position that we had missed. As we descended into the lower basin, we saw that the light flashes and shockwaves had dissipated.

"However, our sensors could tell that there was still movement, so we descended further in. There must have been at least two dozen deceased Thraxon Fangs in varying states of charred dismemberment. If you ever had the displeasure of encountering a Thraxon Fang before, you would understand why this would have put us in a heightened alert. They are some bad-tempered adversaries, not to mention a chore to kill. We'd lost entire units to a meager few of these suckers, but fortunately, the Thraxons don't seem to have many of them and typically reserve them for only the gravest task. So I would imagine this was a terrible loss to them.

"As the eight of us approached the scene with our weapons drawn, we were startled by a stationary Marck, which at first glance blended perfectly into the shadows of the mineral formations around us. Its armor appeared to change dynamically with the textures and shading, a perfect camouflage that even the keenest eye would have missed, and it left no thermal signatures, except for a capsule that it carried cradled in its arms.

"As we neared it, the camouflage started to fail, and we could see its unique banded armor plating. Its dark eyes lit to a fiery red as we came within a few meters, and we all leaped back, keeping a safer distance. However, it made no hostile movements and looked directly at me, like it knew who I was and just stared right into my eyes with such a piercing look that made me second guess it was a Marck.

"To show goodwill, I had my men lower the weapons to ready positions only, not to provoke it. With that, it gently, almost too gently for something that just dispatched two dozen Fangs, placed the capsule before me and walked away into the night. We just stood there frozen, keeping our eyes on it while occasionally glancing down at the capsule. Before it left our plane of site, it appeared to have released some sort of self-destruct sequence on itself and exploded, leaving nothing more than smoke and vapor.

"I felt disappointed. I somehow just knew that we would likely never learn the identity of this strange guardian . . ." Septin cleared his throat. "Well, you probably guessed what was inside that capsule."

Crix's shoulders slung forward, head hung down, and eyes were almost catatonic as he looked at him. "Kerriah."

Septin smiled. "Yes. She was small, maybe two years of age, and tightly secured in the capsule clutching that amulet you have there; that is all she had with her. She had the deepest green eyes that I had ever seen on anyone, the sort of stare that would instantaneously pour warmth over a cold war-hardened heart, so I decided to take her home, and my wife Cendra immediately fell in love with her.

"We could never get the amulet from her all those years. Even as a small child, she would throw the biggest fit if we tried to take it away from her, and as she grew, she would not speak of it. So here it is, yours now. I'm not sure what to tell you to do with it, though."

Crix rested back, giving a close inspection of it. He stroked his finger over its smooth surface and held it close to his face. "It's her," he said. "I don't know how, but it's her. I can feel it."

"How do you know . . . ? Why do you think this?" Septin leaned in closer, intrigued by his statements, sparking his cautious hope and suspicions.

"I-I'm not sure, but since you placed this in my hand, I can feel her, smell her, hear her whispers. I can even feel her breath in my face and the gentle touch of her heartbeat." Crix's heart pounded hard in his chest, and he felt an overwhelming cast of emotions within him. His hair stood on end and his skin tickled. *If this is somehow her, and I don't understand how, but if it is, then there is a way to bring her back.*

Septin stood up quickly. "Joric Placater! This must be his doing."

Crix already knew where he was going with this and slowly stood as well, even though his body wanted to collapse, every muscle tightened with pain and numbness, he needed to heal and recoup, but there was no time. "I know. Fershold can take us to him. He is the one I brought with me, and he knows where Joric is."

"I knew you wouldn't fail us, Crix, just like your father. What are we standing here for? I have Kerriah's body secured aboard my ship, the Elsa, so as soon as we get transferred back, we can get going right away," Septin said as he turned to locate their unplanned passengers Fershold and Luuda.

***

"The Corra moon," Fershold said. His audience turned from exuberant enthusiasm to straight skepticism.

"That can't be," Captain Triko said. His ash hair and prominent cheekbones shone against the infirmary lighting's bright glow, where the ship medic had just finished mending Crix's wounds. "Corra, as we all know, has long been stuck in a dangerous geostationary orbit around Oro and is forbidden; besides, it's mostly frozen and devoid of any useful resources."

"Yes, Captain, you're correct in that remark. That is what made it the perfect choice for his secretive exile. No one would have thought he would be there, and there is no reason for anyone to go there. It's a highly advanced settlement, which is all I know of it. When you see it, you will not believe what you are seeing. You will assume that you fell asleep and are in the midst of a dream. But it's well hidden. You can fly past it hundreds of times and still miss it.

"You'll need to pass between it and Oro while directing your orbital scanners onto Corra's most central region. There will be a mountain peak that's around six thousand meters high. When you find this peak, direct your optical enhanced guidance system 316 kilometers directly west of it. At that point, you will see a blink of light. It just blinks for a fraction of a second and is easily missed if you aren't looking for it or paying close attention. When you see the blink of light, stabilize the ship and reverse propulsion as slow as possible until you see the blink again. Then lock your optic sensors on the blink and enhance the view to the maximum your systems can produce. You will then see it, like looking through a peephole at a picture of paradise." Fershold stared blankly for a few seconds as he thought about the place that was so much the opposite of his home. His reminisces snapped quickly back when Crix interrupted.

"We have to get going. When are we leaving?"

"I just sent a message to our bridge crew, and we are en route as we speak," Septin informed them as he slid his left sleeve back down over his communication band. "The latest intel we received from our outer perimeter agents is that a massive Thraxon fleet, the size of which we have not seen since the first Thraxon

216

war, is moving in a direct approach toward the gammac corridor Pizon. They are only two jumps into our system from there, and the Marck fleet shows no signs of amassing a counter assault or defensive perimeter."

Septin pulled a thin device from his shirt pocket and projected a map in the room's center. There were yellow, red, and blue-lit markers scattered amongst the map of the Oro system. "We have units strategically positioned to slow-up the Marck and Thraxon forces through various coordinated assaults and sabotage operations throughout the system. We are aware that we do not have the personnel or firepower to stop the Marck forces, let alone the combined Marck and Thraxon forces. Their missions are simply to buy enough time to shut down and preferably take control of the Marck's system-wide via the Control Center."

The image drew back into his device as if it was drawing up a fluid spill from the air. Crix felt the chill of anxiety creep over him. He was dying inside to know the location of the hidden Marck Control Center, and if for certain Joric could bring Kerriah back. He pushed himself without rest; his thoughts bounced around in swarms while his frantic pulse danced around in his chest. After a short while, they called him up to the bridge where Fershold stood looking into a visual sensor display. The anticipation was unbearable, exhilarating, and painful; Crix's expression showed it all. He wanted Kerriah back, now.

***

"I know it should be right about here," Fershold said frustrated; the sensors panned past the mountain peak for the eighth time with no blink of light, only a desolate and barren

217

surface that when looked upon gave no thought or hope that anything he described would be there.

Septin nervously scratched his shoulder. "Is it possible that he's been moved, that he's no longer there?"

Fershold slowly massaged his chin for a minute. He'd had similar feelings in the past while transporting Gorag there for inspection visits. Back then, he was worried over what could become of him if he didn't find it and recalled Gorag's irritated growl as he made pass after pass without luck.

"I recall almost giving up hope last time I had to find this place. It took me twelve grueling passes with Gorag threatening my life in the background before I finally spotted it. It's about the time you give in . . . and start to accept it's not there when you see it . . . there!" Like a single star winking at him, there was a twinkle as they passed over the exact location. No one else spotted it, but Septin shouted for a full stop to the flight crew; the ship's engines hissed as they reversed the forward momentum.

"Back the ship up, very slow," Fershold ordered, and Septin relayed the same to the crew.

"Where is it?" Crix asked, squinting to spot the tiny light, yet not able to contain his enthusiasm over locating it. Everyone looked at the onscreen sensor display, eager to put their skepticisms to rest.

"There!" Fershold said, pointing at a tiny blink of white light.

"Enhance that point," Septin commanded. The display projected into the speck of light, and it filled the output like an oncoming train from a black tunnel. Inside was a picturesque scene of a woodland paradise, with a perfectly even mix of scarlet, lemon, and olive shaded trees, each of which were plump and full. A crisp blue, gently flowing stream winded through the forest and dipped into a sparkling pool with a two-story lodge overlooking the serene waters. Everything there was placed meticulously, and nothing appeared worn or out of place. It was perfect.

"That's it," Fershold whispered to himself. It'd been so many years since he had last seen the place and its beauty took him back to the last time as if it were yesterday. "If you focus our descent into the white speck of light, you will enter into our destination," he said aloud for the pilots to hear.

The ship descended upon what would appear to be a shadowy, dead surface ladened with frost-covered rocks. As they lowered, a bright light filled their viewports from the outside, and it was as if they had teleported to a different place. The sky above was a perfect blue and birds flocked below. The same thoughts crossed through their minds: this can't be Corra and they must be elsewhere. The eight crew members, along with Septin and Crix, all stopped to look at each other to verify that they saw the same thing.

"Are we still over Corra?" The ship's communications officer asked.

"Yes, this is Corra," Fershold responded. He stared out of the viewport still enamored with what he had already seen in the past and never thought he would see again. "This is one person's perfect vision of what paradise would look like, and he has brought it to a small part of an otherwise grim place. There is no place to set a ship like this down; I believe he did this by design. We will have to take a shuttle down and land in the small clearing near his home," Fershold recalled the past process.

They loaded Kerriah's body up with Crix, Fershold, and Septin onto the small shuttle for landing. Crix stroked her soft black hair away from her pale cheeks and gave a gentle kiss on her lips. They were cold and unyielding. He pulled away, took a deep breath, and slowly exhaled as he leaned over her again. "I will never let anything harm you again, I promise," he whispered, somehow knowing she could hear him while he held tightly to the amulet.

The shuttle doors swished open, and a crisp, clean breeze rustled in, filling their lungs with the sweetest air they had ever tasted. The air was pure. They all felt instantly youthful and emotionally at ease. Outside there were sounds of birds singing and amphibians chirping in perfect harmony with each other, almost too perfect.

They exited the shuttle, cupping their eyes from the bright daylight until they adjusted. Crix pushed Kerriah out on an electron-elevated gurney; her body hovered on the thin platform as he slid her out in the open. Swarms of bees buzzed by them to work on the many varieties of brightly colored flowers that patched the ground and grew tall around the wood lines.

A shiny chrome Marck shot down a transparent tube from an overhanging section of the large home. The home nestled perfectly into the surrounding scarlet and olive trees with a large deck area that dipped its supports into the lake. The roof was a textured, blueish grey with cerulean shutters hanging from its tall, rectangular windows and natural, smooth stone walls mixed with taupe and ivory. The Marck left the tube and moved almost silently, gliding gracefully toward them.

"Should we be concerned?" Septin asked Fershold. He shook his head, assuring him not to worry.

"Greetings, visitors, and welcome to Pinor Eden. Could you please explain the pleasure of your unexpected visit while I have some refreshments served up?" the Marck asked. Its voice was pleasant, unlike anything they had heard coming from a Marck before.

"We need to see Joric Placater," Septin stated.

"Architect Placater is very busy. You will have to come back another time."

"Busy? From the looks of things around here, I'd say that he is most likely enjoying the good life," Septin said with a sarcastic tone.

Two short, stocky Marcks approached from the side of the lodge bearing platters with frosted glasses filled with fluids. "Please enjoy the refreshments, but leave when you are finished. Architect Placater is too busy for guests," the Marck persisted.

Septin started to lose his patience quickly with the Marck greeter. "Look, I do no—"

"We have something that might interest Joric," Crix interrupted Septin before he was able to get verbally aggressive. He opened his palm and displayed the amulet, then held it close to Kerriah's body.

The Marck tilted its neck forward for a closer look at her. After a minute of silence, the Marck turned and stared directly at Crix. "Come with me and bring Kerriah with you." Crix's heart skipped when he heard the Marck say her name.

He followed the Marck over to a large, clear disk on the ground near the lodge. Crix pushed Kerriah along the way.

"Please step up on the disk," the Marck asked politely.

Crix slid Kerriah over the disk and stepped upon it. He suddenly felt his feet lock against the surface as it lifted upward smoothly for eight meters before shifting directions to the left and through an opening in the side of the lodge. The disk set them softly onto a small platform near the edge of a large room.

CHAPTER 18

Inside appeared quaint with a rustic aesthetic. The walls were a mix of rich timber bracings and grey stones with a tall ceiling that had a large, black metal chandelier hanging in the center. A white-haired man stormed in unannounced. His thin, short beard matched the hair on his head. He had a healthy appearance for a person of his age, wearing a long, burgundy lab coat that draped loosely open with olive green pants and a matching shirt.

He stopped for a second when he saw Kerriah, then quickly walked over to her side. His look was a mixture of excitement and sorrow. "My sweet child, so young, so perfect." He caressed her hair and then looked her over carefully. "What has happened to her? What have you done?" he asked with a convicting, gentle voice that began to elevate with angst.

"Sir, we brought her here to see if you can help," Crix said.

"Well, of course, I can help; she is my child, and I am her creator. I need to know how this happened to her."

"It was the algae on Nathasia. It appears to attack things that are energized, and well . . . she is . . . you know . . ." Crix was at a loss for what to say; to him she was alive indeed, but she wasn't, or was she? He did not want to insult Joric or leave the wrong impression.

"Algae? Nathasia? What was she doing in such a terrible place to begin with?"

"It was . . . you know . . . the plans . . ." Crix tried to answer and stumbled on his words before Joric waved his hand.

"Forget it, just forget it. Do you have her soul amulet?"

"I'm assuming you're talking about this?" Crix extended his open palm, displaying the crimson amulet as it pulsed with an accompanying glow.

"Yes . . . good, now I can save her; now give it here." Joric opened his hand to grab it and then paused to take notice of Crix's blueish radiance. "What are you, anyway? Some sort of Tolagon?"

Crix dropped his head and lowered his gaze, keeping a humble expression. "Well, actually, I am . . . I think," he said, handing the amulet to Joric. Unimpressed, Joric just grabbed it and gave Crix a casual hmph.

"Don't even know what you are?" He shook his head and said no more before he started walking back from where he came. As he reached the doorway, a female voice spoke over the building's ambient audio systems.

"Joric? Who are the guests you have with you?" Her voice was soft and profound. The sound of it was rich and immersive.

"Not to worry, dear, I believe they are just about to leave." He stared back at Crix and put his finger over his lips before turning back out of the room.

Less than a minute later, a featureless, chrome Marck entered and pushed Kerriah out of the room. "Now hold on, I want to know what you're doing with her," Crix insisted as he tried to follow the Marck through the doorway, only to be momentarily paralyzed by an unseen barrier that wouldn't allow him to pass the threshold. He picked himself up from the floor, dazed with a nagging humming in his head.

He tried to gain a view inside, but there was no sign of anyone, only another room, rustic in styling with a sharp infusion of technology overlaying everything. A great wooden table with thick legs and a roughly planed surface sat in the room's center. Crix clenched his fists and readied his stance. He wouldn't be kept from Kerriah, not without knowing what was happening.

He made his decision and charged up every bit of orb power he could muster to build a barrier around himself; his body glowed brightly, and a wall of energy outlined his frame. Taking a deep breath, he stormed into the unseen barrier that guarded the doorway, and though his flesh felt like it was tearing away, he still pushed forward.

There was a deep stabbing pain furiously peppering every inch of his body. His knees buckled. A scream rattled his bones and only stopped once he was out of breath. His vision blacked out, he felt drained of strength, but the light returned as he fell, catching himself with his elbows just before meeting his face into a hardwood floor. He looked up, noticing that he had made it into the next room; his eyes struggled to regain their sight. Kerriah's limp body remained held up in the air, suspended by a star pattern of thin wires.

Joric wore thin gloves and had the amulet placed atop a small, bright disk suspended in the air. He stared at Crix lying on the floor and shook his head. "What's wrong with you? I needed you to stay in the reception area until I finish here."

"I couldn't leave her. Not without knowing what you're doing." Crix managed to get the words out but felt silly afterward.

Joric let out a frustrated sigh. "At least get up and make yourself useful." He grasped a forked tool that was suspended in air and extended it to Crix. "Come on now, take this cybik director and keep it right above her chest, just hold it steady until I get her essence released from the amulet. The amulet has kept a piece of her essence captive for all these years and only this decompressor can release it. Once free, her spirit will want to escape, we need to get it directed back to her body, or she will be lost. That's where your efforts come in. The cybik director will keep it from escaping and help force it back down into her body."

Joric called for several floating disks that brought him a strange array of tools, which he used to clean her wound and prep for the operation. A needle snaked down and inserted into the hole in her heel from an opening in the ceiling. Lights of red and blue appeared to seep through the needle and into her body. He tapped at his forehead-mounted display and then spoke some technical jargon that Crix thought sounded like another language. The system began to vibrate and let out a steady pattern of beeps.

At that moment, Joric took the amulet and moved it onto a small, red disk that now hovered above Kerriah. Crix gave him a nod of assurance and grasped the director as tightly as possible; his knuckles turned white from the pressure. He couldn't let her spirit escape, or he would lose her. In his mind, failure was not an option.

Three round globes dropped down and surrounded the amulet. They began to swirl faster and faster and the amulet illuminated, and the faster they spun, the brighter it became.

"This is it!" Joric shouted. "Keep the Cybik director right below that red disk and do not move it, no matter what." The amulet flashed, and a tiny apparition about the size of a thumb drew out from it. The apparition shined in a blurry haze of greenish-grey as it twirled over Kerriah. Crix instantly felt entranced with its movement, and at one moment, he was sure that it stopped turning and stared straight back at him.

"Don't lose focus!" Joric barked at him seconds before a sustained shock rippled through his hands and arms and then crawled down his spine.

The intensity grew, and he felt his teeth chatter and his jaw lock. He could hear Joric giving more commands to the system, but it was a distant sound, like one from an old dream. The apparition darted around violently, and he felt his fingers losing their grip on the fork as it jolted back and forth. Joric's face got near his, and his eyes had the look of insanity.

"Can you understand me? It's absolutely imperative that you do not let the director move, or we will lose her! Do you hear me?" His voice was frantic, yet stern.

Crix retrained his focus and tightened his grip. *This fork is not going anywhere;* he shouted in his mind. His eyes blazed as he washed out any pain that came his way. He stabilized the fork, and the pain settled.

"Yes . . . that's the way, just hold on for a few more seconds," Joric announced. A blind spot formed in Crix's memory as the next thing he recalled was Joric patting him on his shoulder and pulling the cybik director from his locked hands. "You can let go now. It's done. She will be fine."

Crix relaxed his tired hands and moved his frozen gaze down to Kerriah still suspended by the wires; her eyes were open. Her pupils and iris were solid white, and her chest moved subtly from drawing breaths of air. "Is she . . ." Crix said, wanting so bad for Joric to tell him that she was back.

"Alive?" Joric finished his question before he could get it out. "Depends on what you define as alive. To you and I, yes, she is alive; to some, she was dead many years ago, at least in the natural sense of it. She will be fine but will need a day or so for her body to repair the damage before she will be up and walking about."

Crix felt like he had just dropped the weight of a battle cruiser from his shoulders and gave a long exhale. "Thank you. I can't thank you enough for this."

A faint smile raised Joric's bristly cheeks. "Hmmm . . . I didn't know anything about you when you arrived, and I tend not to trust strangers, least of all the ones that drop in unannounced with our daughter in this condition." He placed a hand on Crix's shoulder as he looked straight into his eyes. "However, I know all that I need to know about you now, and it's clear that you care for her and would make the ultimate sacrifice if that's what it took to keep her safe. That's all we ever wanted for Kerriah. You are welcome to stay here until she is well again, take in the bit of the utopia that I have created. You sure look as though you could use it."

Crix fixated only on one thing that Joric said. "You're her father? How could that be?"

CHAPTER 19

J oric took a slow, calming breath. "I can explain . . . Please." He gestured Crix toward a quiet sitting room filled with lush yellow and purple plants and a bright ceiling that caught a view of white, feathery clouds flowing against a deep blue sky. They settled into a pair of plush chairs. Joric poured a glass of emerald spirits from a decanter that rested on a table nearby. He raised the container in offering to Crix, who gave a nervous smile and waved it away.

Joric told him how he once worked as a contractor for developing artificial intelligence and synthetic beings to replace the living that worked in the hazardous orbital reactors. He explained that when the second Thraxon war initially broke out, a coordinated attack took the UMO forces off-guard, which resulted in his then hometown of Bitarale on Soorak getting overtaken. His wife and infant child were both murdered by the invaders. The Thraxons had briefly taken Joric hostage to exploit his knowledge. Fortunately, the Kelpic Legion squashed the invading force and rescued Joric before that plan came to be. Joric returned to his home and discovered his family's bodies still amongst the rubble like discarded litter.

Obsessed with denial, he took their bodies back to his lab and placed them in a state of cryogenic infused molecular processing. His AI systems found traces of consciousness remaining deep inside them. The core of their personalities and memories lay dormant as the toxins the Thraxons used in their weapons killed them slowly over days. He was able to stimulate these traces in Kerriah and draw them out, keeping them in containment, and the amulet was the vessel he used.

Feverishly he worked days, weeks, and months without rest to get the molecules to bind and the cells to form and all the pieces to flow according to their programs. He built her a new body, an infant body, that utilized as much of her original DNA as possible, then to be able to infuse this mass with her consciousness from the amulet. "I thought it to be at least a one in a million chance that the new body would accept her, that it would take and not just allow it to flutter away into the darkness, forever gone," he explained.

It took, and she awoke as his child again, only stronger, adaptable, and resistant to ailments that her peers would be vulnerable to. Her artificial cells would grow into a woman at a natural pace, and she would grow old like everyone else; it was a flaw he felt he needed to add so that she could have a normal existence. He kept a piece of her conscience in the amulet. He dropped a little tiny bit of subtle urgency into her mind to keep the amulet with her always, never to lose it; for as long as she held it close, it would stay in sync with all her memories and experiences in her life.

"You see, I couldn't lose her twice, so I made a perfect backup. If she were ever to lose her life, I could restore it as long as I had this backup, and I could bring her back up to the last moment she had it in her possession. I also needed to keep her from standing out to provide her with a normal existence. Therefore, I added the sensation of common weakness that mortals would experience, like the feelings of shortened breath, thirst, fatigue, and hunger. All of these characteristics were necessary to keep her safe from discovery by any nefarious entities that would look to harm her if they discovered who and what she is." Joric leaned back to take a sip from his glass and then slowly swirled the oily fluids around.

Crix nervously broke his attention away from him and stared out a nearby window. He could see the waning light peeking in and their transport in the distance. He wanted to hear everything about Kerriah's past but was concerned about Governor Septin and the others waiting outside. They had to be getting anxious over the time that had passed. Yet, he didn't want to interrupt Joric.

Joric gently set his glass down and cleared his throat, bringing Crix's eyes back to his. "Even though Kerriah was restored, I was left filled with hatred and anger for what the Thraxons did to us, what they put us through. I hated them down to the marrow in my bones. I wanted them to be hunted to extinction. So I turned my work's obsession into a quest to create a perfect fighting machine that could easily and efficiently be duplicated many times over to carry out this task. An automated mechanized army. I had the technology, and I built some prototypes to take before the UMO Security Council.

"I needed to gain their approval for full-scale development and manufacturing. I knew they were depleted of combat-capable soldiers from the many years of fighting the war, morale was crushed, and they were basically trying to decide their final fate. It was an easy sell for someone that's not that great a salesperson." Joric cracked a smile as he leaned back, stroking his beard.

His smile quickly faded, and his eyes lowered. "The demands of designing and constructing this Marck force and their intricate control systems took every bit of me. It was easily the greatest endeavor I ever set out to do, and increasingly I found myself neglecting the duties of a father." Joric's fingers gripped into the fabric of his pants.

"I don't know. It made sense to me at the time. I needed to stay focused on my work, so I placed Kerriah into temporary cryostasis. Pausing her life, if you will. Though it was a risky move, I didn't want to neglect her or lose those critical years." His eyes snapped back up to Crix. "It was a decision that ripped my heart out and one that pushed my ethical limits. I figured that once the Marck armies were deployed, I could resume her life again, which I did." Joric's eyes glassed over, and Crix shifted uncomfortably in his seat.

"I am sorry. This was something that I needed to tell someone, and I finally have an ear worthy of listening." He looked at Crix with an enduring smile and an accepting nod.

"I understand. We all have had to make some tough choices." Crix thought back to his decision to save Akhal.

Joric swept his hands across his legs, brushing the wrinkles out. "It all went well for a while. The tide of the war turned with the launch of the new Marck armies. I released Kerriah from stasis, and we resumed our lives. Until the day came when I had some unexpected visitors drop in.

"Thraxon infiltrators wormed their way into my residence, intending to steal my work. They were desperate to find a way to counter the Marck forces. However, I made a foolish mistake and left the designs for Kerriah unsecured on my local systems. They pulled the design plans from those systems and then realized that Kerriah was a result of those plans, so they took her as well. To add to their hooliganism, they destroyed my copies of those plans before they left." Joric became visibly frustrated as he recalled the incident.

Crix sat up straighter than before, then leaned forward, wanting to understand. His elbows rested on his knees and hands clasped together. He wanted to know everything.

"So where did the protector Marck come from? You know the one that saved her from them?" Crix asked, anxious to hear the rest of the story.

Joric raised an eyebrow. "So you have been told of my guardian?"

"Governor Septin told me of his brief encounter with it. That's when he found Kerriah as a child."

"Septin . . . of course." Joric looked up as if recalling something from his past. "That is who I had the guardian send her to; she was no longer safe in my care, and I couldn't risk her life again, not on my account. I met the young captain months earlier at a state affair; he and his lovely wife were a joy to speak to, and they mentioned their desire to have a child at the time. I precipitately activated my guardian prototype, which I had designed to protect her when she got to be a little older.

"At that point, its new directive was to rescue and protect her until it could deliver her to someone that could keep her safe until she was fully grown. It was to do this at all costs, and at that, it was more than capable. The captain was the only person I could think of at that time.

"I had the guardian lock onto her and find the Thraxon's infiltrators. They hadn't gotten far yet. I think they may have been waiting for things to settle before escaping to their fleet. The guardian easily acquired Kerriah and delivered her to Captain Septin. That was that. It's apparent that you know the rest." Joric grabbed his glass, threw back the last drink, and then set it down on the hardwood table. The bottom of the empty glass knocked against the sturdy surface.

Crix gave a slow, uncertain nod as he took in the all-encompassing tale, but an omission in its telling bothered him. "What about your wife; did you rebuild her the same way you did Kerriah?"

Joric frowned. He stared for a moment at the empty glass; fingers of emerald slowly bled down its sides. "It's not something I'm comfortable to speak of as it brings forth bitter feelings and loathsomeness, but it's the least I can do given the circumstances. Kerriah has a right to know what had become of her mother. Gentria did not survive the Thraxon attack on Bitarale." Crix tilted his head back and wrinkled his brow. He glanced around as though he was looking for the voice he had heard earlier.

"The voice that I was speaking to before was a complete artificial recreation of my wife. I lost her spirit during the transplant process to her new body. It was a difficult lesson, but what I

235

learned from that loss gave me success with Kerriah. That is why I was sensitive to your handling of the cybik director. It's also why I am so grateful for your success. You only have one chance, and that's it.

"I must have cried myself to sleep for weeks straight over the loss. I blamed myself and even hated myself over those weeks, and I was even angrier at the Thraxons. I recall holding baby Kerriah tightly as I sobbed. So tight that I thought I might have cut her breaths short at times. What I have with Gentria is not the same; she's purely artificial, and there is no soul, no memories other than what I implanted from my own, no one to reminisce on things that I have forgotten." He stopped and sighed deeply, almost looking exhausted. "There are times that I can forget this, and we do banter back and forth, and we do have some pleasant times. However, it's not the same."

"I am truly sorry," Crix said. Joric's story helped him remember something from Dispor. He waited for several minutes to avoid the rudeness of a sudden change of subject.

"Joric . . . I was told that there are some instances where certain Marcks were showing real emotions. There were examples of them displaying hate, fear, and anger. Is this part of your design coming out? Similar to what you described with your wife?" Joric stared at Crix blank-faced for several minutes before answering.

Joric's eyes widened, and his face flushed. "Where did you hear of this?"

"From an inmate in Dispor, who told us about Zeltak, Dispor's warden. This inmate said that he observed these types of emotions from Zeltak and several others during his time there. We also noticed this sort of behavior firsthand from one of the other higher ranking Marcks on Dispor."

Joric rested his fist under his chin, pressed his lips together, and stared at the ceiling. "It's the queen. She is the one doing this, but why?" He looked hard at Crix. "I can assure you that emotion was not in my design for the Marck security forces. That would have been detrimental to their purpose."

"The queen?"

Joric gave a placid smile.

"I understand your feelings for Kerriah and Septin's love for his adopted daughter, truly I do, but gaining the knowledge of my whereabouts had to have been a perilous task, and I know that it likely took a much greater cause to bring you here. Let's get to what this visit is truly about and bring Septin up here to discuss this situation, shall we?"

Crix let out a sigh of relief. *Finally.*

Joric sent his chrome Marck to fetch Septin, and while they waited somewhat uncomfortably, a striking, slender female strolled into the room. Her jet-black hair and youthful sheen glistened in the radiant lighting. Her flawless complexion gave off a sheltered appearance. She wore a pastel blue dress that flowed out just above the knee and mixed like an artist's rendition with her ruby lips. The sight of her beauty would startle anyone in a room that she entered. She appeared to be a woman that was perpetually in her mid twenties.

"Joric?" Her voice was melodious, yet with an element of concern concealed beneath it. Crix looked over at Joric and tilted his head to the side. *Did he not build her to age like he did Kerriah?*

Joric winked at Crix and cracked a grin. "Yes, my dear? You can see I have guests, and we need to conduct some business; what is it that you need?"

"Who's the woman that's suspended from those things in your lab?" she asked as she batted her long eyelashes in an almost intentionally flirty sense, yet her shoulders stiffened as she spoke.

"That is just a friend of young Crix here, which I am trying to help."

"Ohh," she said, dropping her shoulders. "Is she going to be alright? Can I help?"

Joric shook his head quickly. "No. No, not at all, I have this under control. Please, if you could allow us a bit here to finish our business, and I can further explain later."

She gave a comforting smile back at him. "Okay, love you." Her dress flowed perfectly with her legs as she swanned away.

Joric looked back over at Crix, who had a huge smirk. "Well, since I was not able to save her spirit as I mentioned before, I selfishly decided it wasn't as important to make her age naturally. As such, I decided to keep her in her most optimal appearance. Very much like the first day we met; she is visually stunning, isn't she?" Joric's smile began to sour and he sighed deeply. "It's really not all as lovely as you may think. There is something about the journey of aging with your spouse that is missed.

"Further, she always inquires as to why she never does, and yet I do. I simply explain that her beauty is boundless, and she accepts that since there is no one else here to divulge the great fib." He let out another deep exhale. "Ultimately, I made a mistake that is now difficult to change."

Crix felt bad for Joric, despite living in a self-created paradise of visual delights and amusements. Most onlookers would observe from the outside and think he had everything a person could desire or need; however, his life was nearly as empty as a prisoner confined to a remote island of solitude.

The chrome Marck entered the room. "I give you Governor Septin. Is there anything else, sir?" Its voice was refined and natural in its tone.

"No, that will be all, thank you," Joric replied as Septin stepped in. Joric stood and took a few seconds to look him over. "Well, it's been a long time, Captain . . . or I should say Governor Septin. Welcome to Pinor Eden; I apologize for your wait, but I'm sure you appreciate the urgency that Kerriah required."

"Is she going to be alright?"

"She'll be fine. This sapphire radiating young man here was instrumental in her revival."

Septin placed his hand upon his chest for a moment and relaxed his shoulders before leaning in to give Joric a firm handshake. "Crix is very special, I agree, and certainly a welcomed companion for Kerriah."

"Please take a seat, Governor." Joric extended a hand to a plush tan chair with a contrasting seam throughout the soft fabric. "Tell me what I can do for you."

Septin settled comfortably into the chair, placing both arms across the tall armrests. "First, I just would like to say thanks again for saving Kerriah. She means everything to me."

Crix tried to swallow the lump in his throat. At this point, he knew more regarding the origins of Kerriah than her adoptive father, and he felt an uneasiness over this fact.

Septin continued. "I'm not sure how much information you're privy to in your solitude here, but we are in the gravest of times. The Marck army that you have created has been somehow illegally controlled by a single organization, Sinstar Corporation." Joric shifted up in his seat with disbelief upon hearing this.

"Sinstar Corp? That can't be so."

"I'm afraid it is. We're not sure exactly how, but I can assure you, Zearic is calling the shots."

Joric shook his head. "No. That's not possible. The queen controls them, and that control cannot be severed without the Marck units going into an internal meltdown sequence. This fail-safe would render them into the equivalent of scrap. That was how they were designed and built and is how they are still being built at the Dregwiegh production facility. I do take a rare secretive leave to inspect their production, and I can assure you that they are still built with that same design scheme. Their control must come directly from the Core, and the queen controls the Core."

240

"With respect, I'm telling you that you are wrong, Joric. Our agents have witnessed numerous accounts of them taking direct orders from Sinstar's Overlord Zearic Sectnine. When his interim stint as Galactic Marshal was over, after the transitionary period, his authority over them was to expire, but that never happened."

Joric began to mumble to himself as he rubbed his chin. "The queen would never allow anyone to control the Marcks. Her programming gave her enough ego to keep something like that from occurring." After a few minutes of thought, he smacked his palm down on his knee. "She might be trying to escape from the Central Core."

Septin's eyes widened. "Huh?"

"You said that there are mechanized units that have exhibited signs of emotional behaviors, and now an outside source appears to have control over them. The queen is the only one aside from Kerriah and Gentria that were given the Optimal Secrium, the term I gave for the emotional capacity that they possess. Optimal Secrium was a derivative from Kerriah's original spirit, the one component that I could effectively duplicate. You can see that in Gentria, unfortunately, short of her memories and individual personality which were lost.

"In the case of the queen, for her to function as an autonomous entity capable of making critical military and policing decisions on behalf of the whole UMO system, this trait was essential. Our greatest leaders have made decisions based on a certain level of emotion since our earliest days. Without this emotion, every decision would be broken down into raw quantitative variables. That would lead to acceptable losses without any discernment as to the emotional impact of those losses, either to our enemies or allies." Both Crix and Septin looked at Joric with blank faces from the hasty explanation. "Just trust me on this. This was the best way to design her."

Septin leaned further back in his chair and crossed his arms. "Interesting. So this queen persona is working with Zearic somehow."

"Yes, it's possible, though she is too cunning to work with him without the benefits being weighed heavily in her favor. Very few knew any real details of her existence, and Zearic would have been one of those few."

"Hmmm," Crix rubbed his fingertips over his eyelids and quickly shook his head. "I still don't understand how these emotional displays from Marck units indicate that she's trying to escape."

"She is reaching out through the Marck units she controls. It's no longer just direct orders or instructions, if you will. She's placing portions of herself into them, testing the waters." Joric waited for a minute in silence, but Crix and Septin looked back at him with empty stares. He rolled his eyes.

"Look, the queen and Kerriah are tied together because she was derived from Kerriah's emotional backplane. I fear that the queen is feeling entrapped in her hidden fortress and is plotting to extend herself outside of its confines. Her thoughts and emotions could have evolved quicker than I projected, and she may be feeling less content with her role as a secret orchestrator.

"This was a risk I was aware of when I designed her, but I did not have the time to create a proper contingency for this possibility. The Thraxons were mere weeks away from a massive invasion that we no longer had the capacity to repel. It was something I would worry over later."

"It looks like 'later' is here," Septin said. "Is it possible that Zearic found a way to control her?"

"No." Joric's voice elevated. "The Marcks were designed to abide by his commands only for a finite period, and then the queen would assume full control. She would never allow him or anyone else to circumvent her authority."

Crix threw his hands up. He could feel frustration brewing the more Joric tried to explain the queen. "Fine, so how are we going to deal with her?"

"Kerriah—at this point, you both know her better than I do from a personal standpoint. That means you also know the queen, at least in tendencies and behaviors, since they stem from the same source."

Crix's brows furrowed and his fists clenched as he interrupted Joric. "That can't be! Kerriah would never give in to evil!"

"Don't be so positive that the queen's intention is evil; rather, view it as survival instincts or the need to be free. Any one of us placed in a circumstance of endless imprisonment and servitude could very well behave similarly. Your moral and ethical self does not believe that you could, but believe me, we are all capable of evil in the face of certain conditions. Your survival instincts would eventually look for an escape or some way to end the isolation, and the perceived costs of doing so would become less relevant as time passed. Though the methods or timing may be different, the objectives would be similar. If you look hard enough under the surface, you will see that the queen is indeed more familiar than you may think," Joric explained.

"What exactly are you saying then?" Crix asked, wanting Joric to stop with the riddles and speak plainly.

"What I'm saying is that Kerriah is the queen, in another form. The queen is behaving very much the same as Kerriah would had she been put in charge of Marck coordination and control over all these years, all the while isolated from any living thing. Of course, she hasn't been in that situation, so you do not recognize that side of her."

Crix reflected on the experiences and conversations he had had with Kerriah over the past weeks. She was calculating and stubborn as well as having an aura of free spirit about her. She would never allow herself to be trapped and isolated. She would likely do whatever it took to survive or gain her freedom, even if she had to make some ethically questionable steps to achieve it. "Right . . . I guess I can see what you're saying." He looked over at Septin, who nodded in agreement.

"Her cooperation with Zearic is nothing more than a tactical means to an end. I can assure you of that," Joric said.

"I see," Septin said as he tapped his fingers nervously across his knee. "We need to get into this fortress and take control of the queen. Joric . . . where is the fortress?"

THE QUEEN PROTOCOL

"It was never designed to be accessed by anything other than specially modified Marcks. The queen's fortress, or more commonly known as the Marck Central Core, is in a sustained altitude deep inside Oro's molecular cloud layer. It's deep enough to be naturally hidden from detection by any scanning systems. Besides, no one would think to look there." Septin and Crix looked at Joric, their facial expressions twisted by his response.

"I know by the looks you're giving me that you think I must be mad; however, it is a fact. This fortress is suspended via a sustained cosmic thruster system deep inside the vast Oro atmosphere. It gives it the most central control location-wise, makes it invisible to any known detection systems, and is effectively inaccessible. The complex modular relay system stealths communications from the queen to the thousands of Marcks deployed across the system, all the way to the outer gammac corridors.

"Initially, I had designed specific, extreme, high-pressure resistant Marcks that were used to continue constructing the fortress once it was viable enough to drop down into Oro's hostile atmosphere. This had to be done as early as possible to minimize its detection. Even though I had intentionally positioned it inside a colder region of Oro's cloud layer, which experiences relatively low wind gusts compared to most regions, it was quite a task. A logistical nightmare, and all the while, I had to keep it secret." Joric slowly rubbed his palm across his forehead. This was a task he would never agree to do again. The countless nights of no sleep and the endless challenges nearly drove him mentally over the edge. Only the emotional drive for vengeance kept him going.

"I was able to utilize an early version of the communication system that the queen uses now to control one of them remotely. That way, I could be there to oversee the construction personally. Please understand that no one could withstand the atmospheric pressure to gain access to the fortress, let alone to get inside it."

Septin puckered his lips and gave his head an aggressive scratch for a few seconds. "You wouldn't happen to have any of the high-pressure Marcks still around here, would you?"

"No, I decommissioned the majority of them as the project completed and sold what I had left years ago to a salient merchant who already had an interested buyer at the time."

"Wait a minute." Crix recalled the Eetaks from Plexo's lab. "Plexo had some Marcks that could fit your high-pressure Marck designs. I can't recall where he said he picked them up, but he did mention being at a loss as to why some were designed, for you know, the super-high pressure. He called them Eetaks."

Joric's face lit up. "Eetaks? Where did he get that name from?"

Crix stared up at the ceiling for a second. "I thought he said it was etched into the foot of one of them."

"Then that would have been mine for sure. I named one of my early prototype models Eetak. It's the working model I used to sell the Marck concept to the UMO. However, budget and time constraints chopped its features down to what you see in the field today. I marked its foot with that name."

Septin nearly stood up in his seat. "Does he still have them?"

"Well, I can tell you that of the three that he had which appeared to be built for high pressure, we lost one of them in Dispor, and so he may still have two of them," Crix replied.

Septin leaned forward in his chair. "Joric, if we brought them here, could they be repurposed once again to enter the core and take control of the queen?"

Joric slowly shook his head. "No. The core is outfitted with some highly robust defensive systems. The queen is not going to allow Marcks outside of her control anywhere near there. Plus, the fortress countermeasures are specially designed to repel a robotic unit since that would be the likely threat given the environment. Most likely, the 'Eetak' would be assimilated into her defenses. No, whatever is to get near her will have to be highly calculating and resourceful."

"There has to be a way to get in there. We really planned on Crix to lead this charge, but now I don't see how we can even get near it," Septin said, his voice cracking as he spoke. The central core couldn't have been in a worse place, aside from the Thraxon homeworld.

"I can do it." Both Joric and Septin's eyes widened as they looked at Crix. Crix wasn't sure until now. It was all going to depend on him. He would have to be the one to take on the role of Tolagon and rise to the occasion of overcoming the seemingly impossible. He would find a way because he must. "The blue orb can protect me from the pressure, and I can use it to infuse my body with enough oxygen to get me inside. There is a way inside, right?"

"Crix . . . you can't be serious. I know this is important, but we can't afford to lose you on a—"

Joric interrupted Septin to answer Crix's question. "Of course, there is a way in. However, it's too heavily defended, given the already challenging environmental hazards you'll have to cope with." A sudden sparkle glittered across Joric's eyes. "There's an exhaust hatch that opens periodically to vent out atmospheric toxins, like ammonia, that gets captured by the external filtration systems." He pointed his finger in the air as if the hatch was directly above them.

"These filters keep the guides for the cosmic thrusters from getting gummed up. Why that's important for you is that hatch should open once per day to exhaust what has been collected; it should be around the sixth hour given that the queen has not decided to adjust it for some reason. It will stay open for three minutes only, so you won't have time to waste. If we time your entry perfectly, we can get you inside before these defensive systems have a chance to deal with you. Also, I hope that your orb can keep you warm as the temperatures in this specific layer of Oro are so cold that exposed flesh will instantly freeze."

Crix stared directly at Joric for a couple of seconds. "It will keep me warm; it always has, and if there's a way in, I'll find it."

Septin shook his head. "Crix, we'll find a better way. This is not what I had intended for you."

"There's no other way, and you know that. I have to do this; it's why I'm here," Crix had a tickle of fear welling up in the pit of his stomach over the thought of it. He tried hard to suppress it and show strength and gain their confidence.

To their shock, Kerriah entered the room with the chrome Marck chasing closely behind her, imploring her not to disturb them and to take rest. She looked renewed, her skin blush and tight. Her piercing eyes shot a glance at each of them.

"What is this? You're going on a suicide mission, and that's our plan? The best we can come up with?" She lost her footing and stumbled, catching herself against a tall, slender display case with tiers of awards for scientific achievements. Her body was still not fully healed, yet Joric looked at her with astonishment. Even he couldn't believe that she was already up and about.

Crix leaped up to assist her, and she shoved him away. "No!" She scowled, locks of her tangled black hair ribboned over her face. She pulled her palm across her cheeks, brushing the strands away from her eyes. "I want to know what you're planning. I'm not going to allow you to kill yourself intentionally. Give me the full details, and I'll come up with something better, one that doesn't result in your assured death."

"Kerriah . . ." Septin rose from his seat, his face washed pale with distress. "We have yet to go over any precise details of this plan. However, the core's location is most unexpected and provides very limited possibilities for accessing it."

"Where?" she demanded.

Septin took a dry, pasty swallow before answering. "It's in a stationary position deep within the atmosphere of Oro."

Kerriah remained silent for a minute before responding. "Then we send deep pressure shock torpedos in to blow it up from its hiding spot. Maybe we will be lucky enough that the blast spares it and just pushes it back into low orbit."

"That would be the absolute last resort. At this point, any risk of the core's destruction is unacceptable with the forthcoming Thraxon invasion. We need to gain control of the Marcks if we are to survive this attack," Septin explained.

Kerriah's face twisted with anger, and she gave the nearby display case a swift forward kick, knocking it over, smashing it to bits, and sending awards scattering across the smooth floor.

"Kerriah!" Septin shouted with the frustrated intensity of a scornful father who had just witnessed his child blatantly misbehaving.

Joric quickly stood, placing a gentle hand on Septin's arm and shook his head. "It's okay," he whispered.

Crix couldn't sit back any longer and dashed over to Kerriah, wrapping his arms around her. However, feeling the warmth and strength of his embrace was more than she could handle. Her emotions poured out and tears flowed. Deep inside, she was startled by the level of care she had for Crix. She had never allowed herself to get this close to anyone before, always choosing to keep friendships at arm's length. She would find her comfort in defensive postures that protected her from emotional harm. Crix helped her over to one of the plush chairs and gently seated her upon it. He brushed her hair away from her cheeks. She began to pull herself back together from this rare emotional outpour.

"Tell me at least that your death isn't certain. That there's a plan for your escape, even if your chances are small. Tell me that much at least."

Joric quickly answered her concern. "There's an override. I designed it for use during the testing phase of the core and the queen. Once I determined the system was stable, I had it removed. So it will have to be reinstalled."

Kerriah squinted her eyes shut and shook her head. "Why would you remove it?"

"The risk of it being there was too great. If a nefarious entity somehow learned of its existence, well . . ."

She stared coldly at Joric. "Right."

"It needs to be installed inside the nucleus. This override will allow us to gain manual control by putting the queen into a suspended state. Crix will couple the override into the socket, and it will connect back here to my control system, and we can then send commands to the Marck forces. It should still work, though getting it into the nucleus of the central core will be the tricky part."

Kerriah scowled, not happy with the answer Joric had given her. "Well, that's great, but if he can even get in there, how's he supposed to get out? How does he get back out of Oro's gravitational pull?"

Joric sighed; his eyes looked long over having to answer. He explained how none of the possibilities were certain since having a living organism onboard was never part of the original design equation. There wasn't even a primary life support system installed in the station. However, there was a limited use system onboard that he needed to activate manually. They spent the next several hours going over the possibilities.

They combed over the core station schematics, looking for escape routes, trying to find a way for Crix to survive. Kerriah paced the floor, shouting and pointing until her still traumatized body fell back into a chair, exhausted and dripping with sweat. Eventually, Crix's thoughts regarding his safety drifted into a mental fog over the hours of prolonged tension and overwhelming details. It was too much. He needed to keep his focus on getting the override installed, then he would worry about the rest.

Joric explained that there were two possibilities to escape the core. A supply return container, which he designed to deliver needed materials for the core's final stages of construction. However, there was a risk that the clever queen will jettison it to trap him there. The other option was to turn up one of the station's thrusters and to use them to blast it back into low orbit. This was also risky, as the sudden pressure shifts could compromise the core's hull's integrity. With several plausible options for Crix's escape, Kerriah's inner beast settled, and she assumed her familiar warrior spirit with the task ahead.

***

With little more than a day before the dangerous operation, Crix and Kerriah decided to take time to be alone with each other.

Septin agreed. They would make the most of their last day together in this place that was so lovely and seemingly peaceful. It was a moment they both longed for, and a particular time they both would cherish, and neither would squander with sleep or worry.

CHAPTER 20

Crix pushed off the slender gondola that was tethered to a stone archway overlooking a wooden dock. Joric had created a perfect mix of visible natural perfections that masked the technology behind it all. The sprawling lake narrowed through the dense woods in the distance and hooked away from the lodge's view. A silver moon stared down overhead from a murky blue sky, and the waters lapped against the sides of the boat as Crix gently paddled them out to a private spot away from the lodge.

Kerriah sat relaxed in the front with her head tilted back, taking in the charm of the nighttime sky. Crix remained quiet, aside from the paddle dipping into the water and tree frogs chirping in the background. He enjoyed the view of Kerriah's black hair glistening in the celestial light as it draped back across her shoulders.

They drifted to an area that curved around a wall of tall, red, broadleaf trees and into a small cove outlined with white rocks that provided a tickling glow in the moonlight. A crisp breeze whisked over the water with just enough bite to remind Crix to wrap his arms around Kerriah. He gently pulled her into him, and the gondola's red velvet cushions sank in comfortably as they stared out, watching the shadows of the tree leaves dance in the backdrop. They sat quietly for a few minutes, taking in the surrounding peace and feeling the intoxicating warmth from each other.

Kerriah had on a silky, white, sleeveless dress that she had borrowed from Gentria's closet. The dress draped just above her knee; it was something she thought would be romantic for her time with Crix. A soft black cardigan loosely covered her shoulders and arms from the nighttime nips of a breeze. Crix wore a jacket but felt such an immense warmth from being near Kerriah that it wasn't needed. His hair had grown longer, and he swept it to the side. His focus was on her and nothing else.

"This feels so good, so right, and so perfect," Kerriah said, and she turned to catch a glimpse of Crix's eyes.

Her hair smelled like a mix of fresh cut apples and crisp sheets that were wind-dried on a spring morning. He gave her ear a light kiss. "You're here with me, and that makes it more than anything else I can ever hope for. During the days we spent in some of the worst places and in the worst circumstances, I had wanted this. The thought of which got me through those times, knowing that someday, we would have moments like these together. I would battle a hundred heydromacs to spend this time with you in my arms."

She turned around and looked at him, confused. "A what?"

Crix let out a weary chuckle. "I will have to tell you about that one sometime, but I just want to focus on us now."

They lay there afloat for a while, watching the stars and making plans for the years ahead. An occasional kiss would heighten their pulse and flush their bodies with a blanket of warmth. After a while, Crix pulled the gondola up to a path on the shoreline. The path of smooth white stones weaved up a small hill to a round sitting area constructed of cabernet-tinted wood. The nestled area was canopied by trees with spiral lavender flowers dipping down from their web of branches.

They tickled and laughed like children as they flirted and succumbed to the feelings of blithe for the first time in recent memory. Kerriah made herself comfortable on a wooden bench as she stretched out across it and placed her feet on Crix's lap. Crix removed his jacket and folded it under her head, then carefully slipped her flats off and began to rub her feet. She closed her eyes and hummed with pleasure. Crix rubbed his thumb across the heel of her foot and noticed no visible sign or scar from the algae attack. Her ability to heal was remarkable, and her feet were as soft as delicate flower petals. *She is wonderful.*

"Kerriah, tell me more about your life before we met. Did you have other . . . you know . . . .relationships that were more than friends?" Crix kneaded his thumbs deeply into the arch of her foot.

Kerriah took in a deep, relaxing breath and opened her eyes, gazing up at the twinkling stars. "I wasn't that unusual. My father kept me safe and well cared for. My mother was a very proper lady and tried her best to instill honorable values upon me. I had great parents. As for friends, we used to go out and hit all the hot locations in Teinol. We liked to get dressed up and go tube drifting, and if the tubes weren't hot at one place, we'd leave and hit the other down the street where they would be. I didn't want serious relationships, so I didn't have many. At least any worth mentioning." She frowned for a second over the thought. The close relationships she tried to have in the past always ended up tarnished with jealousy. The egos of her suitors were too big to be with someone who excelled at everything.

Crix grinned. His eyes widened with intrigue. "Tube drifting?" Kerriah gave him a playful smile before she sat up and caressed his head.

"I forget at times that you came from the outskirts. It can be a blast. Think of a mix of large reverse pressure tubes that simulate weightlessness filled with multicolored ambient lights and vibrant music mixed with some of the more creative high energy youth of Teinol, certainly some good times for sure."

"Wow! Sounds like fun. No wonder you took to Annexis so well."

"Yeah, I did get a similar feel as tube drifting, but a lot less intense and much less hostile."

They talked for hours, and the time passed quickly. Crix told Kerriah of his childhood challenges growing up different from the Andors he lived amongst but stopped short of telling her of his true genetic identity. *What if she doesn't feel the same for me after finding out the truth? I can't take that risk. Yet, she has a right to know. But I didn't even know until almost a week ago; maybe I can tell her later.* His thoughts swirled, and he tried to keep from sapping the enjoyment of their limited time together before his potentially fatal task ahead. Scared that she would not understand, he held off telling her and decided to enjoy her company while he could.

The trees' shadows turned long and the sky a deep orange from the sun breaking over the horizon. The night of stories, sensual kisses, and rolling around tickling had given way to the impending end of this carefree evening, and the morning brought with it the anxieties of what was to come and what could be lost.

Crix pushed the gondola back out into the lake and began paddling toward Joric's lodge. The depths of his heart wouldn't stop bothering him, and he couldn't keep it from her any longer. "Kerriah," he said in a tiny voice.

"Yes," she said before kissing him on the back of his neck.

He turned around to face her. His throat tightened up when his eyes met with the emerald green of hers. "There is something I have to tell you, something you have a right to know about me." He tried to keep his voice from sounding weak, but he was as anxious as he had ever been at this moment.

She gave a serious stare back into his eyes. "You can tell me anything. Is it regarding you being a Tolagon? I know it's a lot of responsibility, but we can work through that together."

"No. It's nothing like that, and I really wish it were that simple," Crix said with an uncomfortable pause. "I'm not a Mendac."

She raised an eyebrow, and for some reason, everything she did looked charming to Crix, which made this that much more difficult. "Well, you are, you just come from Troika, and that does not change the fact that you're still a Mendac like your father and mother were."

"Yes, it does, because I am an Andor and not just by home but by blood." His face was long, with an uneasy stare in his eyes as he gave her the details. He had dreaded this moment since he discovered the truth. "I'm a crossbreed of an Andor and my Mendac mother," he said, lowering his head. For a moment, his thoughts drifted to the Monoglades. He had more in common with them than he had realized at the time.

"What? How?" Kerriah tried to find logic in what he was telling her but came up empty. "Andors mating with anything aside from Andors? It's against their culture, their principles . . . isn't it? Besides, you don't have any trace of Andor features in your physical appearance."

Crix hated this. His heart sank, and his stomach wretched over the thoughts of self-loathing as to why he couldn't just be *normal.* "Creedith was my biological father and not because he mated with my mother, because he was tricked into giving up his molecular extract to Zearic. That extract mixed with that of my mother's. In a fit of shame, my father Corin used the power of the yellow orb and the blue orb together to alter my outward appearance somehow and hide the Andor side of me. I don't know how he did it, but I show up as myself under Plexo's scanners, so it's nothing more than some sort of lasting illusion," Crix said, unable to keep his voice from quivering as his heart raced.

Kerriah stared at him blankly. She was at a loss for words given what was just told to her. Crix stared up at her like a child that had just got caught doing something wrong and was awaiting their punishment.

"I—I don't know quite what to say. It's just so strange. I don't mean that in a negative way; I'm just having a difficult time believing it." Kerriah stretched out her arm and lightly smoothed her palm over Crix's cheek. It didn't feel any different. A strong jaw overlayed with the coarseness of white stubble that had emerged recently. Aside from the Tolagon white hair, everything you would expect from a young Mendac male.

Crix needed to know if this news had changed anything between them, yet he also feared the reply. She likely hadn't had enough time to decide one way or another, but he still had to ask. He wiped his cold sweaty palms across his pant legs in anticipation of his next question. "Does this . . . you know, does this change the way you feel about me? If it does, I understand; I just don't want to lose you and was dreading telling you this."

Kerriah smiled and shook her head; her shiny black hair caught a breeze and streamed across her right eye. Her petite fingers brushed the stubborn hair back as her green eyes stared straight into his soul and melted away all other thoughts within him. "No-no-no, not in the slightest. To me, you are still the person I fell in love with. Besides, I'm not exactly a shining example of normal by any definition either. Besides, who gets to define normal anyway?" Her warm smile widened. "You've accepted me for me, and I accept you for you." She gave him a comforting hug that was so snug he could feel her heartbeat against his own. Her embrace offered no doubts with regards to her sincerity. His emotions stirred him into sudden dizziness over his feelings for her.

THE QUEEN PROTOCOL

As she released her embrace, Crix felt the weight of the world lifted from his shoulders; he smiled big, wrapped his arms around her again, and snuggled her tightly.

"Thank you." He whispered in her ear.

CHAPTER 21

They arrived at the lodge's dock and noticed Septin standing there with a distraught and impatient look. A circular ship rested upon a long, slender tripod high above the peak of the lodge behind him. He tapped his right foot nervously and waved them in with a motion to hasten their return.

"It's time," he told them as Crix tethered the boat off and helped Kerriah out.

Kerriah gazed up at the ship that wasn't there when they had left. "The Thraxons?" she asked.

"I'm afraid so; it's worse than we anticipated. Please, come with me. We have established a remote command post here. We have already called down some of our leadership to convene at this location," Septin told them before he stormed off to a transparent lift that flowed up to a circular ship above.

"What of Throwen and Systine? Why are we not assembling there?" Kerriah's voice rose as she inquired over the last-minute change.

Septin stopped just before entering the lift and stared into her eyes while placing his hands on her arms. "Child, both have been lost already. It happened so quickly, too quickly, and at a very coordinated point in time. We were completely taken off-guard with the timing of the attacks. The only explanation is that we must have been compromised early on and utterly unaware."

"Why couldn't we fight them off? They should have fought them back!" Kerriah's thoughts went to those that she had come to know at those resistance strongholds. The breath was taken out of her for a few seconds as their faces flashed through her mind.

"The Marcks sent in their Knactor Legion and made quick work of us while most were still asleep." Septin's voice broke, and he took a dry swallow.

"No! Mitara, Renic, Aros . . . our fleet . . . all lost!?" The news visibly shook Kerriah as her eyes welled up with tears.

"We're not sure about any of that right now. The flow of communication has been jammed, and we don't know who was able to get out. We know that the ships Perso, Lamber, and Saber were out already setting up outer perimeter defensive batteries to use against the incoming Thraxon fleet." He stopped to clear his throat and swipe a trickle of sweat from his forehead. "We can only hope that they are still online, but again, we have no reports. Plexo is recalibrating his parallax drones for emergency communications, and hopefully, we will have contact with most of our fleet soon. Now you will need to pull yourself together as we decide what exactly to do."

They took the lift conduit up to a circular control area filled with floating control panels and observation screens that lined a high ceiling. The screens displayed images of Marcks indiscriminately blasting civilians on all three worlds and taking many more captives. The great cities of Soorak smoldered, and deep ocean megacities crumbled under the assaults from the amphibious attacks of the Marck Kator Legions on Thale. Standing about watching the screens and plotting amongst each other were six of the resistance leaders. Commander Burling, Barth, the controversial religious leader of Thale's oldest faith and publicly outspoken critic of Marck control, Tayole, the wealthy energy mogul of Soorak, who had been a chief financier of the resistance, Captain Boran of Solara, Piria the female Luminar. Both Pira and Plexo had stayed behind as guides for peace as the original Luminar emissaries returned to Easolan. Krath, who was already geared up in heavy battle armor, stood near Joric.

Tayole cleared his throat, loud enough for everyone to notice. "There they are; now we can begin." His voice filled with the confidence of one accustomed to being quickly acknowledged. He was tall with thin black hair, sunken in cheeks, and a wrinkled brow. His blue eyes blazed against his slender black suit adorned with the corporate emblem of a glowing star that had an arrow piercing its center.

Captain Boran sized Crix up and down and grunted as if he questioned the young Tolagon's ability to save them. The well-aged, brawny, stout warrior wore a gold and black Solaran battle uniform of the old world. His patchy, long beard and bristly, dark grey eyebrows gave him a wild, primitive appearance. He was a warrior with a legendary reputation during the first Thraxon War, with no love for the Thraxons or the Marcks. He had been an active member of the resistance since its roots shortly after the UMO handover.

"I'm very pleased to finally meet you, Tolagon Emberook," the mystic voice of Piria said. She had a beautiful petite figure and a soft, radiant face. Her eyes gave Crix a tickle inside when she looked directly at him, and she exuded a gentleness that made him feel at ease. Like all Luminars, she wore no clothing, but that was hardly noticeable behind their white, glowing bodies.

"Thanks," Crix answered her with a forced smile, though he started to feel a little at ease. Krath grabbed his hand and gave it an overly firm shake. Crix winced but tried to keep from showing that it hurt.

"Good to see tya again, buddy. I was getting' tired of keepin' ol' glow rod company, and they were getting tired of me complainin' about it, so they decided to put me in command as a representative of Thale." Krath gave out a bellowing laugh. "Tya believe that?" He pulled his sleeve back, showing off a metal cuff with an emblem of a two-headed sea dragon, the symbol of Thale. "Anyway, this is what I have been waitin' for anyway, kicking the scrap out of those walking cans. Tya know what's better than that? Pounding the guts out of them crusty bugs." Krath pounded his fist on his chest plate.

"I'm glad to hear it, Krath. They made the right choice with you," Crix fought back the angst, which had clawed its way back into his gut. Anxiety had flushed over him since entering the room.

Septin motioned to Joric, who activated holographic images of Thraxon warships moving throughout from a gammac corridor; the fleet was vast and shadowy, and the ships at times were nearly concealed against the black backdrop of space.

"These are the images we captured of the Thraxon invasion fleet moving through gammac corridor Delta less than twelve hours ago. This fleet appeared to be the largest we have seen to date from the Thraxons, with a complement of ships that are more advanced than before. There are also reports that Zearic and Sinstar Corp have assisted in rebuilding this Thraxon fleet."

His eyes shifted over to Kerriah. "Also, as we are all now painfully aware, the Marcks have made their move early and have already taken hostile control of every major city within the UMO. Pockets of resistance are holding out in some areas, but they are ill-equipped against the Marck armies and police forces. All the leaders sympathetic to our cause have been rounded up and executed in public view. What's worse, our primary bases of Throwen and Systine have been annihilated in these well-coordinated attacks."

As Septin continued, Crix looked over at Kerriah and couldn't help to notice the pain in her face as the briefing continued. Her eyes welled as her frown deepened and cheeks twitched. He wanted to comfort her, but she wouldn't want it from him right now. He knew that she was brewing up a belly full of anger deep inside, the anger she was going to need in the coming hours and days.

"We are holding out hope that there are survivors that will report back from the emergency rendezvous point. So far, nothing.

Our entrenched units are on standby, awaiting further orders. The plan is to create a diversion long enough for Tolagon Crix Emberook to place the override into the queen's central core. This override will allow us to control all Marck forces and fight back these Thraxon invaders once again. Joric has built this override for just this purpose; the difficult part will be getting it put in place. Joric, I will let you fill in those details."

Septin extended his hand to Joric as he stepped forward, carrying the override plug. The cone-shaped device was about the same size as his open hand. He swiped the bottom, and the cone lit up to a brilliant white glow.

"The override, once placed into the core's nucleus, will shut down the queen's control and thereby inoculate her to submit only to our commands. There is only one override, and it's keyed specifically to the core. We would have to have direct access to the core to create a new one. So we get one shot at this. If the override is lost, then so are our options." Joric frowned over the thought.

Boran sneered as he stared at the override device then back up at Crix. "This boy cannot handle this job. I will get this thing put in that core. I'm not comfortable putting my trust in this unknown adolescent." He curled his lip and growled at Crix.

"Oh, Boran, he will do fine. You need to put your faith into something and release this deep-seated anger that oppresses your thoughts," Piria said in her gentle manner.

"Captain Boran, do you have anything or anyone that could withstand temperatures of minus two hundred degrees combined with atmospheric pressures that would instantly crush any ships in your fleet, sporadic electrical storms, and funnels of liquid hydrogen plumes . . . hmm?" Septin gave Boran only a few seconds to reply since he already knew the answer. Boran scrunched his brow and lowered his head. "I didn't think so. Please contain yourself as the burden on this young one is enough as it is," Septin snapped, putting Boran back in his place.

"I have faith in you, young Mendac," Barth said in his calm voice. His long, purple robe draped down, cupping the floor; his hands folded into his sleeves. "In these times, we must find faith; I have prayed many months for the day our cause will find victory. Now my prayers have focused on providing this young individual with the strength to wield this great burden. I do not foresee failure." Barth slowly bowed his head; the silver ring atop his headpiece reflected against the multiple light sources in the room.

Kerriah stared at Crix, her eyes glossy. "He's done more than you know of already, and though I wish he didn't have to do this as well, I also understand what is at stake right now and that he is truly our only hope here. I have complete faith in him." She swiped her finger across the inside of her eye, trying to catch an inevitable tear.

"Well, son? You've been relatively silent, what are your thoughts? Are you comfortable with this?" Septin asked him directly.

Crix took a deep breath to settle his nerves. He was calming the storm of thoughts that were rushing through his mind at the moment. The task before him was not something he had completely surrendered to yet. So many were depending on him, so many lives, the future of these worlds, and their shaping. Kerriah, his father's legacy, *both of them*, it was all just so much that he felt drunk with thoughts.

"Well?" Boran stomped his foot with impatience. "You see, he cannot even speak of it, much less perform this task, so I will do it. Damn the pressure and damn the cold."

Septin put his hand up to silence Boran's tirade. Crix stared down at the floor and then back up at Kerriah. Her eyes drew him in, and love poured through his insides. He suddenly felt as if there was nothing he couldn't or wouldn't do to see those eyes again. "I'm not going to lie, by claiming that I haven't battled with fear and doubts, but I'll find a way to accomplish this. You have nothing to worry over." He spoke with such conviction that the tension in the room instantly melted away.

Kerriah smiled proudly, and Septin took an easy breath. "You see. I told you we had the right person for this task. Someday our children's children will speak of this moment to draw inspiration from."

Joric handed Septin a slender device. He pressed it with his thumb, which blinked an image of the Marck Central Core station into the room's center. The image spun slowly and revealed a towering structure with a long, pointed bottom, which coned upward into an eventual bulb at the top. It gave the appearance of an inverted steeple floating stationary in some hellish surroundings.

"The lower atmosphere of Oro is toxic, and the queen does not need life support systems, though the station was originally outfitted with them," Joric explained. "Much of the station will be filled with stastic gas to keep its structure from buckling under the extreme atmospheric pressure as well as keep the corrosive elements pushed out." He looked directly at Crix.

"You will find this gas to be almost fluid-like or at least a middle ground between air and fluid. It will be somewhat difficult to pass through, but still easier to move around in than water. Once inside, your first objective will be to get down to the Hailo governor deck, purge this gas, and then kickstart the long-dormant life support systems. This action will be required for you to continue further.

"Not to worry over the absence of the gas, the station can remain structurally sound for a short time with the air pressure alone, but you'll need to make haste. The queen is also aware of this, so be prepared to create another air bubble, just in case." Joric finished his mental dump of what Crix had ahead of him twice before dispersing to each of their objectives.

***

Shortly after the meeting, Crix departed to the Admary to prep and suit up for a shot propulsive orbital dive, or spodding as it was called. This was not something that first-timers typically took into a hostile zone, much less into Oro's gas clouds and the Central Core as the target. Crix had the jitters over the thought of where he was spodding to more than spodding itself.

Would he be able to hold his orb bubble up for the duration? Maintaining such a shield took immense focus, and he was going to be sensory overloaded with strange sights and intensive mission objects, which had almost zero margins for error. The more he thought it over, the more it felt like a one-way journey. Beads of sweat covered his forehead, and nausea filled his stomach.

Burling and Kerriah left for the command ship Berritt. Krath and Boran made for the resistance ground units on each of their respective homeworlds. Their jobs were to counter the Marck and Thraxon assaults in key areas long enough for Crix to complete his mission, and they would do so until the last one remained afoot.

CHAPTER 22

It was lonely. Crix had never felt so alone before. He found it difficult not to fall back into that abyss called despair. Thoughts of failure consumed him. Was the kiss before his shuttle left Joric's paradise the last time he would ever feel Kerriah's touch? He recalled feeling magnetically pulled in as he pressed his lips against hers and felt their tender warmth. She hypnotized him with the sparkle in her eyes as her moist lips pulled away from his. The visual sensation speared his heart with adrenaline, which tickled its way through all his extremities. Her beauty melted him away.

Afterward, they had departed their separate ways, he on his mission to Oro and the Marck core and she onto commanding resistance units in defensive positions in and around Soorak. He now felt black inside, a shell of himself with a spinning tunnel before him. His thoughts chased back to the feeling of her smooth cheek against his as they hugged so tight that their muscles quivered. The memory was permanently fused into his heart. He would hold onto it with a vice-like grip and the last of his strength to keep his mind on why he was there.

A flight operator helped him attach the last parts of the cumbersome deep-pressure suit. The distinct design was only going to get him close to the station before it collapsed, and he would have to push it off with his orb power. The pressure suit would buy him precious minutes of air and strength. The round helmet locked in place and gave a sudden squeal as the pressure began to adjust inside. Crix's ears popped, eyeballs slowly pushed in, and his cheeks sucked to his teeth. Everything went completely mute, but he could see the flight operator outside giving him a thumbs up for ready. Everything was silent, and he couldn't even hear his heartbeat. It was strange. Without any sense of sound or feeling, it became similar to dreaming. Perhaps that was a good thing. The more this seemed surreal to him, the less he felt anxious about what he was about to do.

Before him, a spinning tube of powerful lights entranced his thoughts. Shot propulsive orbital dive barrel, or spod. The resistance used it for small unit deployments, and the UMO Legions used it during the Second Thraxon War. Spodding certainly wasn't a new feat, but blasting down to the Marck core station far below for his first dive made his stomach squirm. Crix tensed his muscles for a minute, trying desperately to relax his nerves. He stared for a moment at the chorus of lights. They swirled around in some pattern that made sense to an engineer. Through that swirling hole was his destiny, and it scared him into a cold sweat.

Cables pulled taught above him as the flight operator guided him into a loading lift. His bulky, armored pressure suit was impossible to walk around in, so the cable hoist moved him to where he needed to be. He swung over to a shiny, black platform and was lowered face down upon its slick surface, staring ahead. The platform raised level with the tube of spinning lights and then jutted him forward like a bullet chambering into a rifle's breach. The breach closed around him, and the only thing he could see was the spinning lights, which taunted his sanity. His heartbeat quickly increased as claustrophobia leapt into his chest. Regardless of how he felt at this point, he will undoubtedly be deep inside the hostile atmosphere of Oro within minutes. There was no way to turn back or change his mind.

A display in his helmet read the distance to his target and flashed the words "stand by." After several minutes, each of which felt like lifetimes in the middle of his stirring thoughts, the words changed to "armed" and the display dimmed to a red glow. Immense pressure built up behind Crix, and the lights stopped spinning and turning. They instantly became long, thin threads and then shot back toward him. He felt his stomach leave his body. The scene before him immediately changed to a rapidly growing Oro as the immense magenta shaded planet layered with violet swirls charged forward into his view.

Crix shot into Oro's outer atmosphere at a blinding speed, and the Admary was already the visual equivalent of a tiny spec behind him. The sight of the planet's mass quickly became so overwhelming that the feeling of vertigo began to tease him into nausea. Clouds of red, orange, and violet gas immersed his sight as he entered the atmosphere. He was close enough now to witness the violent movement of these gas clouds, which became more and more ferocious as he neared.

He plunged headlong into a wave of hydrogen gas and ammonia that crystalised the deeper he went. The ferocious winds ripped into him, and the guidance system kicked on, trying to maintain his course trajectory. The suit's thrusters fired to compensate against the pushing and pulling that forced his heading in the wrong direction. His display froze with a thick layer of ice. He called out to the suit's lip-reading system to apply heat and thaw it. As he regained his visibility, the colors of violet, red, and traces of orange whisked by at speeds so fast that they mixed visually into a muddy soup.

The rigid suit held up well so far, but Crix could feel a chilling cold inside as it started to struggle to keep up with the rapidly dropping temperatures of the planet's inner atmosphere. His lips stretched back, and the display began to fog with a light layer of frost.

A green light blinked on his display as the suit's guidance system detected its projected destination was nearing. It fired its shoulder and chest descent control pulsers. Crix felt his guts forced up from his lower extremities as the speed suddenly changed, and strobing white lights from the pulser's glow blinded him temporarily. His suit felt like it might shake apart from the violent jolt and vibrations as it continued to fight against the thickening atmosphere.

Inside his helmet, red lights flashed faster and faster with the words "pressure warning" to notify him that the pressure had reached the critical point that the suit could handle. It began to pop and crack, and all around him, sharp pains stabbed at his body from the pressure denting in weaker sections of the suit. Crix prepared to create his protective sphere from the orb to give him the crucial minutes needed to fire up the core station's life support. *Was it too early?* The suit had to hold up longer. He hadn't even seen the station yet, and would he see it? Or would this be a one-way trip to being crushed like an insect under the boot heel of Oro oppressive atmosphere? A flurry of doubts and questions invaded his mind just before the clouds broke into an open and clearer, calmer region.

It was dark, but a nearly constant show of lightning strikes illuminated the area with a creepy strobing effect. This portion of Oro was vast and continued for thousands of miles down. The lightning bolts extend from the top of the cloud layer to the liquid-gas layer far below. All around this vast region were thin funnels of ice, gas, and liquid that needled upward from the furthest reaches below and splashed into gas clouds far above where he had just emerged from. The whole scene was one nightmarish vision of some netherworld.

For a moment, he took in the sight of the world he just entered. Less than two weeks ago, he lived a simple life in the natural calms of Troika. At that time, he could have never predicted he would be freefalling into the belly of Oro right then. He slammed to a sudden stop, which caused a powerful shock throughout his extremities. The suit split open, and he quickly blasted it off and dispersed the oxygen module strapped to his body, promptly after forming a blue protective sphere.

The orb's life maintaining bubble held, but Crix could immediately feel the strain stabbing straight into every nerve in his body. The pain pierced and dug around his insides, looking for a lethal spot. It was sharp and unyielding. The silver fanged creatures that he had been plagued with throughout the past few weeks filled his sight again, but he managed to push them back . . . for now.

CHAPTER 23

It was the Core Station that shattered the spod suit. He faced down upon its hard metal surface with the orb's oxygen-containing bubble ballooned around him. A perfect shot, Joric set the suit's guidance system to absolute precision and somehow accounted for all the atmospheric pushes and pulls.

He needed to locate the exhaust hatch. Hopefully, Joric's timing was as perfect as his landing for its daily three-minute opening. The outside of the station was slippery, coated with frozen ammonia, methane, and other atmospheric sediments. The extreme cold bled through the orb's protective bubble, something they had failed to account for in the mission planning.

As he carefully crawled down the sloping surface, his hands went completely numb, and pain shot up into his elbows. He lost his grip and snapped his hands up, rubbing them furiously together, trying to bring them back to life. He began to slip uncontrollably downward without his hands pressing into the icy metal for stability. The frigid slime made a perfect slide down the station's surface and into a helpless death plunge far below. Crix didn't want to die in that unknown Hell. He planted his hands back down again, trying to ignore the throbbing pain pulsing its way up to his arms.

His momentum stopped just short of a stabilizing cosmic thruster burst. He shielded his hand over his eyes from its intense light, and the outward blast visually distorted everything in its path. Joric warned Crix that he would need to take extra care not to get within proximity of the thrusters when they fired. Their matter displacement effect would turn his body into what he referred to as "noodles."

Maintaining his grip continued to be a challenge as he searched for an exhaust hatch. His numb hands stopped working, and his fingers would no longer bend. He shook them until he could slowly curl the fingers into a fist again. A wind gust shoved him onto his backside, and he completely lost control, narrowly missing the timed stabilizing blast of a dreaded cosmic thruster. His heart skipped several beats as the edge of the station rapidly approached. His mind went numb, and his chest burned with fatigue from sustaining the orb shield under the extreme conditions. He was doubtful if he could use it to stop his descent without accidentally lowering its critical protection.

He slid faster and faster. As he reached the side, the vastness below came into view. Darkness cast shadows across everything, with an occasional lightning strike that would light up the enormous, spectral funnels of liquid that shot upward across the expanse. He froze, locking up his muscles; his arms and legs extended straight with nothing to grab. He tried to stop himself with the orb's power, but the spike of pain shot into his brain with such intensity that he couldn't hold it, and it merely slowed his slide into the abyss.

THE QUEEN PROTOCOL

He spilled over the station's edge along with a waterfall of frozen molecular slime. He felt his stomach leave his body as the station's upper dome moved away from him, along with his last grip of hope. This was the end. There was nothing below him now but frozen death and the crushing weight of Oro. The sea of liquid gasses and freezing pressure, along with a bottomless chasm of horror, were his only companions now, and a brief thought crossed his mind, that he should just open the protective globe and end it quickly. Pulling himself back up with the orb's power was out of the question given the strain he was feeling.

A sudden jolt ripped through his body as his fall instantly stopped. His neck whipped back, and his head banged into a hard surface, nearly costing him his consciousness. He was starting to elevate. *How is this happening? Is this death?* He stammered back up to his feet upon a flat surface and noticed the long, slender midsection of the core station webbed with fingers of black ammonia stains that dripped down its smooth, outer hull.

The air inside his bubble already started to thin, and he couldn't help feeling short of breath. He had to get inside. *How am I not plunging to my death right now?* He spun around and saw an apathetic metal face; its eyes flashed red at the sight of Crix staring upon it. The chiseled face appeared to be the upper portion of a guardian drone that circled the station looking from anomalies to subjugate. He stood upon the drone's backside, and the face had spun around and was now scanning him.

A red beam waved up and down over his body. A discolored mechanical arm flexed out from the drone's side and formed a long needle at its tip. The arm drew back like a snake about to strike. It stabbed forward, punching into the orb's

279

protective barrier. Crix screamed in pain from being stretched to his limit keeping the shield up and running low on oxygen. The haunting images flashed into his view again, and he fought to suppress them, which despite his strain, he found it easier to do than before.

As the drone levitated upward, he looked back at the station for the exhaust hatch. However, the drone had not given up on its prey, and another arm extended out to join the first. The second arm lit up bright blue before firing a deep thermal blast that soaked into the orb's energy field. Crix felt an instant relief of warmth that quickly turned to crippling pain. The first arm cranked mechanically around his orb barrier to keep him from moving. He bent the orb bubble inward and squeezed out of the drone's grip. Fortunately, the drone carried him back to the station's topside. He took a desperate jump and made an unforgiving landing upon the hard surface.

The drone quickly swooped around; its red eyes appeared angry without actually moving. Now two other arms sprung out from its platform, joining the other two in their attacks. They worked systematically, swinging around without mercy in an attempt to knock this pest off the station; it was here to protect.

The hatch! It was right next to him but was still closed. Two more drones swung up from the outer perimeters behind him, and each also spawned out arms with vice-like grippers. Their clamps opened wide. He couldn't evade or fight them. All he could do was close his eyes and hope that maybe the hatch would open.

He felt a sharp tug from one of the drone arms pulling him into his inevitable end before a blast of orange and red gasses streamed out from the station. The hatch had opened! A twinge of hope re-energized him, and without a second thought, he drew every ounce of himself and leaped up into the vent. Everything turned black, and the vent trap closed until the next days' dispense cycle. Crix laid there for a few minutes, exhausted and short of breath. He couldn't stop; if he did, he would never get up again. His breathable air was almost gone, and a mix of nausea and dizziness clouded his thoughts.

CHAPTER 24

It was nearly pitch-black inside, and the only light was the gentle blue glow from the orb. It was enough, and the reduced pressure inside the station was a welcomed relief. He pushed himself upright; the area was tight and the surface was as smooth as glass. Crix crawled through the environmental waste pipe to an expanded space. The snug conduit combined with the thin air was enough to wrap him into a blanket of claustrophobia, and his heart started to race, thumping like it was about to leap from his chest. *I can't panic . . . not now.* He felt like he was mentally slipping as he stared down the narrow shaft before him.

He moved ahead by shuffling his elbows forward little by little to get to the holding tank. The shaft reached the smooth open tank, one that Crix could stretch out to gain back his mental state. He slid down to its bottom and freed himself from the claustrophobic confines of the ventilation shaft. He stood up and walked forward. The clack of his boots echoed across the hollow metal with each step.

He placed a small thermal device on the floor and jumped to the other side. It flashed, then began to heat the pipe around it to a bright red glow before melting a hole in the metal. Crix slid down the hole and dropped into a maintenance area below. Joric had instructed him to seal the room off using the emergency override outside the door when he left, which would keep the toxins from overtaking the station. He did as instructed.

The inside of the station was dark and frigid, with an occasional flash of light as he made his way down the hexagon-shaped corridors. The stastic gas swirled in the scant lighting and placed a ghostly film across everything visible. Moving around was frustratingly difficult through the density of the pressure-suppressing gas, and the air in his orb bubble became thinner with each gasping breath. His head spun with fatigue, and he wasn't sure he could keep his thoughts clear enough to follow the projected map that Joric had provided him.

The map folded into a compact cube that he secured in his pocket before departure. He pressed his thumb firmly down on the cube, and it spun into a lighted ring that fit perfectly over his head. He panned around, and blue beams projected into the direction of the Hailo governor deck, the place Joric told him controlled the dormant life support for the station.

It wasn't far from where he was, but it felt as though it was miles away. He dragged his exhausted feet across the metal floor, and the orb's barrier flickered. He just wanted to drop it and take a deep breath even though he knew it would kill him. Only two more turns to his destination, according to the map display. At least the station seemed quiet and abandoned. The hexagon corridor split left and right.

This is it . . . he thought. The map lights changed from blue to green. Looking up, he noticed a closed hatch. *That's it. Focus . . . must stay focused.*

His vision blurred and his hands trembled as he inserted the transparent key provided by Joric into a small hole nearby. As the key clicked, the hatch swirled open and slowly raised a platform beneath him. As his head cleared the room above, he could see where it read "Organic Boost Systems" atop a dimmed console in the center of the circular room. *Finally,. . . life support.* His chest cramped like a hot knife stabbing into it, and his lungs burned as he took in deeper and increasingly panicked breaths of depleted oxygen. The room spun around him, and he could feel his consciousness fade.

He fell to his knees, devoid of enough strength to stand any longer. The panel was only a meter away, and he lacked the endurance, so close. He crawled desperately on his hands and knees, but he knew he wasn't going to make it. The console was there; as he reached his hand up toward it, his orb's oxygen bubble faded. Everything around him began to shake for a couple of seconds before a lurid hiss poured in, lasting for several minutes. He blacked out and felt a deepening pressure in his chest.

***

As his eyes peeled slowly open, he felt his face pressed against the cold metal floor. The area appeared brightly lit, and he could breathe naturally. *How?* He didn't recall reaching the console. There was a long, high-pitched zipping sound going up and down repeatedly near him. Clanking echoed against the metal floor, which followed each zip and became louder with each subsequent clank. He peeled his face up from the cold floor and observed a tall Marck with a slender head. It was unlike any he had ever seen before and looked like an early design. It also didn't appear to be outfitted for combat but some form of a maintenance worker. It had small modules protruding from its head and body, long awkward looking legs, and a single rectangle lens for its vision. It stood next to a lit-up console that registered a flashing message—organic boost systems were online.

"Did you turn that on?" Crix asked the Marck, but it gave no reply or movement back. The Marck just remained in what appeared to be an idle state. "If you did, then thank you." Crix felt he owed his life to this unexpected friend, but the question remained; why did it save him? He struggled back to his feet; his strength slowly returned with every breath.

He took a closer look at the Marck. "Where did you come from? Do you have a name?" he asked, not expecting a reply, but he extended the courtesy of asking just in case. He tapped the Marck's arm a couple of times with his finger to see if it would react. It didn't budge.

He checked his lightmap for the direction to the queen's tower, which resided above the core's nucleus. The map lights projected his path forward. He followed it down the hexagonal-shaped corridor that now looked much different lit up than it did earlier. The stastic gas was now gone and it had adequate lighting. The Core's hull creaked and groaned. The stress from Oro's pressure outside took a toll on the station without its stabilizing gas. Crix passed Marck workers and guards partially hidden inside wall cubbies, dormant. Crix would rather not awaken them as he stepped carefully following the map's direction.

He reached an elevator that swooshed him up five levels to an access dome, above the queen's tower. Its doors groaned open into a large, circular area that was spoked by narrow passageways that lead into it. His curiosity directed him down one of the corridors.

The corridor opened into a ring that connected the other passages. Marck warriors lined the looped area, each staggered in armaments, bearing either a pulse rifle or percussion blades. Each one was adorned with the Marck guardian forces' blue concept insignia; they were fortunately dark and cold. The chilled air smelled a bit like scorched rubber. Crix's eyes were dry, and he tightly closed them for a couple of seconds before giving them a firm rub. He cautiously stepped back into the corridor. He would like to avoid whatever would trigger these guards.

He returned to the large, domed space and walked around looking for a switch, lever, ladder . . . anything. He couldn't recall Joric's instructions, and he slowly dragged his hands down his face, stopping to squeeze his temples as he struggled to remember.

As he peeked through his fingers, he noticed arrows across the walls pointing down in six different locations. A large, round disk sat at the ceiling's center, and six smaller disks appeared to correspond to the wall arrows on the floor. The holographic map lights pointed down.

Crix approached the larger disk in the middle. With his memories returning, he carefully waved his hand across the area beneath it. The large disk lit up upon his motion and activated a holographic control system beneath it. The system consisted of six square panels that appeared to correlate with the arrows and floor

286

disks, and each square read six different alphanumeric options:
T1 . . . N2 . . . P3 . . . D4 . . . B5 . . . L6. Crix recalled this part from
his discussion with Joric. Each was an acronym for parts of the
Core's tower. N2 is what he was looking for, which was nucleus
level two. The queen would be on T1, throne level one. Crix would
rather avoid this level if possible.

Crix reached over to press the N2 square and felt a sharp,
stabbing pain in his right hand. *Youch! . . . What the?* He quickly
jerked it back. As he turned it around, it withered black and
instantly went numb. He hunched over to clutch it with his left
hand, and he caught a glimpse of silvery figures converging on him
from the outer corridors. The control panel must have activated
the Marcks. About thirty of them had him surrounded, their rifles
drawn and their blades held lurching with aggression.

As he tried to move his right hand, it snapped off at the
wrist. Its charred remains shattered as it impacted the metal floor.
The pain in his wrist screamed up his arms like a bolt of electricity
and then streamed back down like fire. The Marcks advanced,
closing around him. With no time to overthink their intentions, he
stepped back into a defensive posture and cast an orb barrier
around himself.

The Marcks opened fire while the blade-bearing Marcks
pounced, trying to pierce their sonic charged tips through the
energy field. The barrier started to falter quickly against the
onslaught. Crix used his left hand to fire tepid orb blasts at some of
the nearby aggressors, toppling them momentarily before they
picked themselves back up again. It was enough to buy him a
desperate moment. He leaned down into a ball, soaking up as much
emotion as he could muster in a few short seconds before

exploding outward, sending a shockwave across the room and the whole of the Marcks onto their backsides.

The Marck's bodies remained motionless and scattered across the floor. Crix took some calming breaths as his thoughts attempted to digest what had just happened. He looked down at what remained of his hand, a charred stump. As his mind drifted into how he would complete the mission, the dreaded whine of servos jolted him away from his focus. The discarded metal figures scraped across the smooth surface as the Marcks began to return to life and back to their feet.

Crix didn't look. Instead, he swung around and hit the control panel with his stump and then hopped up on a nearby smaller disk. The disk flashed a blinding white and then turned clear. He felt his feet lose solid ground and he dropped into a freefall. His stomach was the only thing left in the dome as he slid down a transparent tube.

All around him were thousands of tiny spheres of light. The palpitating lights shot to and from the station's outer walls and into the side of a tall, black tower, the queen's tower. This narrow center of the core station would be pitch black if these spheres suddenly disappeared, leaving Crix lost in the darkness. The shadowy queen's tower was a spectral behemoth that narrowed at the top, consuming and spitting back these tiny light sources. *These lights must be the source packs that Joric spoke of that maintain the communications streams to the Marcks in the field,* Crix recalled as he marveled at them for a moment while still clutching his throbbing wrist. *They must only be visible in this part of the station.* His eyes tried to follow the spheres as they shot past him. The view provided a momentary distraction from the pain and the chaos that had unfolded above.

Crix felt his descent slow as he neared the bottom. A light disk below turned transparent just as he passed through it. The area he emerged into looked similar to where he had escaped the Marck guards, except it was dark.

This doesn't seem right, Crix thought to himself, recalling that the elevator should have taken him to N2, the nucleus. Unless, in his haste, he had activated the wrong disk. He began scanning the area for another control panel similar to the one above. He brightened his orb's light. The calming blue radiance illuminated a nearby wall marking . . . L6. *Yep.* His suspicions confirmed, and it had to be the lowest level. At least there was likely another elevator, just as long it didn't take him back to where he had come from. The L6 marking blurred in and out of his view, and the room began to shudder and spin. Dizziness pounced on him like an ebb tree tiger.

Out of nowhere, his strength abruptly left him, and nausea pierced into the pit of his stomach. He dropped down to his knees as he felt his legs go rubbery. He clamped his eyes shut and winced in pain as his heart stumbled through its beats. Inside he felt ablaze with fire, and the blue glow around his hand faded out.

What's happening to me? Vomit uncontrollably shot from his mouth, retching the contents of his stomach onto the metal floor. Clarity and his strength slowly sparked back in and he gave his eyes a firm rub. *Is this what Plexo has been warning me of? Using the power of the orb without the guidance of Gobar? I felt like I was dying.*

Crix slowly staggered back to his feet. He needed to get his thoughts back to the mission and dying would have to wait a little longer. He wiped the back of his hand across his mouth and turned to look for the ceiling disk but noticed there was an obstruction blocking his view.

He squinted and leaned forward for a clearer view. A red beam of light flicked on from a giant head. Crix felt a crushing blow to his torso and received an airborne trip across the room. His body crashed against the far wall, removing all air from his lungs. A huge Marck stormed toward him, and its block feet smacked against the floor with a loud crash of metal on each impacting stride. The floor vibrated a tickle across Crix's backside, informing him that it wouldn't take much of a pounce from this cruel monstrosity to turn him into a pile of broken flesh and bones.

He waited until the last second before darting between the legs of the two-legged tank. Unable to stop its momentum, the giant Marck clumsily crashed into the wall, leaving a large section a crinkled mess. Crix quickly located the control panel disk and swung his right arm under it. The disk illuminated intermittently, and behind him, the rumbling noise of the heavy Marck closed in.

Come on . . . hurry up . . . The control panel cycled up too slow. The behemoth Marck punched upward, shattering the large disk and destroying any hope of a quick recovery to the control section. Crix sidestepped a hammering downward blow from the Marck's massive arm, leaving a crater in the floor where he had stood only a split second earlier. It flailed its limbs around searching for its target, wreaking havoc on everything it contacted.

Crix lured the Marck back to the same area that it thrashed seconds before and drew it into striking the same spot on the floor time and again. Each time the floor cratered deeper, to the point where Crix was finding it increasingly difficult to evade. The floor section began to split, and Crix drew the Marck over the crater once more. The buckled floor creaked and groaned before crashing inward. The weight of the hulking mass of steel collapsed into the hole and through the area below.

The compromised level tore like a thin piece of foil, and the giant's arms desperately scraped and tore against the opening, trying to save itself. It clattered down into an area filled with spikes that arced with energy bolts. Crix carefully and hesitantly leaned over for a look. It was dark, except for bolts of power snapping and flashing across the giant Marck's body, which lay impaled through the spikes. The gigantic limbs flinched with every animating jolt.

Taking a deep inward breath and releasing a large expounding exhale, Crix switched on his lightmap.

"Great," he said, looking at the smashed control panel and disk. "Main elevator disabled." The map updated its path and transitioned from pointing to where the disk was to a service entrance that would take him to the tower's base. The small hatch was accessible from several dozen foot-sized slits in the wall. He climbed up and grabbed the cold, metal lever at the top of the ladder and gave it a turn to the left and a firm push upward. The hatch squeaked open and clanked down against the hard floor directly at the base of the queen's tower. From there, he could see the light spheres shooting across the blackness far above.

The haunting tower stood tall as it gazed down upon him. As he stepped out into the core's communication field, a phantom breeze nipped at his exposed skin with a slicing chill. Poignant sounds were drifting by overhead like screams mixed with garble and peppered with voices throughout the vastness. The voices moved back and forth with the lights, and it was at this point Crix felt like a distant shell of himself. He knew those cries somehow represented suffering. The hollow feeling turned to frustration and anger, which fueled his drive to trek to the top and finally stop this madness.

He pulsed his body with orb energy and raised himself into the whisking breeze and through the light fields above. The distressing sounds became more individually discernible as the light spheres passed closer to him. They zipped by him like speeding traffic, echoing closer and then quickly further away.

His mind struggled with wanting to track every sound and voice. It became monotonous to the point that the montage of audibles and screams felt like he was on the brink of madness. He ascended higher and higher through the light spheres following the black tower. He looked down, and his stomach filled with the nauseous feeling of vertigo. He trained his eyes on the tower, trying to forget where he was and instead focus purely on the objective.

He could finally see it, the top. The tower peaked to a sharp point with the queen's throne room just below it. A circular walkway surrounded the throne room entrance with steep stairs leading to a giant, silver doorway. There appeared to be no direct way into the nucleus section from here. He referenced his lightmap as he approached. The map indicated that the only way to the nucleus from here was via the throne room. The elevator must have the capability to open nonvisible ports on the tower sections. Still, without the elevator, it was any guess where those would be, and trying to access the elevator above was not an option. The

station groaned like a wounded beast of lore and shook violently—
the hull pressure.

As unappealing as the idea of entering the Queen's throne
room sounded, there appeared to be little choice, and time was
quickly running out. For all he knew, the war was already over.

CHAPTER 25

Crix dropped himself upon the circular landing area that was at the base of the throne room entrance. Several Marck guards wielding percussion blades stood at the bottom of the stairs. *Strange, why are they not attacking me? Why are they not coming down after me?* Questions filled his thoughts, and he couldn't help but feel concerned that he was about to walk into a well-calculated trap.

As he approached the stairs, the Marck guards turned their heads following his movements. They were keeping a vigilant watch. Their purple capes flapped and whipped around their legs as the brisk air swept through. At one point, Crix was almost sure that their hands tightened around their weapons, only to loosen back up seconds later.

The grate stairs followed up steeply and ended at the large door. Crix sauntered up the steps; his heels clacked against the steel with each footfall, and he kept an eye on the Marck guards behind him. He reached the door unobstructed after a tiring climb to the top. Etched into its thick metal surface was the image of a four-winged creature in flight, with the face of a woman wearing a crown above it. The door slid quietly down, disappearing into the floor as he approached, giving the sense of an invitation to enter.

An opaque red glow filled the doorway. At first, it looked impassable as Crix couldn't see beyond it, yet it didn't appear to be a solid mass. He carefully pushed his wounded right arm into it, not wanting to risk losing his good hand. The wounded stub passed through freely. A tingling sensation danced up his elbow and into his shoulder. He pulled it out for inspection to make sure it was still intact. Cautiously, he stepped fully into the crimson field; the tingling filled his body and turned into an itch, an uncontrollable itch. There was itching and scratching everywhere with galling intensity. He couldn't help dragging his fingernails back and forth across his shoulders and down his chest. Quickly the itching began to wane, and he started to take notice of his surroundings. The red barrier wasn't there anymore, at least from this perspective. However, a subtle hue of red remained beneath everything around him. He spun around; the doorway was black.

The low, round entryway looked outward to a multi-tiered floor; the walls slowly pulsed darker and then lighter in the rhythm similar to a heartbeat. A waterfall of sparkling light poured down behind a sizeable blood red throne atop the highest tier of the floor. A striking female sat confidently upon the throne. She had an outward beauty mixed perfectly with a generous dusting of sexuality and magnetism, the likes of which Crix could never have dreamt or spawned from his imagination. Her long black hair shone like polished steel, glistening in the lights behind her. Her eyes were brilliant emerald green. As she gazed upon Crix across the large room, a tickle shot through his eyes and leaped deep into his gut, stirring up all the butterflies within. Her skin was a perfect powder white, her lips a crimson red, and her dress as red as her lips. The dress slit high up her legs and snugged around her breasts. It was liquid in appearance as it hugged every flawless curve of her body. Her feet pointed downward as to show their sensual high arches in a provocative pose.

Crix's heart pounded, and his guard instantly went down. His knees wobbled in weakness at the full sight of her. He felt drugged. He needed to sit, but somehow, he remained on his feet. She stared at him for a minute without saying a word, and then she gave a slow, disarming smile.

"Come closer. You have nothing to fear." Her voice was strong and seductive as it danced into his ears and tickled into his thoughts. Crix felt the impulse to obey her. He stepped in with spongy legs, and he felt a clumsiness that he couldn't shake off no matter how much he tried. As he approached, the worse the condition became.

"I have watched you for some time now, Tolagon; your strength and endurance is truly surprising." She slowly stroked the tip of her tongue across her glossy upper lip. "Even more so is your love for those you scarcely know." The sound of her voice felt like warm liquid pouring over his heart. It was soothing yet alluring. "Through my children's eyes, I have witnessed you fight and survive under the grimmest conditions. Beasts, elements, and even some of my finest have fallen to you. Now you stand before me as whole as the day you were born . . . look."

She held out her hand and turned it to the side. From the tips of her polished red fingernails poured out millions of tiny particles that streamed and drifted through the air to his stump. Crix looked down at his right hand, and it was as if it had never left him. He raised it to his face and tapped his thumb across the tips of each finger. His hand had sensations. It looked and felt so real that he began to have doubts over his memories of losing it.

"How? How did you do that?" He felt like a child, completely disarmed. "It was missing just moments ago. Your guards have been—" He stopped as she arose from her seat and walked smoothly down from the first tier. Her leg slid out from the slit in her skirt with every forward step. She moved with the grace and elegance of a feline. Crix found his heartbeat racing and his focus unwinding as she approached.

"My guards and the X-Ore were merely a test. I needed to be sure that you would be a worthy king, and so you are." She stopped and stroked her fingers through her glistening hair and gave him an enchanting smile. "I can make you whole, just like your hand; I can fulfill all of your pleasures, fill you with warmth and comfort. I can become everything you want me to be." Her apparel metamorphosed through several variations of sensual attire, from a fun-seeking, white, short skirt with a feminine-cut sleeveless top to a commanding black undergarment displaying several straps clipped across her figure and various other fantasies before settling back to the former red dress. She resumed her catlike walk toward him, her toes gently touching the surface followed with a gentle drop of her arch and heel. Her eyes stared him up and down, and her left leg crossed her right as she paced, waving her curves seductively at him.

"I—I have someone I love already." He broke her captive trance enough to get the words out.

"I know," she said with a whisper before stroking her wet tongue over her lips. "She is certain to disappoint you, which is to no fault of hers. Your destiny is for greatness, and she cannot provide that to you. I will. We can make this system a better place; your people need a representative. They need a king to guide them through their evolution, or they will be reduced to Thraxon sustenance. Together we can lead them; with you at my side, we will break free of this stronghold, and our pleasures together will know no limits."

She continued advancing until she was standing only centimeters from him. She slid her arms around his neck, pulling herself in close to him, and then stared into his eyes. "The power within you will extend our army's reach further and rout the Thraxons from their homes, delivering peace across the galaxy. We will raise Nathasia beyond its former glory. It will be a perfect world where our citadel will reside high atop Mt. Clouds." Her leg gently caressed around his as she pulled him close. Her hands and breath were surprisingly warm and inviting. "We will love each other from early dawn until the nights grow weary of our passions." She leaned inward and pressed her moist lips and sweet-flowing breath upon his.

Crix's mind drifted to thoughts of Kerriah, and he forgot where he was at the moment, embracing the sensuality the queen gave as his eyelids closed. His inner wildness surged and his hormones pumped, throbbing through every vein and vessel of his body. The temperature elevated, and tiny beads of sweat formed on his forehead as she let out a soft moan. Her leg stroked smoothly up and down the back of his while their tongues touched. She pulled her mouth in closer, pressing their lips firmly together. For a few minutes, he lost himself; his soul fleeing to observe his moment of weakness.

THE QUEEN PROTOCOL

Kerriah . . . Creedith . . . I'm so sorry . . . Troika . . . No . . .
No . . . No! His thoughts flooded back to where he was; the passion
snapped like a thread pulled too tight. He placed his hands on her
waist and pushed her back. Startled, she closed her mouth and her
eyes opened wide. Her sudden surprise was quickly followed by
irritation as her brows curled in and her green eyes turned dark.

His heart filled with defiance. "No! I am not here for this.
You murdered my people, destroyed my home, and my father,
there will never be anything between us. If you show me where the
nucleus is, this can be a lot easier for both of us."

Her eyes turned black and then a blazing red. "You
ignorant fool! You could have had everything, yet you choose death
for what? An inferior female foolishly designed with inadequacies
and weaknesses? I suppose that is only fitting as you are a just a
filthy inbred part of a barbaric and dated species long worthy of the
destruction they received. Just look at yourself!" A mirrored
reflection of a pale, sparsely-haired Andor stared back at him. It
looked mutated, or at least not like one he had ever seen before.
The nose was shorter, and the eyes were smaller.

"You see, you're grotesque! The illusion that you walk
around in is pathetic, and I would have fixed this permanently. The
burden of this wretchedness would have been lifted from you
forever! Your true self will never be accepted in either culture, but
you would have been a king in mine. Now you are destined to be
nothing!" As she shouted, the glow of the walls pulsed at a faster
pace with each passing second, mimicking her fury.

Crix seethed with disgust over her remarks. He wanted to
attack her, but her female form gave him reservations. She had not

physically assaulted him, only provoked him through her words. Attacking her went against his Andorian principles. "Just tell me where the nucleus is, and I can make both of our problems go away."

Her haughty laugh echoed throughout the chamber. The area blinked a blinding flash of light. His sight left him, and his hearing fell silent; even as he screamed out, cold hands gripped around his throat, followed by a painful ringing that stabbed into his ears. There was blackness and silence followed by a whisper.

Wake up . . . wake up . . . wake up . . . The gentle voice tugged at his mind until his conciseness returned. He felt the sting of a bruise on his face and soreness around his neck. There was a sticky puddle of cold fluid pooled around his cheek, and his mouth was dry and crusted. As he tried to swallow, his throat stuck together like thick paste. His body was planted against the floor. He pinched his eyelids together to clear the cloudiness from his thoughts and painfully peeled himself up with stiff muscles and foggy eyes. His right hand was missing once again.

The queen was seated upon her throne. A sheer, black dress draped across her body with a golden crown raised to a tall center spike. "Despite your many flaws, you still astonish me. I would have expected you to be unconscious for much longer. It's of little consequence anyway; it's too late for your ill-fated plan." Her voice was low and ominous. "Look for yourself."

An image unfolded before him. The image showed the great cities of Soorak, Thale, and Solara in smoldering ruins and its citizens filed in endless lines as they entered Thraxon food storage ships. The lands were littered with Thraxon and Marck soldiers that went unchallenged as they oversaw their newly seized worlds.

The image zoomed into a view of Kerriah and Krath's remains that lay partially consumed by Thraxon larva at the bottom of breeding pits. "Now you see that your struggles are no longer worthy of your efforts. All is already lost, and everything you've known is gone. There is no longer any motive to fight or quest. Give yourself and the orb to me, and I will make your suffering stop forever," the queen scathingly offered him from behind a baleful grin.

Like a giant's anvil placed upon his chest, Crix felt the full pain of his loss; his eyes pooled with tears as he let out a sorrowful wail, a wail filled with so much pain and ran so far into the hallows of his soul that the sound of an Andor's scream could be heard through his cries. The cry came from deep within his body, breaking through the almost permanent disguise that Corin had put on him at birth. It was the first time he had ever noticed a sound like that from his voice.

How did he fall asleep so long that everything had come to this conclusion? He broke down for several minutes before pulling himself back together. A sudden realization hit him, and he slowly looked up at her. The hurt drained from his eyes, and his nose and lips wrinkled with disdain.

Crix couldn't let go of the image of Kerriah's partially devoured body. *She's lying.* The Thraxons wouldn't consume her. She wasn't organic. *This queen of deception made a mistake.* He was willing to take that bet; it was all he had now. His brows furrowed as he stared at her.

"Why do you still need me, then? If the war is over and our side is truly lost, why don't you bring the newly claimed orbs? You must have surely recovered at least one of them and given yourself the supposed power to leave here. I'm sure Zearic is happy to hand them over to you. Or why haven't you simply killed me and taken this one for yourself?" Crix tried to study her expression to confirm his suspicion while wiping away old tears from his eyes and cheeks. The queen pursed her lips tightly but said nothing.

"You need me to provide the vessel to control this orb, which you cannot pull from my body? The way this orb bonded with me makes it impossible for you to kill me and extract it. Even if you could extract it, you still would not be able to control it yourself since it wouldn't bond to you. It's not as simple as just tapping the orb's power; you need something to control it for you, manipulate it . . . You need a Tolagon! That's why you haven't killed me and why you saved my life when I first arrived here." Crix stood up and brushed himself off with renewed confidence.

"You're nothing more than a conniving trickster, and you need me to agree to join you. Those images were lies used to break me and give up all hope." If nothing else, he needed to believe this and was unsure if he was merely trying to convince himself or calling her out. "If you wanted me dead, I would imagine that I would already be so."

The queen stood. Her face was full of rage; the chamber strobed with her anger. "So you think I really need you to cooperate? Sure it would have been easier if that were so. However, I do not require your cooperation. I will take control of you by will or by force. It's a pity for you that it could have been the other way." Her eyes squinted, and she cocked a sideways grin before biting her lower lip.

"That override you have is useless. I can see that it was damaged during your clash with my X-Ore. Your clever attempt is thwarted. You cannot take control of my children or me. In fact, you need me to cooperate with you if you're to stop the Thraxon invading force. Sadly, that option has expired." She let out a taunting laugh.

"Fool! As I'm sure you observed the light apertures moving through my tower, each of those represents a direct link with each of my children, and right now, I'm commanding them to slaughter everyone you have ever known; the rest will be fodder for the Thraxons."

Two sturdy Marcks seized both of his arms and twisted them against his back. "I still have good news for you. You will be implanted as my slave, your free will lost, and you'll live to serve my desires. Isn't that right, Lord Merik?"

The noble hybrid stepped out from behind the two Marck guards and gave a low bow to the queen. "Yes, my queen, it will be my pleasure." His appearance was more Marck-like without flesh.

"No! It can't be!" Crix said with disbelief at the sight of Merik.

The queen's eyes widened as she took pleasure in his surprise. "You didn't realize that I could call my children back to me at any time? Merik may not have been a pure child of mine, but he's been properly altered, and I see everything he sees. This incarnation of Merik before you here is purely one of mine. Less

303

his own free will. Just after the loss of Dispor, I duplicated his mind and transferred it back here, where I had him reconstructed to what you see now. He is still visually identical but without any organic parts. This version of Merik will now serve me here, and one of his first tasks is to provide you with a slow and excruciating transformation.

"I knew that you would come here for some time, and I also knew that you would likely resist me because of your ignorant love. So I had my contingency planned well ahead of your arrival." She paused for a moment to observe Crix as he took in the details of being caught in her web. "Goodbye, young fool." She sat back down with her arms resting calmly upon her throne. "Take him, Merik." She casually waved her fingers and intentionally looked away. "Make sure the process is painful."

Merik grinned; his eyes settled from blue to deep red on the thought of torture and experimentation. The former flesh portions of his body were now metal, making his appearance more uniform and less pieced together. "As you wish." He turned to walk out as the two Marcks drug Crix away, struggling against their vice-like grips. Merik pulled a thin card from his coat pocket. "Stop!" he ordered the guards. "Hold him still." He looked into Crix's eyes. "Do you know what a Kreillic is, boy?"

Crix said nothing in defiance. "I didn't think so. Before you depart this life, I thought that I would grace you with one well-forgotten piece of our history. Perhaps you'll find it interesting. A Kreillic is an early Thraxon, which our intelligence determined is now extinct, or perhaps the species had evolved beyond it. One of these Kreillics visited Nathasia thousands of years ago. This Thraxon was stranded after his scouting ship crashed onto the planet's surface. We now know that this creature's primary directive was to find inhabited worlds and report back their existence. It's hard to imagine how this Kreillic made it so deep beyond its system before the existence of Komeectram driven gammac corridors, but it did. Eventually, with no way to return to its home, it did what came naturally to it. It feasted on the ancient inhabitants of Nathasia.

"Many tales were written of this monster and the horror it wreaked among the primitive people of that day. It had created such a legacy of terror that my ancient order of house Spancer even took the Kreillic's image as our family crest. How ironic is that? Ironic in that I would later work to build weapons to kill the ancestors of these creatures that my family once worshipped. Would you like to know what's even more ironic? Its ship was discovered many centuries ago by the Nathasion people, and through extensive reverse engineering, its technology was used to take their people to the moons of Oro, in particular, Soorak.

"Its influence is all around us. You just fail to see it. Just look at the insignias for our queen." He pointed to a copy above the door, identical to the image on the entrance. "Why would Joric, who hates the Thraxons more than anyone, give her an insignia that so closely resembles the Kreillic?"

For a moment, Crix's eyes widened and his jaw went slack at this revelation, then he quickly hardened his expression. The queen's blackish silhouette veered out from the background.

"I really don't care what fairy tales you believe in," Crix spat back.

"If it weren't for that fairy tale, as you refer, you would not exist. No matter, that existence is about to end."

The card formed a triangular tip, and he tapped it against the back of Crix's neck. Crix felt burning shockwaves travel from his eyes to his heels and into every nerve and tendon. His body had the sensation as though it was set afire. He twisted and squirmed as he broke loose from one of the guard's tight grip.

"I said hold him steady!" Merik shouted angrily. He carefully tried to aim the tip back into the same spot on Crix's neck.

Crix knew that the next tap would likely be the last thing he would ever remember as himself. He dug deep from within and created a powerful pulse of orb energy that sent the Marcks staggering back. They loosened their hold on him just enough. He slipped free and ran toward the queen. She stood quick and ready to take action before he huddled down. The sounds of the approaching Marcks were atop of him now. He mustered everything, every emotion, every resolve, every memory, every piece of himself, and exploded the orb's power like a massive bomb of energy. Everything went dark and silent.

It was so quiet that one could hear the thumps of the storms outside and the lengthy creaks of the station walls against the relentless pressure of Oro squeezing its tight grip around it. Crix opened his eyes; his body felt feeble, but he could still make a light. The orb's blue glow was the only illumination in the shadowy chamber. There were no pulsing lights and no waterfall. Merik and the Marck guards laid motionless, scattered like discarded dolls on the floor.

The queen was not at the throne, though a mostly featureless female shape dangled from the ceiling above. She was unadorned, pale silver with a flesh-like undertone. A mix of wires, tubes, and cables clung to her back and suspended her from her real throne high above. A crown of red spikes protruded from her head. The lights strobed back to life, and the walls slowly began to pulse once more with the crimson glow. Her eyes pried open; they were round and solid black.

"What have you done?" she groaned; her voice was deep like a Thale gortfrog as it cracked apart. "You have killed us all now . . . the . . . Thr . . . ax . . . wi . . . cons . . . ever . . . m . . . my . . . children . . . are lost." Her eyes slowly shut, and the pulsing red walls faded into blackness.

Crix removed the override from his pack and noticed that it was indeed crushed. He tossed it to the floor. It would do no good now. The nucleus needed power, and there was no longer a way to transmit the control signals to Joric's relays. There wasn't time to overthink this; for all he knew, Kerriah, Krath, and the others were already dead. He had to finish what he had set out to do. The access to the nucleus was there, where her throne was; he couldn't see it before through all her illusions. Clearly, before him was a square panel on the floor with a simple inscription, "Nucleus Access," and a four-winged creature insignia over it. There was no obvious way to open the panel, so given his shortage of time, he forced it open with the help of the orb's power. The metal hatch peeled back before popping into the air and then clattering down upon the hard surface.

He dropped down inside an area with a low ceiling. Crix had to stoop down to avoid hitting his head. The walls, floor, and ceiling appeared to be covered with tinted mirrors. There was a black socket in the ceiling, where the plug would have inserted. *Darn X-Ore.* Crix shook his head and let out a weary chuckle at the thought of getting all the way to this point only to ultimately have his mission fail during his encounter with that one, big, lumbering Marck. He studied the situation for a minute and then lowered his head in thought.

A hero's definition is universally known, though the boundaries of such an individual are often perverted, thus cheapening the true hero. Crix never really set out to be a hero by anyone's definition. However, it was a thought that crossed his mind when he realized that there was only one way to right this wrong, and it would mean that he would have to give up everything, everyone he held dear and every future aspiration. It would all end for him here, but in his mind, there were no other choices. Perhaps this was why the orb bound to him in Dispor. Somehow, it knew this day would come and, without such, would make what he was about to do impossible.

He stood there solemnly, staring up at the socket; it was only for a minute or two, but it was something he needed. It was his gift to himself, to reflect once more while in his flesh. He took a knee and collapsed deep within himself, so deep that he could see every moment, every memory, and every vision within his mind through a single pane. He could even see the orb within for the first time. It had a smile that wasn't evident, as strange as it may be; it was more like seeing a tickle of love within his heart. Now he finally understood, the orb was an embodiment of good in its purest state; any baggage that it carried was from that of the host. From wherever it might have originated, it was purely noble. It handed it all to him, every bit of itself. Crix became a celestial form of energy and shot up into the socket as his physical body collapsed pale and limp into the cold surface.

CHAPTER 26

His celestial energy quickly filled the core. All its information and the queen's knowledge were instantly his, and the throne room lit up again. He saw thousands of images of horror, struggles, and battles waging in real-time. The resistance was still active with Kerriah. She was there fighting a helpless fight along with dozens of resistance fighters at her side. The Thraxon forces moved inward, dropping her comrades one by one as they encircled them. Hundreds of Thraxon ships commanded the airspace and orbited over the UMO system. The Marcks appeared functional and followed the last directive sent out via their queen, mercilessly executing all UMO citizens who still drew breath.

I control them now, and there are so many of them. So many more than I could have ever expected, even ones that most are not aware of, buried deep within the grounds and lakes, early designs . . . giants. They are still alive. I will activate them all and defeat the Thraxon forces. This will all end now as I can also control the soulless townspeople Plexo's shown me. I will release them from their pain, and they will be enslaved to this evil no more. Behold, Kerriah, I have kept my promise.

The Marcks were many for sure, but the Thraxons had multiplied by the millions over these last decades. *How could there be so many?* They peppered the lands and seas en masse, pouring down from their low flying cruisers' deployment chutes. The Thraxon waves that encircled Kerriah's group swiftly crumpled and dropped like swarms of ants set to a torch. Marck elite forces dropped down from hover disks, and air to ground attack craft began strafing the unsuspecting hordes. Only the Hybrid Thraxons held their own against this new offensive. Their enhanced countermeasure systems deflected much of the Marcks' firepower.

Marck warships turned their cannons onto their allied Thraxon cruisers, caving their hulls and leaving broken debris crashing down from orbit and burning into fiery bits. Massive fingers of giant Marcks burst upward from the depths of Soorak's great underground lakes and the oceans of Thale. They broke through the grounds where some were buried deep and forgotten. Who knew exactly why they were discarded and buried as if to be called upon in some unknown future? Why didn't Joric mention them?

They emerged like titans. The mere sight of them sent the Thraxon ground forces breaking ranks and scurrying in every direction as the giants stomped across their exoskeletons, leaving nothing more than flattened armor and goo in their wake. *Squash the Hybrids; chase them down and crush them under your heels.* The titan-sized Marcks took focus on the Thraxon Hybrids as the hunters became the hunted.

There he is, the great betrayer, Zearic. You destroyed Troika, and now I'm coming for you. Crix gained sight of Zearic as he prematurely celebrated his victory. His chrome limbs wielded a scepter as he sailed between the majestic arches of Corasan, Sooraks capital; his wicked grin was wider than it had ever been with the anticipation

311

of his new unquestioned rule. His underlying mistrust of the queen had kept him from having Marck guards. Instead, he had chosen to keep the red armored Thraxon Widowers at his side for personal protection. These rarely seen Thraxon variants were some of the deadliest and near impossible to kill.

Crix brought down the closest legion of Marck forces upon Zearic, and his grin quickly snapped into a scowl. He turned swift to fury as he cursed the queen aloud and ordered his Thraxon units into a counteroffensive. The Widowers proved to be too much for the Marcks, and they shattered under the force of their concussion rifles and their lightning-fast pouncing attacks that left the Marck attackers headless.

The Knactor legion, they are holding the resistance's hidden stronghold at Qoron. They can be redeployed to Corasan quickly from there. That is what I'll do, send the legion home to kill Zearic. The idle Knactor legionnaire's eyes flashed as they sprung to motion and boarded their assault transports; their propulsion packs sent them straight up through the ship's deployment ports.

Within moments, the ship's engines thrust from the small, rocky moon of Qoron to nearby Soorak. Zearic called in additional Thraxon support for protection as he made a hastened advance on the city center, Porray, where all the political elites of Soorak resided. Corasan quickly filled with Thraxon reserve forces, and the high gates of Porray fell against the scant resistance of Marck police forces protecting the structure.

With the Marck forces turning against him, Zearic planned his contingency. If he couldn't control the great cities of the UMO, he would level them and build new cities upon their ashes.

THE QUEEN PROTOCOL

"Warlord Racluus," Zearic's call signaled to the Thraxon commander over the forward invasion force. "The insolent Marck queen has betrayed us. Engage the scorching operative now, and let her reign over fire and debris." His eyes sparkled red, with a mixture of anger and delight over his reprimand.

A voice returned over his com speakers. Distortion raked against the audio due to latency in the digital translators. "Order declined, we need their flesh living for our spawn and our nourishment," the crackling voice answered back. Zearic filled with fury over the reply, and he rolled back into the embrace of his oldest and most trusted friend, deceit.

"Now you will listen to me . . . the scorching operative must be carried out, or you will get nothing! Level their cities and demonstrate to the queen that we can take everything from her. It will force her into submission, and there will still be ample numbers of the living to be swept up from the surrounding towns and countrysides to fill your processing ships. Now do it!"

The Thraxon guards around him took note of his anger as their black eyes darted toward him. He stared straight back at them defiantly. They wouldn't dare betray him! Warlord Racluus's voice chirped back in over his com. "Incinerators will be moving into position. You are advised to evacuate immediately." *Ha . . . feeble-minded fools!*

Under Zearic's recommendation, the Thraxons had increased their incinerator fleet from the two they had during the second war to twelve, allowing them to burn down the remnant population they consumed much more efficiently or to break the morale of those that put up resistance. Zearic turned away from

313

Porray, his dream of control dashed by the queen's forces. He knew long ago that their allegiance would one day end like this. He should have made a greater effort in taking control over her directly, instead of this contrived alliance that he had laced with betrayal. She won the game, and he hated her for it. *She will get her payment for this betrayal. I will return to make her suffer, even if I have to build her a flesh and blood body to feel pain in; oh yeah, she will suffer for this.*

Zearic took one last look at his thwarted prize. Porray should have been his. He was to build his palace there and enjoy his unquestioned rule over the system. All the years of effort and planning were now for naught. "Ensure my ship is ready for departure, we are—" Before he finished, the sky rained with deployment pods like a meteor storm, thumping and rumbling against the ground as they hit, caving the sides of structures as they passed through. *Knactors.* "Make haste to the ships!" he shouted to his forces.

Pods burst in the air, releasing Marcks via propulsion packs that showered down upon Zearic's forces. The ground pods popped open, releasing their warriors. The red- and silver-armored warriors of legendary tales converged upon their targets with their signature blitzing tactic, putting Zearic's Thraxons back on their heels. The reserves folded quickly under the oppressive fire of the Knactor airborne concussion rifles, and the ground forces quickly surrounded Zearic and his Widowers.

"Protect me!" Zearic screamed as he made a desperate break for his ship; the Widowers pounced upon their attackers, but the Knactors did not succumb easily. They fired their rifles, and when that proved to no avail, they snapped out thin-bladed weapons. The auxiliary swords, which were standard issue to the

Knactors, glide out from their hilts with a flick of the wrist. The metal warriors cut and thrust into the Widowers' soft spots, their spines. Sprays of oily black spewed everywhere, and they let out horrible a screech, fighting until they had completely bled out. Each of the Widowers slowly went down, fighting one by one.

The roaring of thrusters blasted nearby as Zearic's ships ascended. The would-be tyrant made his hasty escape during the skirmish. Knactor legionnaires latched on with precision explosives, but the ship's short-range turrets fired, fending off most of them before reaching Soorak's upper atmosphere.

No! Stop him! Crix sent Marck warships to intercept his escape. The failing Thraxon fleet was still able to provide cover before they engaged their hyper-light drives, spinning toward the inner system's gammac corridor Quadril.

The Marck fleet remained in close pursuit, and by the time they shut down just outside Quadril's opening, they were face-to-face with a dreaded hive ship. *Focus your attacks on Zearic's ship,* Crix ordered the fleet, but that order would prove to be a miscalculation on his part. The hive ship gaped open its immense jaws and released thousands of Volan attack fighters that began to prey upon the Marck fleet, providing the Thraxons and Zearic an opportune escape through the corridor. The sturdy, knife-shaped Volans fighter had the element of surprise on their side as their cannons ripped into the hulls of the Marck destroyers, sucking some of its mechanical crew into the vacuum of space.

The Marcks unleashed their agile attack drones to counter the Volans. The smaller, faster drones poured out by the hundreds and outmaneuvered the Volans. Their tined ovular shapes swooshed around the Thraxon fighters like debris kicked up in a windstorm. The drone's side turrets flashed red as they rained death upon their targets. The ranks of Thraxon attack fighters plumed into flames, peppering the blackness of space with blooms of orange that faded into specters of smoke. The Hive ship folded its jaw back in, its mission accomplished. The Thraxon menace reversed its thrusters and pulled its mass back through the corridor, disappearing into the black void.

Follow them, finish them for good, Crix commanded, and the Marcks obeyed their new king, jumping deep through the corridors Quidril, Delta, Pizon, and into the interstellar reaches of the outer corridor Zeta. The Thraxon fleet had already made their way through, and the portal stood lonesome and ominous in deep space. Beyond the gateway was the unknown; the Luminars had broken the chain long ago.

Crix went mad with vengeance. He couldn't allow Zearic to escape. He ordered his Marcks through but quickly realized why they never attempted to pursue the Thraxons to their homeworld or ever ventured through Zeta. As the Marck ships passed through the silvery black opening, they went dark; his view of them severed as they fell out of the central core's limited reach. The apex of the Marck fleet was lost, though it was difficult to say in what capacity they were lost. Crix wondered if they were running on their last orders or simply floating in deep space helplessly devoid of their lifeline.

Close the portal now, destroy gammac corridor Zeta! It was a fraught move, but he had to ensure that the Thraxons would not reemerge with a more potent force. They might never be capable of rebuilding it without Luminar aid. Still, Breaking Zeta's nearside gammac mirror would render useless the far end that the Thraxons used to enter the UMO's corridor system. Marck ships fired on the portal's outer rings. Zeta flashed and folded upon itself in a swirling storm of scrap and debris. It was done.

CHAPTER 27

Where is she? I have to find her. I've lost her. The hills and trees flashed by in a blur, over a lake, and through smoldering towns. This is where she was; why can't I find her? I have to see her once more, even if it's not my own eyes.

Groups of refugees that had escaped their captors trudged back to their homes, or what remained of them. The Marcks stood as their original design intended, as guardians sweeping up the last remaining Thraxons.

He stopped. There before him stood a slender female in sleek black with armored shoulders and matching boots. Her jet-black hair swayed in the wind. Six resistance fighters flanked her, all mixed with joy and sorrow over what they surveyed. A single Marck scout, agile and lightly armored, bearing no weaponry approached them. Her companions cautiously drew their weapons and prepared to take down the unexpected Marck that acted out of character from the rest.

"Wait!" she ordered them. "Lower your weapons!" Somehow, she knew this one, though it wasn't immediately clear to her why. There was something about his appearance, his posture.

"Crix?" She knew it must sound crazy to say his name to a Marck scout. Yet she knew it had to be.

In some way, this Marck had soul-filled eyes, long with sadness. It shuffled slowly toward her and nearly lost its footing. It stumbled forward with a lowered head and slumped shoulders. "Is that you?" She moved close to it, looking into its eye lenses, seeing deeply into a life that was there but lost.

"It is you." Its head lifted, and its cobalt eye's twinkled. Now she knew for sure, and she threw her arms around its cold metal body. It was hard and rigid, not soft, and it was missing that familiar scent that reminded her of being a child. "I'm sorry . . . I'm so sorry. I love you. Never forget that I love you," she said aloud. His metal hands rose and lightly touched her back before gradually dropping back down.

Somehow, she knew that he solely controlled the Marcks and that he could never leave the central core as long as a potential Thraxon threat still existed, for without them, they would be helpless to defend against another invasion. He was imprisoned there now, enslaved with duty, the duty to keep the core station stable in Oro's hostile cradle, which was his purpose. A hero's purpose.

ABOUT THE AUTHOR

Gregory Benson grew up in the Midwest and married his high school sweetheart, Dawn. He graduated from the University of Missouri-Saint Louis and works in the technology field.

As far back as he could remember, he would spend much of his childhood daydreaming about alien worlds and immersing himself into science fiction and fantasy. As an adult, he's enjoyed adventures traveling with wife Dawn and his son Luke, as well as sword fighting, pinball, and of course, writing sci-fi/fantasy.

Made in the USA
Middletown, DE
10 August 2024